IN A VERTIGO OF SILENCE

IN A VERTIGO
OF SILENCE

A NOVEL

MIRIAM POLLI

SERVING HOUSE BOOKS

In a Vertigo of Silence

Copyright © 2014 Miriam Polli

ISBN: 978-0-9913281-6-1

Cover design: Allen Mohr

Cover photograph: "Passaic River Fog" by Mark Hillringhouse

Serving House Books logo by Barry Lereng Wilmont

Published by Serving House Books
Copenhagen, Denmark and Florham Park, NJ
www.servinghousebooks.com

Member of The Independent Book Publishers Association

First Serving House Books Edition 2014

For my husband, Jim Katsikis, who made everything possible.

In memory of my dearest mother, whose love has filled me with constant motion, and in memory of my sister Loretta, who did more than name the moons for me.

ACKNOWLEDGMENTS

When a book takes twenty or more years to write, it would be near impossible to thank all the people who encouraged you along the way. A novel grows from a moment in life, a word, a thought, almost too complex to state here, yet at the core there are those who urge you to continue. Deep gratitude goes to Helen Morrissey Rizzuto for being there from the beginning; talented writer, devoted teacher, careful reader, and life-long friend. Her knowledge has brought so much to me. I thank Lorraine Ramer for her friendship and her unwavering confidence in me, and to my remarkable daughter, Alexandra Katsikis Rutherford, who encouraged me and nagged me to write as soon as she learned what words could do. I wish to thank my daughters Laurie Iannucci and Suzy Agostino for being there for me, always, and for their huge hearts. And to all my incredibly beautiful grandchildren for filling me with sheer happiness, plus a special mention to my grandson, William (Billy) K. Lawrence, our own English professor who read this before the countless revisions, and urged me to continue. I wish also to thank Walter Cummins for inviting me into Two Bridges, a most dedicated, cogent writer's group, and particularly for his knowledge of all things publishable.

Two dear friends, no longer with us but never forgotten, Joan Beer for being the first to tell me I was a writer at the young age of ten, and for Pam Conrad whose confidence in me filled me with wonder. And to John Gardner for giving me the push I needed.

TABLE OF CONTENTS

EMILY
1950
CHAPTER ONE

Cooled spaghetti floats in a pot of starchy water. Emily sits on the floor near the stove. Mother screams at her to take off the bracelet, but there is no bracelet. She paces, cries, carries on; you will not be allowed to sleep until you remove that bracelet. Her mother's burgundy high heels snap at the floor around her. She stoops before Emily; her full skirt flows like a tent of terror over Emily's small knees. Her eyes are wild and smudged with mascara. Take off that bracelet, she demands. Emily searches her arms for the bracelet — she offers her, clean, small trembling limbs yet Mother will not touch her. Only later, when she is filled with sorrow, will she touch Emily, smother her to her chest, to the nape of her neck, to the familiar scent of Shalimar, fostering an illusion of security.

You will not have your dinner until you take off that bracelet. It is priceless. Your father gave me that bracelet, take it off I say.

Emily is tired and hungry, she looks at her bare wrist and tries to imagine a bracelet . . . perhaps she can draw one? Color it in . . . make believe . . .until finally she stands and unclips the imaginary bracelet. Carefully holding it at arms length, she walks towards her mother and places it on the kitchen table in front of where she sits. Mother looks down at the bare table and lets out a satisfying groan.

Sometimes it happens. A murmur or pang, a prod of memory. My senses take me there: I skip along Broadway Boulevard. The repetitious clunk, clang of the elevated train roars above my head, dulling the car horns and the squeal of city buses opening and closing their doors. It is a gray cold day in November, and Babcia Marishka made me wear my brown woolen coat. It has frogs for buttons, and a yellow plaid lining that shows when the hood is down. Babcia said it might snow. This meant leggings, galoshes, and mittens attached to the sleeves of my coat with metal clips, all of which I had forgotten in school.

Though the streets are barely familiar, I feel reassured as I pass Feldman's drugstore and Umberto's open vegetable stand. "Mr. Feldman's daughter is going to college. That's where you'll go one day," Babcia talking on a walk home.

I heard her tell Mother that Umberto's second wife, Carmela, was pregnant again. "Poor thing," she said, in the same sympathetic tone she used when our neighbor, Mr. Ohare, was found dead on his bathroom floor.

Outside the hardware store, there are red wagons and sleds. One resembles the one Mother surprised me with last Christmas. It has a knob at the helm with a small rod through its center. I remember Highland Park, Babcia's gentle shove. The wild sensation as I sailed down the hill, my body cut through the wind. Clutching the rod so tightly my arms began to tremble. Paralyzed with fear and excitement, ears burning with cold, I held my breath until I reached the bottom. When I looked up at the top of the snow hill Babcia was all smiles. "Yes?" her voice riding the wind drifted down to me.

"Yes!" I shouted back, "More, More!" and began to climb the hill again.

Broadway is a frenzy of traffic. People rush in and out of shops, inch their way between parked cars then zip across the boulevard. Exhilarated by this new sense of adventure, I walk on, stopping to look in a store window whenever I like, tapping my new brown penny loafers against a steel cellar door, pleased by the small echo that follows my tapping. In the window of the five-and-dime there is a small jewelry box with a ballerina unwinding. A man inside the five-and dime picks up the jewelry box and turns the key on the bottom. Unable to hear the music, I pretend she is dancing to the Russian-Polish lullaby that Babcia sings to me, and I begin to hum the tune. Intently, I watch the ballerina, my humming spurring her on. Seeing my reflection in the plate glass, I begin to twirl. I twirl freely, openly, not like the ballerina whose arms are stretched in a heart above her head, but in my own way, my head tilted, ear to shoulder, my arms down, palms up towards the hot sparks of the screeching train above me. It is odd, strange, but as I twirl I become mindful of me, not only of my skin, hair and eyes, but also of my own singularity. In this small kernel of time my own existence swells inside me—an existence that I would later come to recognize as both wondrous and terrible, both remarkable and unremarkable in its obscurity.

Pausing, I rest against a steel girder that holds up the train platform. Sparks from the metal wheels shower fireworks, coppery, pink and gold. The train slows, clunks its way into the station. The sweat at the back of my neck begins to cool. I feel buoyant, swaying in a floating dampness. The world slowly moves around in circles, coming into focus. It is then that I notice the woman sitting in the store window. She is wearing what I think Mother would call expensive rags. Her head is tied with a blue and gray scarf, knotted beneath her left ear lobe. Her blouse is multicolored, gold and silver threads run through it. Her skirt has colored panels of green, red, and black satin that hang to the floor. Her feet are bare and look as though they are suntanned. Her toenails are painted bright red, and there are gold rings on two of her toes. She is sitting on a chrome-back kitchen chair. The floor of the window is lined with black felt, and a rust-colored curtain hangs behind her. She carelessly flips through magazines, occasionally looking up to watch the passersby.

When I move closer to the window, she puts the magazine down and smiles at me. Her toothy smile, large slanted teeth, dark near the roots. They remind me of the small tiles carelessly set against the edge of our bathtub collecting soap scum, the ones Babcia scrubs with what she calls her horse's toothbrush.

The gypsy woman beckons me. A red long fingernail gestures me closer, waving amid the emptiness of the store window.

She disappears behind the rust curtain and appears in the doorway. "What is your name, little girl?" She asks. There is light in her eyes. I am unprepared for her. I remember Babcia Marishka's warning to not talk to strangers.

"Emily," I say.

She places her hand on my shoulder and urges me on. "Come," she says, "come meet my dark child."

I hesitate, but my curiosity peaks. Behind the rust curtain there is a small room with a hot plate resting at the side of the sink, a small table, and a single unmade bed. A young girl with long black hair sits on the soiled ticking of the mattress, her legs crossed beneath her. She is dressed very much like the woman, long earrings, fringes of silver that tinkle whenever they touch her shoulders. She doesn't seem to have much interest in me. She is looking down at her empty lap.

Stacks of corrugated boxes and a dark green suitcase with scales of peeling leather bound with a heavy rope and knotted at the handle occupy the corner.

The gypsy woman pats a spot on the mattress next to the girl and directs me to sit. The base of the sink is covered with a wrinkled floral material. Moving the curtain aside she removes a tin from under the sink and offers me an assortment of hard candies. I take one but don't eat it. She speaks to the girl in a language I have never heard. Her tone seems harsh, but the girl just moves slightly and utters a word. The woman looks at me, her eyes, thick, black like watermelon seeds floating in liquid.

"I can tell your future. Would you like to know what will happen to you tomorrow?"

Silence. I don't know what to say.

"How would you like to know what your daddy will bring you for Christmas?"

When she says the word daddy, it is more than her accent, daddy is a foreign word to me; one I am unaccustomed to hearing. "My daddy's dead," the sound of my voice fills the room. Knowing I will sound like Mother, I say, "Mother said he died before I was able to focus my eyes properly."

I touch the piece of candy in my coat pocket, and think about eating it. The front door rattles every time the elevated train passes. I can feel myself getting restless, gathering up this adventure. Uncertain whether it should end, I look behind to the door, towards the street. The glass window in the door is covered with stained glass paper like a cheap church window. Light reflects through the window, scattering spots along the cracked linoleum floor. Unaccustomed to speaking to strangers, I say quietly, "I have to go now."

"Have another candy." The gypsy woman offers me the tin. This time I look for one that is tightly wrapped. I put it in my pocket, next to the other one. The woman says something to the girl, her tone again harsh. The girl sighs, looks up from her lap, and opens her face to me. Her deep eyelids reveal large tiger-amber eyes. The skin under them is darker, shadows of half moons band her eyes. She seems older than her body.

"I love your shoes," she says to me. Her voice is swelling and lofty. "I would be happy to try them on," then her tone turns, "can I pleasssse?" Her arms spread out towards my feet. I look down at my brown penny loafers. Her bare, soiled feet appear from under her skirt. I am embarrassed and afraid to say no, so I remove my shoes. The girl puts them on. She says something to the woman, then stands and walks to the sink and then towards the front door which is trembling from the passing of the train. She is happy in my shoes. She smiles and walks firmly back and forth across the length of the room, heels hitting the floor in an exaggerated motion. There is an exchange of words.

"Would you like to speak to your daddy?" The gypsy woman asks me.

Would I like to speak to my daddy? No one had ever asked me that question. "How?" I ask, remembering Babcia saying that when someone dies they live with God until he finds another place for them. And that sometimes they come back as butterflies or spiders.

"Your father may be dead," the woman says, "but it is only his body, the house of his spirit, that is gone. You can't touch him, but you can speak to him. Not everyone knows that."

She stands tall and smiles, hugs herself like she is remembering something good. "His spirit..." She pauses, hesitates, looks upward, "His spirit is always with us." Then she begins to wave her arms, drawing wide elaborate circles, crossing them at her chest. Her eyes close, and hugging herself she says, "I feel his presence." Her body sways from side to side. "Emily." She says, "Emily, he's waiting to talk to you."

A curtain of colored beads hang in the doorway near the sink. When the gypsy parts the beads it sounds like ice cubes falling into mother's glass. "Come," she says, "I will show you. Don't be afraid."

The girl walks into the room with us, and then goes through a door that has a thick panel of frosted glass. The gypsy directs me to sit at the small round table. The oilcloth covering the table has a cigarette hole in it. She mumbles something to herself and walks back into the front room. From where I sit, I can see the girl behind the swirls of frosted glass, her movements are fluid as though she is underwater. I watch her for a while. She must be sitting now — all I can see is her head moving slightly, her head taking on the shape of a seahorse. I am alone, waiting for the gypsy to return, watching the slight movements of her head.

In my mind Allison sits next to me in school. She shows me a mother-of-pearl pen shaped like a seahorse that her father bought for her while traveling in Boston. She talks incessantly about her father. When she asks about my father, I think of grandmother's brother Felix, a concert violinist; newspaper clippings from Poland and Hungary, a black and white photograph of him in a tuxedo, casually resting against a steamer trunk pasted with exotic travel stickers, his violin askew under his arm; all framed and hung on the wall opposite the bed where Marishka sleeps. I visualize Great Uncle Felix, whom I have never met, awkwardly carrying the trunk, its fine leather straps and gleaming brass fittings clumsily slipping downward through his hands. I tell Allison my father is a violinist, he is touring Europe, and that the gifts he brings me are too large to bring into school.

Noises echo from the front room. A closet door slams; pots and pans are juggled. A toilet flushes somewhere in the building. A small mirror hangs on the wall; silver metal shows through, scarring its purpose. I push the oddly shaped wooden chair over to the wall where the mirror hangs, and stand on it. Will my father know me? And if he does, what will he say to me? I adjust the barrette that keeps my black curls from falling in my face. Do I look like him? Does he have barely noticeable freckles running along the width of his nose? Are his eyes hazel like mine?

My reflection, caught in a circle of silver. I move to the right and almost fall off the chair. I steady myself by holding the wall. Now there is a streak of silver, a thin line tracking its way up to my widow's peak. I am excited. In a collage of infant memories, so deep, so wildly distant, there are voices, touchings, feelings, all huddled together — worn, so that their meaning is filled with bewilderment — except for one small thread of impulse: *This...I think. This* is it. And I touch my widow's peak, and know it is my father. I imagine him walking towards me, his black widow's peak set against porcelain white skin, his hands deep in a gray tweed overcoat, his green eyes set wide apart so that they appear clearer, sharper. The muscles in his cheekbones move, like a smile coming towards me. Now I am prepared, I think, and shudder at the thought that I will know him if I see him.

"Splendid." The gypsy woman fractures my vision as she enters the room. I drag the chair back to the table. "Soon you will see light. The same light that your father will see. This will help bring his spirit to us."

The girl is leaning against the wall, looking down at her fingers, picking the skin on her cuticles.

Abruptly, the gypsy woman moans, shakes her head as though she has forgotten something. "Oh, Emily." She says, "Emily, do you have money?" She has a mole on her jaw-line, near her earlobe. "Without money we can't reach the spirits, and if we can't reach the spirits, we can't reach your father."

My hands search the insides of my coat pockets knowing there will be nothing there. One hand comes to rest on the two pieces of hard candy. She is waiting. I can barely say the word. "No," I murmur.

Like me, she seems sad, disappointed. "Those terrible greedy spirits. They don't care that you're such a small child."

In the corner, the girl stoops over in a half sitting position, polishing my loafers with the hem of her skirt. "There." I shout, pointing to the two pennies in my loafers, "There, I have money."

The gypsy woman looks to where I point. "Only two pennies." She laughs. "That will never do. We can't insult. . . .but wait . . . ." She says. She walks around the table, her eyes close, her forehead resting in her hand. "Yes...yes...that might work."

She kneels next to my chair. An aroma rises from her, a mix of rose petal and wet cement that reminds me of Sunday mornings at All Saints Church. "Yes, they will do, Emily. Yes. Your shoes. You can speak to your father if you let the spirits have your shoes."

Without warning, the room is filled with a moving block of light. Light radiates from a round ball that sits in the middle of the table, out and up, the light forms cylinders of movement above our heads. The gypsy woman sits opposite me, eyes closed. She chants in a foreign tongue. Her hands are hairless, grotesquely large, with protruding knobby knuckles. They hover above the lights; their shadows loom against the ceiling like wings of scattering pigeons.

Her chant turns into a low long hum, "What is your father's name Emily?" She has to ask me twice. The hum continues as she waits for my response. I am thinking I want to be certain. "Frank," I say.

Her eyes still closed, chanting again. Soon Frank is the only word I recognize.

There is a whirring noise, like a belt whipping in the air. A currency of indistinct sound fills the room. The gypsy says in a long wavering voice, "Frank, is that you?"

Nothing.

"Frank you must speak louder. Emily is here, Emily your daughter. She wants to speak to you." The sounds become less muffled, muted, the whirring slows to a buzz. "He's going to speak to you in a minute, Emily."

We wait. A chill runs through me. My worn knee socks are gathered loosely around my ankles. I pull them up, and they creep back down slowly; goosebumps chill my legs.

In between contours of moving lights and the silence, my eyes search the room for the girl.

At first the voice is inaudible, then for a second it reaches a plateau so loud that I must cover my ears. "Frank." The gypsy woman shouts. "Hurry up, its getting late, little Emily has to go home."

A voice rises out of nowhere; "Hello Emily. I've been waiting a long time for you to come to talk to me." The voice seems lilted, not at all what I expected, more like a woman or that young boy on the radio who sings about his mother's scouring powder. The gypsy reaches over, pats my hand and whispers, "Go on, sweet child talk to your father." I am enthralled with the word father, with the possibilities, the broadness of who he is or might be. I want to say so much but am unsure of what to say.

"Do you remember me?" I ask suddenly open and fearless.

"Oh yes. I remember you well. You were such a sweet baby. You had black curls all over your head. Oh, and then, then there was that little dimple on you chin."

A familiar knot lodges like a bone inside my throat. Suddenly I feel a peculiar urge to weep. To weep the way I know I've wept before, but no longer can remember why.

"Did you like me?" my voice quivers, barely above a whisper.

"Like you? You were the brightest star in my universe."

Even though his voice is odd and uncomfortable, he seems so agreeable, so easy. So I ask, "Why did you go away? Why did you have to die?"

His voice cracks, comes across in waves. "I'm in a much better place." *A better place?* I think, *You left to go to a better place?*

My thoughts are transported, to a time before grandmother came to live with us. I try to stop myself from going there, but it is not in my control:

Woken by a nightmare, its shadow surrounds my crib. Mother enters my room and offers me a sip of her drink. I taste the bitter, spit it out and scream.

"Only bad people have bad dreams, Emily," she says, "what did you do that was bad?"

"Emily, we are losing your father. There isn't much time," the gypsy says impatiently.

Suddenly the heavy humming noise ceases and the lights go out. A shock of quiet surrounds us. The gypsy woman rises from her chair. She blurts words of anger. Her skirt swishes in the darkness of the room, she clicks the lamp switch several times. She mumbles harshly, then kicks open the refrigerator door. A flat moldy medicinal aroma exudes from its dark interior.

"Damn, we've lost our power." I feel her hand on my shoulder. "Come back tomorrow, Emily. You'll be able to talk to your father then." She pats the top of my head, ushers me quickly towards the door and says, "You've made the spirits very happy."

Heading down Broadway in my sockinged feet, I avoid stones, pebbles, puddles of oil and gasoline leaks from cars. It is awkward and tricky yet thoughts of my father transport me easily. I think of the old radio that sits on top of the refrigerator, and realize my father can no longer be that man inside the radio. No longer will I search for him between those glowing amber tubes, afraid that in finding him he will be indistinguishable, obscure, with no real features, like kneaded cookie dough. With this an odd and almost sad feeling swells inside, as if I had gained and lost something at the same time.

When I arrive home my feet are wet, numb with cold. Mother is frantic. Babcia Marishka is still out searching the streets for me. I don't know what to tell mother so I lie and tell her I've lost my shoes. This seems to make her worse. She has to take more pills. For a moment her pills seem more important than I do. She stands by the sink, swallows, holding on to the rim of the sink with both hands; she pauses, motionless, as if any movement would cause the pills not to go down.

She insists on the truth. Where was I? Where are my shoes? I wish Babcia were home. I lie again and tell her someone stole them at school. When she asks who? How? I cannot think of anything, so I tell her the truth.

Mother is stunned by my story. "Those thieves, how could they do this to a small child?" And then, "It isn't fair. What have I done to deserve this? Why must I handle this all by myself?" When I tell her I'm sorry, that I only wanted to speak to my father, she says, "No one can speak to the dead. Dead is dead, Emily. It was all a hoax. A hoax, do you understand?"

When Babcia returns home she is there just long enough to hear the story. She never takes off her coat. She listens to mother then calmly asks me if I know where the gypsy lives. When I tell her they live near Mr. Feldman's drug store, she leaves the house.

Later on, when I take the hard candies from my coat pocket and place them in Mother's old lingerie box under my bed along with my other keepsakes, I hear Babcia in the front room. Her voice tunnels through the railroad flat to the back room, to my bed. She tells Mother the gypsies are gone. Their door was left open; the electricity had been turned off. Mr.

Feldman was there with his flashlight. The only things left behind were some magazines in the store window, and an old mirror hanging in the back room. Mr. Feldman had given them a notice of dispossession three days earlier. They owed him two months rent and had stolen the lock right off the front door.

"This is final Anna." Grandmother said to Mother. A kitchen chair scrapes the floor. "You'll sell whatever furniture you don't want, and the rest we'll make room for in my house. Things are bad now, but they'll only get worse.

"Worse? I'm not worse. Why do you say that?"

"No, Anna, not you. It's the neighborhood, its changing: it's no longer fit to raise a child."

I pull the olive-green woolen army blanket all the way up to my chin. The strangeness of the day weighs upon my body. Mother said I could've been kidnapped. She says I was lucky there were no men there, that I was *only* robbed. Confused, I wonder what gypsy men look like. I feel exhausted, contented, pleased by my boldness; I was unafraid of the gypsy, unafraid of my father's spirit. Without knowing why, and without warning, I begin to cry. Tears roll onto my cheeks; they are quiet tears, the kind I am used to.

Grandmother enters the room, genuflects in front of the bronze crucifix that hangs over the walnut dresser, and sits on my bed. "It's all over now, Emily." She lifts the edge of her soiled apron and wipes my cheeks, "Babcia's here. I won't let anyone hurt you." She smiles. "Oops," a laugh, "I've got some flour on you. But," she looks closer, "it looks like snow."

Babcia always loved the snow. I think of the deep wide sweeping angels she showed me how to make. Her large frame took up the narrow patch of snow between the two apartment buildings, she'd lift herself, lightly — without disturbing her imprint she'd float to her feet as though she were truly <u>the</u> angel. Afterwards she'd looked towards the sky, encouraging snowflakes to fill her dark eyelashes until they looked like white centipedes, and then, mouth opened wide, she'd teach me to eat snowflakes.

I touch my eye to see the snow and a trace of flour is on my finger. Babcia wipes my face with her hands, "From my apron."

"You'll have to wear your old oxfords until we can see about getting you a new pair of shoes."

I never tell her the oxfords are too small, that they push my toes together.

We both pretend to not hear mother's languid voice from the kitchen. "It's worse, it's worse." Over and over, swaying slowly back and forth in the chair the way she's been accustomed to lately.

Although Grandmother Marishka is a large woman, she kneels on my bed with an amazing lightness. She stretches towards the window above me, moves the curtain aside, and raises the Venetian blind. "Did you notice, Emily? Look," she says, "look at the beaver moon."

I don't ask her why it is called the "beaver moon," I just want to sleep. I know she will show me the moon again.

MARISHKA
1920
CHAPTER TWO

It is morning, and raining. Through the small cabin window high over the sink Marishka can see the earth giving up some of its darkness to the sap moon high in the sky. She fills the bottom of Antoni's lunch bucket with drinking water she and the girls pump from the well each afternoon. She is intensely aware of the rain. Familiar, it seems to fit around her like a worn sock. Freezing temperatures have plagued western Pennsylvania over the last month. Now the sound of the rain hitting the window brings warmth and comfort as she reaches for the carving knife.

Slicing into what is left of the ham, she cuts thin slivers, spreading it over a thick piece of bread. The smell of the ham triggers a memory: She is relieved with this baby there is no nausea. With the other two there were endless months of morning sickness. She forks sauerkraut over the ham, then tops it with another piece of bread and wraps it in a coated paper that one of the miner wives has given her. She places the two sandwiches in the top tray of the metal-silver bucket, adds some dried figs and white grapes. Visualizing Antoni's lips puckering from the bitterness of the grapes, she finishes off the bucket with a wedge of cinnamon babka. Since Antoni had been working underground it seemed his appetite had doubled. That first week he'd come home famished, asking her to add something extra to his lunch bucket each day until it grew to its present three levels.

From behind the curtain, a makeshift door to the room where they sleep, she sees movements of Antoni getting dressed. His elbow, his leg, poke against the muted gold fabric; she is reminded of the way their daughter Paulina ceremoniously takes on the job of older sister—wrapping herself up in the curtain, pulling it taut over her open mouth, making animal sounds at her sister Anna. Carefully, Paulina would twist the curtain around Anna's body mummy tight, crying out in delectable glee, as she spun Anna in release.

Marishka lifts a shovel of coal and empties it into the hearth of the old black stove. This small coal stove doesn't do the job. Dampness surrounds them, seeping into the corners and crevices of the high ceiling of the cabin, releasing moisture each morning, as though made active by the movement of human flesh.

She hears Antoni's footsteps, the floorboards creaking behind her. When he goes to kiss her, he misses her cheek and kisses her ear. He picks up the small black shovel he'd found in the outhouse when they'd first moved here three months ago and hands it to her. "Here, use this one," he says. An expression of annoyance on his face.

She forgets to use the smaller shovel: she doesn't know how to pamper herself the way he wants her to. Why should she take more time to fill the stove than is necessary? As a young girl in the old country, working the fields with her mother, she had witnessed pregnant women carrying bushels of potatoes. Their arms extended, hugging the bushels over their bellies, their bellies aiding in their task. Life was reduced to the barest then: She remembers when one woman complained of cramps, the woman thought she had eaten too many kapustas for lunch—and two hours later, deep in the potato field, she gave birth to her first son. It was the harvest of all harvests, Marishka's mother slapping the baby's bottom, the same way she'd slapped a melon to check for ripeness. The new mother reached for her baby; umbilical cord still intact, earth under her fingernails, hands filled with potato dust, she wiped the mucous from the baby's face. Realizing the potato dust dried his flesh, she began to tamp into the earth, gathering more and more dust onto her hand, wiping, spreading the earth over the baby's body. Marishka was barely seven years old at the time, but she still recalled her mother's friend Sonia embracing her as though she had in some way helped to bring this child into the world. The five women formed a circle of hands around the mother and her newborn. "Thank you Virgin Mary for bringing us this joy," they said in a single voice. They laughed as they witnessed the newborn's flesh turn muddy brown.

Women were stronger, less wasteful. No matter what Antoni said, Mariskia knew her body's capabilities — her limitations; she would never be wasteful. Soon there'd be another one to care for, another one to fill her already heavy schedule. How could she waste anything? She stood the small shovel against the coal stove and resolved to fill the oven after Antoni left for work.

After consuming a cup of boiled coffee and a bowl of farina, Antoni, in what has been their daily ritual for the last month, heads for the mudroom where the children sleep. The girls are too young to be left alone while Marishka drives with Antoni to work. He swaddles the girls in two heavy woolen army blankets and carries them into the kitchen. This crude intrusion of being lifted from bed, from the very spot that warmed their bodies, out into a cold dark morning, no longer seemed to disturb them. Anna in her sleep wiggles herself into a comfortable position. Paulina, awake, looking forward to the rocking of the car, languishes in her semi-dream state, murmuring the word "car," pushing Anna's body away from hers with her feet, making more room for herself to snuggle against her father's chest.

The rain is coming down hard. Antoni carries the girls, Marishka holds the lunch bucket in one hand. The water at the bottom squishes back and forth making it difficult to keep steady. In her other hand she holds a flashlight, guiding them in the early morning darkness to the little bridge where Boris's car is parked. Boris had been a good friend from the start; the moment he learned Antoni and Marishka were born in Poland, just beyond the mountain in the village next to where he was born, he became their big brother. Having seniority at the mines, Boris didn't begin his shift until four hours later. It was Marishka's job to drive Boris' car back so that it would be there when he woke.

Marishka learned to drive on Antoni and Boris's day off; it was Easter Sunday when she sat next to Boris in his car. "Watch the way I move the shift. At the same time you push in the clutch." Antoni was with the girls at the cabin. When she and Boris arrived at the mouth of mine 12-D, Boris said, "Okay. Now you try." With great reluctance she got behind the wheel, and after a half hour of bucking the car back and forth, stalling over and over, she managed to move ahead slowly. Boris was patient and showed no signs of stress except for his lighting one cigarette after another. The four miles back to the cabin seemed like hours. The road was rugged, full of potholes. The frame of the old Ford shook violently, causing the car to stall. Weeks later when Marishka felt more comfortable driving she noticed how isolated the road was, only an occasional miner passing now and then. At one point, she thought about being stranded with the girls. She felt herself lose her breath, *I can't do this*, she thought, but knew this was the only way for Antoni to get to work. She wasn't afraid of driving she was afraid of the car stalling and not being able to start it again; of being out in the cold with the children, but then she'd remind herself of Boris; if his car wasn't there when he woke, he would come with help.

The rain is even heavier when she pulls into Boris' parking space. The girls are sound asleep on the back seat. She carries them into the cabin one by one to their beds. Knowing the girls will sleep a while longer. Marishka hurries to prepare a glass of tea for herself and removes the map from under their bed and places it on the mattress. It is not really a map, but she likes the word "map." It was one of the first words she had learned in this country. She unwraps the paintings, carefully unfolding the yellowed bed-sheet from the corners. As a young girl she had begun to write in a journal. Dissatisfied with her way with words, her lack of expression, she tore out the pages and began to record the events of her life in drawings. She was a good artist — she had been told by many in the old country — even by her brother Felix whose ability to paint and compose music had won him a scholarship to the Academy of Arts in Krakow the year he turned twelve.

When finished with the drawings, she had intended to give them to Antoni, yet the more she worked, the more she realized she would never be finished — they would only be finished when their lives were over. Now she thinks she will show them to him after the new baby is born, or perhaps she'll wait for an important birthday.

Antoni knew she was up to something. Late in the evening, on a day when she had more time to work than usual, the fumes from the orange lacquer would linger in the cabin and she'd have to boil up some cabbage soup. Or sometimes Paulina would cry, wanting to draw with a piece of charcoal that Marishka had hidden. Then there were the large pieces of white-textured cardboard the grocer's wife would ask him to bring to her. She didn't know how long she could keep it from him, but she savored the anticipation, the wondrous look she would see in his eyes as he feasted upon her drawings.

At first she miscalculated; the images were too large. She had to scale it down gradually. Now it seemed each time she saw what she had painted, she was intrigued, she found herself reliving moments: Her grandmother's mountaineer home, where she'd stayed with her mother and brother, her wedding night, the mattress filled with fragrant hay, the mountainous fawn-yellow comforter stuffed with bird feathers. She could almost feel the Tatra Mountain air, always cool and crisp. Smell the babkas baking in the oven. Her mother sits on a stool in the outside kitchen churning goat cheese, wearing a blue and white flowered dress, her apron grayed from wear. Over the doorway to the kitchen, above her mother's head, hangs a framed picture of Jesus with his heart exposed.

Marishka removes a water-colored stained cloth from another drawing. Only the first four letters of the S.S. PULASKI are visible as the ship heels and dips its bow into the silver-black waters of the Atlantic. The storm rages for days, decks are barren, lifeboats dangle along the body of the ship like legs of a captive spider. In another painting the sea is still, like a block of ice. The ship, as if planted on the ocean floor, bolts upright, exposing a thin strip of the black painted hull. Marishka on the gray deck stands in between Antoni and her brother Felix. She wears a white, hand embroidered blouse, and a wine colored burlap skirt. The shawl wrapped around her shoulders is royal blue with large cabbage roses. It is the last gift she'd received from her mother. Felix, smaller in statue than Marishka, holds onto a railing, his violin on the floor of the deck wedged between his feet. Antoni's camel-haired Fedora is tilted to one side. In his hand he holds his Polish-English dictionary. The drawing is primitive, flat, as all three seem to beam off into the distance towards the statue of Liberty, towards America.

She recalls the terror she'd felt when they were detained in Ellis Island. Women were separated from their husbands and fathers. Uniformed men speaking another language, words she didn't understand. Some of the shipmates were pushing and shoving. Doctors, nurses, poking, pulling through her thick curls with a fine toothcomb. A large man in blue uniform with a red-tipped mustache had chalk-marked Felix's small black overcoat with the letter H and led him to another part of the building. Poor Felix. The villagers had thought him odd with his oyster pale skin, his small hands and feet, the time he spent wanting to be alone. That night Marishka prayed for him, asking God to give Felix a chance, to allow him to stay in America, but her prayers went unanswered.

Marishka and Antoni slept in a long narrow room. White-sheeted cots were lined up on both sides of the walls, the bunks only inches apart. Down the center of the long room was a thick wall of luggage; carpet and straw bags, wooden trunks, leather and tapestry mixed with corrugated boxes, piled haphazardly, bringing chaos to the sterile white room.

After a day and a half on Ellis Island, Felix was still held in isolation. Antoni spoke to an officer with the help of his dictionary and discovered that the H meant there was a problem with Felix's heart, and that he would be returned to Poland on the next ship. Marishka was frightened she could taste the fear. She sat on the cot and felt herself choke up with tears. "Let's go home, please Antoni." She wanted to return with Felix, return to the familiar, to her mother's arms. Antoni held her to his chest and swayed back and forth; repeating, "It will be fine. I promise you." He had rocked her into acceptance; and as difficult as it was, she knew her place was next to her husband.

Marishka wants to build new memories. She begins to draw herself sitting next to the coal stove; she thinks she will have Anna sit on her lap, and Paulina will stand behind them brushing out Marishka's hair, the way she so often pleads to do. She feels her round tight belly, her sore, hot, bruised breasts. She thinks this one will be a boy. The girls never had hiccups. How odd it was to feel a hiccup in her stomach. At first it reminded her of the movie theatre in New York, of the little white ball on the screen that bounced over the words of a song. But as the baby grew, the hiccups changed. Still rhythmic, but now it seemed that the little white ball had become transparent, more like a bubble floating in liquid, darting about in her stomach, as though it had a life of its own.

Marishka puts down her charcoal stick when she hears the wild dog whimpering outside. The girls still asleep, she has time to feed him. She hurries to the door. He hasn't been around for days. The dog's hind legs, backside and tail are practically hairless, as though only half his body had contracted mange. Some of the sores have scabs, some have gotten smaller. He stands at a distance, almost near the bridge. She can tell by the way he whimpers and moves his backside in a dramatic plea for food that today he is in a good mood. She rushes back to the kitchen and removes stale pieces of bread from the tin breadbox. She struggles with the lid on the jar of bacon fat. Her hands are strong. She has a tendency to seal everything too tightly. When the lid is loosened, she smears a layer of bacon fat over the bread. Today the dog is shy; he will not come close. Last week he'd stood in the iced pathway to their door. He wouldn't accept a bite to eat; he just barked and growled until Boris, on his way to work, tossed stones at him. Marishka calls to the timid dog as she walks towards him. The rain is fine, like a smoky mist. It cushions the sound of his whimpers. "This is for you," she says. "C'mon. For you."

The dog stops whining. His body arches, he scuffs backwards, his rope-like tail hanging between his hind legs like another leg, adding to his grotesqueness. Placing the bread on the ground, she turns around in time to see the two girls in their nightgowns running towards her, Paulina crying out that she wants to feed the dog. "Later," Marishka says. Not really trusting the animal, she throws the last piece of bacon-fatted bread as far away from the house as she can, and the three of them watch as the dog rushes towards it.

It is a rare occasion where Antoni and Boris have the same day off. But on Wednesday they gather at the kitchen table, Boris' silver flask filled with whiskey stands between them. Antoni enjoys these sessions with Boris; the heated political discussions, the putting down of the crew bosses. The pull of relaxation, of feeling free for a couple of hours. Antoni's feet extend, rest on another chair. Boris sits across the table, pouring whiskey into his beer. When Boris starts his hacking cough, it lasts a minute or two. Antoni takes this as an opportunity to playfully slap Marishka on the backside, to interrupt the girls playing, attacking them with tickles. He takes Marishka's shawl from the hook next to their curtained doorway; pretending to be a woman, he wraps it around his waist and bumps and grinds his way across the room. Paulina and Anna play baking on the floor. They have their mother's bowl and wooden spoons and measuring cup spread before them. Antoni dances around them. "Ba da boom; ba da boom," he sings. They laugh and giggle; Paulina becomes so excited she rushes to her father, grips his thrusting thigh and sinks her teeth into it.

By three o'clock in the afternoon they are still talking shop, about the accident list. This week a new safety inspector visited the mines. The men had gathered in the washhouse. The inspector said, "You probably already know that mining is the most dangerous occupation in the country, but did you know that you fellows are working in one of the most dangerous mines in the United States?" He spoke about how many square feet of air per man per minute was needed. "Watch, be aware of worn out cables and safety props, be sure you use your masks properly." He made Boris angry. Boris had been in the mines for 15 years. He didn't need any snot-nose trying to screw up his job. Marishka, making bread, hated talk of the mines. She visualized the small narrow black tunnels; Antoni crouched, kneeling in water, the roof only inches above his head, his elbows and sometimes his back scraping the walls as he'd scooped up the coal. The scars on his back: she had cleansed the long deep gashes, swallowed hard, applied ointment, always pretended they were nothing.

She had tried drawing him in the tunnels, but couldn't. She had never been below. He had never said the conditions were unhealthy—but she knew. She was there once, waiting at the mouth of the mine to take him home. When he stepped out she felt the darkness peel from him. His back seemed to arch upwards, his body shuddering from the light that touched him. After that time she thought of Antoni as some sort of mushroom, growing in the blackness. Once, after a particular heavy rain she went into the woods to pick mushrooms. She dug near the roots of the trees and found the mushrooms hiding in the darkness. Pulling them up from the darkness, she placed them in her spread apron. Walking back to the cabin she felt a small tremor, a movement so much like a shudder. She wrapped her apron close around the mushrooms, almost caressing them, shielding them from the shock of light.

Boris announces he is going back to his cabin to get more whiskey. Anna wants to go for a walk with him. Antoni is feeling good. "Go on Cureczka," he says, "go with your uncle."

Marishka is kneading dough. The dough is yellow and sticky. She may have added too many eggs. She takes a handful of flour and continues to knead. She pulls and pushes the dough; it clings to her hands and fingers like a webbed foot of a wood duck. Antoni is up against her back, nuzzling, kissing her neck. He suggests he bring Paulina over to Boris's cabin. Although Marishka laughs and says that he's had too much to drink, she loves the way he feels against her, the way he moves the collar of her dress, kissing her shoulder. Apparently Paulina realizes that something is going on without her, so she drops the eggbeater on the floor and rushes between them. Just as Antoni swoops Paulina up in his arms, there is a sound outside that enters the cabin like thunder.

Outside, Boris stands with a shotgun looped over his shoulder. His eyes are large, wild. He says, "He could've bitten Anna. He was going for her." Anna is crouched next to the rusted steel drum, close to where Boris stands. She is wailing softly, her face muffled in her dress. Marishka rushes towards Anna. A milky fog hovers over them, yet through its opal density she sees the dog, blown up against a tree stump, blood oozing from his rear end. She hugs Anna tightly in her arms. A strong smell of sulfur lies in the air. She dashes back into the cabin with the children and watches from the cracked doorway. Antoni takes the gun from Boris. Holding the shotgun, he opens the barrel and lets the casings fall onto the ground. He picks them up and throws them, one by one, as far as he can into the woods.

Boris is pleading; "You don't know how it feels — to want something so much — you're willing to die for it." He staggers, catching his balance.

"That dog wanted something. Do you understand? He was ready to die for what he wanted." Antoni swings the shotgun over his arm, and holds Boris by the shoulders, guiding him back to his cabin. Marishka hears Boris's voice, lifting off into the fog. "That's the kind of dog I'd want to be. Brave dog. Good boy."

A few days before the arrival of spring, Marishka prepares a small patch of land for vegetables. Turning the earth, she feels her blood pumping fast through her body, a sense of freedom fills her. She knows that the pumping of her blood will be good for the baby, make the baby stronger.

When she informs the girls that a general clean up of the yard must be done each spring, they cheer, jump up and down on the small pile of dried leaves, and fight over the rake with the broken handle. Marishka watches as Paulina nears the tree stump where the dog died: She squats by the stump, examining it as if looking for traces of the dog. The natural markings of the bark have become stained with the dog's blood. Marishka calls out to distract her, "Paulina, come, look what I have for you."

It is still early in the day when two men drive up. From across the bridge Marishka recognizes Boris. The other man is a stranger. She drops her shovel, wipes her hands on her apron, smoothes her hair back off her forehead and checks to see if the comb in her bun is intact. When Boris's face comes into view, a sudden urgency grabs hold of her, and she rushes the children into the cabin.

It was so simple. Antoni had been in the shaft alone. A pulley snapped and struck his temple with such a force that his body was thrown several feet. They found him wedged in an oval cavity, folded, broken at the waist. Boris said, "He was like a limp puppet."

As the men leave, Boris asks them to wait a moment. He embraces Marishka, and says, "I must go and help them to bring Antoni back to you." She hates the sound of his voice, the way it cracks and chokes words. She wants to hit him, to smash his mouth so he can never speak again, but instead she pushes him away and goes into the house. She heats leftover chicken soup and fills the children's brown bowls halfway. She thinks no matter what they must eat. Yes, the house still must be clean and the children must eat. She cuts two slices of bread and lays them next to the bowls. While the girls have their soup, she goes out into the woods behind the house and begins to tear branches from the evergreens. With her bare hands she bends and breaks the branches, ripping them from their tough bark, the pine needles pinching, cutting into her skin, but she feels nothing. Her hands covered with blood, she gathers the boughs of evergreen and brings them to the cabin door, dropping them on the doorstep. Inside, she searches through drawers until she comes upon her black slip. She cuts her slip into long strips. Outside, she gathers the evergreen branches. Using the strips like ribbon, she ties the branches together. The cuts on her hands are still bleeding, leaving blood on the black ribbons. When the wreath is done, she takes what is left of her slip and ties a bow at the top. She hangs the wreath on a rusted nail outside the cabin door.

Marishka can't seem to bring herself to get out of bed. The baker's wife takes the children for the day, and two of the other miner's wives come to help. Their presence shapes the enormity of her tragedy. She hears them in her kitchen, moving about, touching her things — the oddness of the rhythm they bring to her home, their low whispers make her feel as if she is drugged.

Elsa, who had taught her to speak English, comes into the bedroom and boldly sits on Marishka's bed. She holds Marishka in her arms, rocking her, telling her what a great man Antoni was, and how she remembered the first time they met, how handsome and strong-minded he was. Marishka doesn't like this stranger in their bedroom. She's absorbing Antoni's odor. She takes Antoni's pillow and covers it protectively with the blanket. She wants to say, "Get out." But for some reason she doesn't. She knows Elsa just wants to help, but on one can help.

"Do you remember?" Elsa asks. "You were so determined, both of you, to learn English. He offered to pay me two of your babka's a week. Remember how fat I got? Marishka — please, you must get out of bed."

Her hand gently moves over Marishka's forehead, along the side of her face, forcing her to face Elsa. "Antoni, he's here, watching you. Do it for him." Just as Marishka thinks, *Why must I get out of bed?* She bolts up and rushes to the tin barrel where they deposit their dirty clothes. She gathers Antoni's shirts and pants, his socks and undershirt he took off last night, and brings them into bed with her. She inhales the undershirt, all the clothes, "Please, Elsa, I want to be alone." Speaking into Antoni's clothes, her words are muffled. She records his scent, records the ashy odor, the yeasty scent of his armpits. She cannot believe she still smells him, his essence still alive, she pushes Elsa from her bed. "Please I must be alone."

It is hours later when the other miners' wives return the children to her, when Paulina comes into the bedroom holding Anna by the hand, standing solemnly at the side of her bed, that Marishka feels a small spark. In a widening effort to behave, they do not speak; there is only the involuntary twitching and shuffling of their small feet. Only then, when Marishka sees their small vulnerable faces glowing towards their mother's approval, does she realize that not only has she lost her Antoni, but that they too are to live without him. She motions them to get in bed with her. One child under each arm, she cries, telling them they'll be okay. All three of them hold on to one another, the room echoing with the sound of tears. Hugging fiercely — grasping what is left of what she loves the most; Marishka believes her adrenaline has reached the one in her womb — she senses the unborn infant's mourning; and visualizes all four of them as some sort of crucifix pinned to her bed, one spiritual body moving through a long narrow tunnel, a dark space bloated with pain and love all at the same time.

Two days after Antoni is buried, Boris drives Marishka to Miners Hospital. Five hours later she gives birth to Eva. The baby is premature; she will have to stay a week longer for nourishment. Each day when Boris leaves for work, he drives Marishka and the children to the hospital. The children play in the hospital corridor. In between feedings, she reads to them from an old torn book of fairy tales she finds at the nurses' station. The nurses are surprised she can read. Marishka gives Paulina all her charcoal pencils. The hospital is so poor there are few blankets to cover the baby. One thin flannel blanket doesn't seem to be enough. She places her royal blue shawl over the baby's body; the cabbage roses loom larger than the babies head. One of the roses lies across her chest, giving off the illusion of opening and closing with the baby's quick faint breaths. Marishka feels blinded by the shawl — its presence oversteps some boundary in the bare hospital room. The black and silver rosary beads lie at the foot of the crib. They are for baby Eva, not for her. How can she pray? It would be a long time before she'd pray again — if ever. How could He have just taken Antoni away? She yearns to be back in the potato fields, to be in the arms of her mother. She sits by the baby's steel crib, her mouth gaping in silence. Paulina and Anna play in the corridor. No nurses or doctors are to be found, only the occasional echo of a door closing in the distance.

EMILY
1955
CHAPTER THREE

Marjorie Housmann and her friends always manage to find me at three o'clock. Some days she'd pull my braids all the way to the five-and-dime, but today she says she had a hard time at school and she orders Jenny Corolla to not let go of them. I prefer Jenny to hold my braids because she doesn't yank and tug them the way Marjorie does, she just holds onto them.

When we arrive at the store, Marjorie watches me from outside through the plate glass window, while Jenny and Theresa clown around, bumping against the store window. I walk through the aisles, hesitate by the glassware and the skeins of colorful wools, pretend to look for something in particular. I eye Marjorie from the cosmetic counter. *Go away you stupid witches, Mr. Janowski will get suspicious.* In front of me tubes of lipstick are lined in rows of purple, pink, green, and yellow like flavored lollipops. Just as I slip a marbleized purple tube into my pocket Mr. Janowski shouts, "Get away from that window." My heart races, and quickly I walk to where the sewing notions are and pretend to look for safety pins.

Mr. Janowski walks towards me. "Can I help you find something, Emily?"

"A. . . I need a pin." I said, "A safety pin."

"Just one?" Mr. Janowski with his huge arms and small head towers over me. "We don't sell just one pin." He shakes a package of pins at me.

"It's okay," I say, and start to leave the store.

"No. Wait," he says, as he places his wide palm against the back of my neck. "Come with me. Let's see what we can do about this situation."

My body tingles with fear. I break out in a sweat and feel about to cry. At the cash register, he opens a drawer and takes out a safety pin.

"Here we are. One pin." He smiles. I feel the blood rush to my face.

"Thank you." I take the pin and back away.

"Say hello to your Grandmother. Oh,—and tell your friends not to lean against the window."

The bell on Mr. Janowski's door rings louder than I remember. I run to the end of the block, and when I turn the corner Marjorie and friends are right behind me. I hand the marbleized purple tube of lipstick to her.

"This isn't poppy," she screams at me. "Now I'll have to slap you."

I am cornered against the building, but still move forward to run just as Marjorie's hand breaks against my cheek. "This is a warning," she says, "next time get it right." I stand there holding the side of my face, fighting back the tears as she and Theresa and Jenny Corolla walk, run, and then skip down the street.

When I arrive home, standing on the screened-in-porch I hear the rare sound of laughter coming from the kitchen, and remember that Great Uncle Felix was visiting today. I place my school bag down on the gray slated window ledge next to grandmother's African Violets, and crouch beneath the window to catch my breathe. The freshly watered Violets fill my nostrils with a mossy aroma of wet earth. Rising slightly to peer through the window I see Mother slouching at the kitchen table, while grandmother Marishka sits next to her brother Felix, her powder blue eyes fixed on his face, intent on his every word.

A heaping bowl of chrusciki and a plate of puffed pastries from Montroses' bakery is on the kitchen table. That familiar after-school hunger rumbled on in my stomach, yet I linger, not wanting to go in the house. What I want most is the courage to beat Marjorie Housmann to a pulp. I could still feel the slap stinging, burning my cheek.

The large closed-in porch hugs two sides of the house. Grandmother calls them the 'north' and 'west' porches as if the house were so huge that unless you knew the direction you wouldn't find them. She spends lots of time sweeping corner-to-corner, pruning and caring for the plants that tumble down from the broad otherwise pasty-white ceiling. Once the storm windows are replaced with screens, the West porch turns into our summer veranda. On hot muggy nights I'm allowed to sleep out here. The night air thick with the sound of Cicadas. I would imagine them huge, kindly, as if I were riding their backs, their small jerky movements rocking me off to sleep. Sleeping outdoors began even back in Philadelphia. Despite Mother's protest, Grandmother would take me to sleep with her on the fire escape; she'd roll out the cot mattress on the iron grating and we'd lay there. We never heard insects but sometimes we saw stars. And there was always the traffic, the rhythm of the cars, the fire engines, and the sirens goading us on towards sleep.

Just when I thought I was doing a fine job of hiding, Mother catches sight of me. Her upper body appears through the kitchen Dutch door. "Emily, what on earth are you doing there?"

I stand, straightened my skirt, knowing I'll have to meet Uncle Felix.

"Look at what you've done to your face. Leaning against the window ledge."

Once inside the kitchen Babcia Marishka puts her rough hand against my burning cheek, and gives me a 'we'll talk about this later' look.

Grandmother Marishka had begun preparing for Uncle Felix's visit days before his arrival. I helped her polish the silver coffee urn, and just in case he didn't drink coffee, she took out her favorite gold-rimmed glasses for tea. We had prepared the spare bedroom.

Grandmother taught me how to make hospital corners on the sheets, pulling them tight. She asked me to fluff the down pillow, and then covered it with her best hand-embroidered pillowcase. From the closet in the spare room she removed a large box. She had dusted the blue, faded to gray, box, and put it at the foot of Uncle Felix's bed.

When I asked what was in the box, she said it was something that once belonged to my grandfather, and now it was to be a gift for Great Uncle Felix.

"No. No," she grinned. "You can see it, only after Uncle Felix does." And then she added that in the old country Great Uncle Felix and Grandfather Antoni had been close friends. "They were like brothers," she said, her eyes gleamed, glazed by the memory.

It was strange, meeting Great Uncle Felix, the man in the photograph the man who I once pretended was my father. Without his violin and exotic trunk he seemed plain. His face is white, doughy, and looked, I imagined, the way that tiny man who once lived inside Mother's radio did. Marishka had always said Uncle Felix was frail. And frail he is; his fingertips feel like feathers against my chin.

He hands me a small but heavy package with streams of curled purple ribbons cascading over its sides. Awkwardly, I accept the gift. Looking at Grandmother, her expression is proud, beaming, she gives me a nod of approval, and so I begin to unwrap the package. Inside is a brown leather book with a brass lock and a key hung from a string.

Great Uncle Felix looks at me, his eyes large and round, peculiar, yet kind. "Your Babcia told me you like to write." His English is slow, but exact.

I unlock the diary and turn the blank pages. A scent of jasmine lifts from the book. It reminds me of the Midnight Jasmine soap I stole for Marjorie Housmann. Its fragrance still lingers in the front pocket of my school bag.

"It's beautiful," I say, and see Grandmother eyeing me, so I move close to kiss his cheek. He pulls me in towards him. His body is stiff, and he smells fresh and crisp, yet warm like the pages that come out of my teacher's new mimeograph machine.

"Uncle Felix can only stay the night. He must meet up with the Budapest Symphony Orchestra in Montreal the day after tomorrow," Babcia says proudly.

When Mother excuses herself and leaves the room, Grandmother and Great Uncle Felix begin to speak in Polish. Their voices louder than usual. I know they are talking about me by the way Babcia's glance is so visibly turned from me. Uncle Felix soon validates my feeling, nodding at me as though I was participating in the conversation. When Mother returns to the kitchen, fresh red lipstick dominates her face. Uncle Felix says to her, "It would be all right for your mother to come with me to Chicago for a few days. Yes?"

Before Mother could answer, Marishka raises her voice at him in Polish.

Mother apparently understands some Polish: She wipes the edge of the kitchen table with her used napkin. "Go. If you want to, go," Mother says now looking off in the distance. "Emily will be in school. Surely I can care for my own daughter."

It has been apparent to me for some time; I was not allowed to be alone with Mother. I wasn't certain whether it was because Grandmother Marishka felt Mother was incapable of caring for me, or simply that Mother is incapable of being alone. Whatever it was, I was always pleased by this unspoken decision. I learned early on to leave things alone; not to ask questions that might bring discomfort to the family.

The discussion would continue. One thing that was settled upon was Great Uncle Felix would send grandmother a recording of the concert whether she attended or not.

When Aunt Eva enters the house, she greets everyone with warm hugs. Waiting my turn, I watch as she and Uncle Felix hold one another for an exceptionally long time. It is one of those times when Grandmother stands proudly, her eyes water, her wide fingers clutch her crumbled handkerchief, entwined across her stomach against her spotless apron.

Unlike Mother, Aunt Eva is a big-busted woman, matronly, with a flair for exotic clothing. She has always greeted me with the kind of affection that took her breath away, and this day is no different. Aunt Eva smothers me against the density of her breast.

She unwraps her 'special' homemade cheese babka from the brown paper wrap and pushes her fingers against the center of the cake, testing to see if it is still warm. The table in the dining room is prepared with a lace tablecloth. Babcia presents an old olive oil bottle filled with a clear liquid she calls schnapps. She lines up little shot glasses. Keibasia, cut into small pieces are placed on the blue and cream china. Chunks of goat cheese and olives are on another plate.

Chopin is playing on the record player all afternoon. When Mother says she thought we all had enough of Chopin, we can't agree more. Babcia Marishka says, "Anna, how can you say such a thing? Everyone loves listening to Chopin. She turns to Uncle Felix. "Don't you?"

Mother is flowing over with the festivities; she takes another sip from her shot glass and says laughingly, "Mother, I'm sure Uncle Felix wishes he had brought some of his own records."

Uncle Felix laughs. "I have always thought my sister enjoyed too much Chopin."

Marishka says, "Emily. I want to tell Emily." Turning to me she says, "Did I ever speak to you about Frederic Chopin?"

Mother shifts in her chair. Smiling, she whispers to Aunt Eva who is sitting next to me, "Here we go again, another Chopin concert."

Watching my mother and her sister together, giggling, obviously sharing something from their past, lifts me, gives me a sense of belonging. I've forgotten about Marjorie. I feel washed with love, and think why can't it always be this way. Yet I know it is just a matter of time before Mother will cause some kind of chaos, but I quickly move from that thought.

Marishka hushes their giggles. She pours another round of schnapps and hesitates when she comes to Mother's glass, but then pours and says, "Now let me tell Emily." She places the bottle on the table. "There is a church in Warsaw. . ." I've heard this before. " . . . a beautiful Baroque church. Inside there is a special sealed urn." Her voice breathless, circles around us like one of Chopin's chords. "Inside this urn lies the heart of Frederic Chopin." She sits back in the chair and takes a deep breath. So much bigger than Uncle Felix, she seems the man of the house. "Chopin was born in Poland. His wish, when he died, was to leave his heart in the land to which he had dedicated all his music."

"Yes. This is all true," interrupts Uncle Felix, "but I must say that in the past, I too have grown impatient with your mother's Chopin." He turns to Marishka, "Remember when we were children, how I'd sing out the names of other composers, trying to blend my voice with the movements? 'Vivaldi, Beethoven, Wagner.'" He laughs, "I, myself, do not like repetition. But yes, I too have a special place in my heart for Chopin."

"See." Marishka nods triumphantly to her daughters.

"And once more," Uncle Felix adds, "I am happy to see my sister hasn't changed."

I am bubbling over with warmth, the festivity of family, the laughter, and the memories that would someday be mine. Everyone is laughing at something Aunt Eva says when I blurt out eagerly, "This is my whole family. My whole family is here, together." Suddenly it was as though the chandelier had fallen smack in the middle of the dining table. I look around. The mood changed. Silence. Did I say something wrong? No one speaks. I don't know what to do. Is it because I left out Aunt Eva's dentist husband, George, and George Junior who had his first job after school helping his uncle cut up chickens' parts for his fast-food restaurant?

Aunt Eva looks up at me.

"I'm sorry," I say, "I didn't mean to leave out Uncle George and . . . ."

"That's okay, honey, hush." Aunt Eva says patting my hand. And then in her most cheerful voice she says, "Lets get out the old photographs."

"Be careful with them," Grandmother Marishka says.

I was about to lie for the sake of Aunt Eva: I've never felt Uncle George and George Junior were part of our family. They are distant, so uninvolved. They never visit or share with the family. And whenever I'm forced to visit with them they're always so polite to one another, so perfect that it makes me feel self-conscious. Whatever I'd say or do always seemed out of place.

Suddenly, I feel some kind of grief for Aunt Eva. Even though she has her son and husband, she seems alone. Her devotion to family and her threads of kindness summons an odd sympathy from me. All of this rushes through me as Aunt Eva hands me a photograph of a long dead relative. I scan the yellowed tinged photograph quickly, then place it on the table. Without further haste I throw my arms around Aunt Eva, and press my face into her neck and chest. Silence holds the room again until Aunt Eva releases me from the grip. Aunt Eva is flushed, apparently more embarrassed than touched by affection, she quickly reaches for another photograph.

Babcia continues to conduct the viewing of the photographs as though it is a sacred ceremony. The ones pasted on black paper with their frayed edges are the oldest. Slowly, solemnly she unties the black ribbon, and passes the photographs around, page by page. Eager, anxiously awaiting any questions. The only one who ever really asked questions was me. I always asked about the photograph from Poland where her Great Grandfather sat in what looked like a nice comfortable chair, while her Great Grandmother had to stand alongside of him. "Why wasn't your grandmother sitting?" No matter what I'd ask, I'd love that faraway look Babcia got whenever she'd transport herself back to Poland. She'd say, "That's the way it was—the old country." Always smiling.

But today, with Great Uncle Felix there, it was different. That faraway look had been in her eyes all afternoon.

Later that evening, before Aunt Eva goes home she has to help Mother to bed. It is already clear to me that Mother should not drink.

Grandmother always told me it was my mother's medication, and in being told this, I too came to believe it really was her medication.

When Aunt Eva is long gone and I am supposed to be asleep, I hear Marishka and Uncle Felix in the spare room next to mine. I scurry into my closet, and press my ear up against the wall. They speak in Polish, then English, about people I don't know. They laugh. Quietly, I sneak out into the darkened hallway, and watch them through a crack in the door. Uncle Felix is no longer wearing his suit jacket, revealing his dark blue suspenders. His matching blue tie is still in place. "A model of a well-groomed man," that's what Marishka always said about him. Uncle Felix is about to sit on the bed, and almost crush the box Marishka had placed there earlier. Grandmother quickly saves the box from being crushed, then walks to the other side of the room where I can no longer see her. She continues to talk in Polish to Uncle Felix. I see Great Uncle Felix shaking his head, acknowledging what she is saying. His head hung as though he is staring at something on his lap. The lamplight shines on his receding hairline. His eyelids are deep and clear, and suddenly I realize what causes his appearance to seem so odd, is that he has no eyelashes. I recall the Netherlandish paintings in my art workbook and see Uncle Felix so like one of those paintings, his eyes deep bowls with hairless hoods.

When Marishka comes into view again, she hands the box to Uncle Felix and blocks my view of him. All I see is his shiny black shoes and black socks beneath the wide hemline of Grandmother's dress. Silence haunted by the past fills the moment until Grandmother embraces him, her upper torso arching, she holds her brother to her stomach and cries. Uncle Felix rises from her embrace. He too has tears. He places a camel-colored fedora on his head. Looking into the mirror that hangs over the maple dresser, he positions the hat on his head, all the while smiling through his tears. Uncle Felix then removes it and embraces his sister once more. I can't help but think if Uncle Felix were an inch shorter his head would be nuzzled right against Grandmother's breast, the same way I was each time Aunt Eva hugged me.

Feeling out of bounds like the thief that I learned to be, I continue to watch them through the crack in the door. Making up for time lost. Crying, laughing, grieving for all those years they hadn't been together.

Perhaps it is the small space, the funnel view of what I am witnessing that intensifies the moment. I swallow hard, and begin to choke on unexpected tears. The moment takes me the same way a perfect chord of music lifts me and makes me feel buoyant for an instant.

Sitting there on the cold hardwood floor, it occurs to me that I want a sister or brother. No, I long for a sister or brother. Without being able to verbalize it, I sense what I'm witnessing is the kind of love that floods you with light. The kind of love that fills you with power. A power that can send a Marjorie Housmann fleeing, begging for forgiveness. A power that allows you anything you want.

The next morning, Grandmother Marishka and Uncle Felix walk me to school. Marishka always says it's the fresh air that makes her healthy. She tells Great Uncle Felix that she still walks three miles a day. "I've been so hungry lately, now I know why," she says, "did either one of you notice the Hunger moon last night?"

I know Grandmother is joking, but her brother seems to take her seriously. "The Hunger moon? Doesn't that have to do with not having any crops to harvest? Isn't that why they call it the hunger moon?"

"Yes," she squeezes my shoulder, "but it also makes you hungry. Right, Emily?" We both laugh.

My school is at the end of Schoolhouse Road, six streets from Greenstone Boulevard, where our house is. Knowing the embarrassment of walking to school with a Grandmother at your side, Grandmother usually walks only the four blocks, then turns down Merrick Avenue, leaving me to walk the last two streets by myself. But on this day, I feel the opposite of embarrassed, if anything I feel a glimmer of pride being with Great Uncle Felix and Grandmother Marishka. When we get to the Merrick Avenue, Grandmother bends to kiss me goodbye, but I say, "Why don't you walk me to school?"

Grandmother looks both surprised and pleased. "Okay." She turns to Uncle Felix, "Can you go a few more blocks?"

In his competitive spirit, Uncle Felix says, "Anytime. Anyplace."

They talk about a concert in Rome. Uncle Felix calls it a musical extravaganza. "The Budapest Symphony Orchestra is only one of the many orchestras invited to play." He says.

Near the school yard I see Marjorie Housman walking with Teresa Corolla and Jenny Murphy. They are giggling and laughing, pointing at me. I pretend not to see them. Feeling a bit defiant, and not caring about the consequences, I walk on with my nose tilted upwards.

When I leave school at three o'clock, I try slipping away without Marjorie Housmann seeing me. When Marjorie calls my name I feel as though D-day has arrived.

"We're going to Janowski's today, birdbrain. Let's see if you can get it right. Move your ass." Marjorie says leaning against a parking sign that reads SCHOOL BUSES ONLY. Jenny Murphy stands next to her, waving for Theresa Corella to join them. I start to walk in the opposite direction. "Hey, Pollack. You hear me? Move your backside over here."

I feel the short hairs on my body rise; bloated with fright, I yell, "No," amazed that the word came from my own mouth.

"No?" Marjorie spit.

Theresa Corella says, "Let me get her," and Marjorie lowers her voice and whispers to them.

Two blocks from the school, and out of breath, I stop to rest against the bank building. They are nowhere in sight yet I know it can't be this easy. When I turn the corner Marjorie grabs my upper arm and throws me against the building. I feel my head, like a ragdolls, flop against the cement blocks. The three of them surround me. "Now," she says. "Just for saying 'No,' you're gonna have to get us three lipsticks today."

"Yeah, you little bitch," chorus Jenny and Teresa. I force myself to think of Uncle Felix and Babcia in that slot of light. *No,* I think, *I belong somewhere. So what if I don't have a father. I have a family.* The thought is like a single glowing cell moving through my body, a magnificent cell that seems to empower me. "No, Marjorie," I say. "Never again. I won't do it."

Marjorie strikes me several times before I feel my own arms strike back. The more I hit back the more powerful I grow. But not powerful enough. Theresa grabs at my blouse,

ripping and popping the two top buttons. Arms flying, feet kicking, scratching, hair pulling. The skin on my face and arms is hot with bruises. I try to get close enough to Marjorie to bite, but her long arms keep her at a distance.

Babcia Marishka is seeing Great Uncle Felix off at the airport, so I slip through the back door, knowing Mother would be up in her bedroom. I hear the singer crooning some love song from the radio Mother kept by her bedside. I stuff my torn blouse under my mattress and then wash my face with cold water. I have to think of a story to tell grandmother when she asks about the bruises on my face.

That day isn't the last day I have a problem with Marjorie Housman. There are a few more fights, but Theresa and Jenny have backed off, giving my resistance greater strength. My problem with Marjorie Housman really ended when she moved. Her father had to take a job in the state of Washington. The day before Marjorie leaves school, I hear that Great Uncle Felix is growing a mustache, so I paid a visit to Janowski's and stole a mustache comb for him. While there, I think about taking a tube of poppy pink lipstick for Marjorie Housman, one last good-bye present, but don't.

PAULINA
1932
CHAPTER FOUR

Paulina and her younger sisters were in the attic of the small Victorian-style house where they'd lived for the last six months. She huddled in her coat, and watched the snow fall past the oval bubble-glassed window. Her forehead pressed against the cold windowpane, she saw the cemetery clearly; the snow was thick and covered the tombstones quickly. She had spread out an old quilt on the rough narrow wooden planks. Her sisters were on the blanket, wrapped in scratchy tweed sweaters their mother had knitted. Eva sat Indian-style, her tin box of crayons by her side, finishing a poster of a victorious President Roosevelt. Next to Eva, Anna stretched out on her stomach, reading, quietly smiling at Little Orphan Annie.

Two floors below, Paulina heard her mother working in the kitchen. Soft muffled sounds of the radio flowed up to the attic.

Turning from the light of the window, to the contrast of the open dark attic, Paulina became intensely aware of her sisters: a colorful block of quilt — a field of contentment. There was a delicacy, a genuine innocence, a thinness of air that she wanted to preserve a while longer

Anna started moaning, complaining of a toothache. "Tell Mama," Paulina said impatiently. "She'll take you to the dentist."

"I'm not going to the dentist ever again." Anna whined holding her hand against her cheek. "The last time he hurt me."

Paulina shrugged and combed through her wheat colored hair with her fingers. An aroma of pork baking in sauerkraut flowed through the cracks of the poorly insulated attic. "I hate Sundays," Paulina said, as she moved to the quilt, wrapping her coat around her legs, tucking it between her thighs. She lifted a black crayon and began outlining the map of Europe that Eva was now coloring. Lying on her stomach Eva moved on her elbows to make room for Paulina. She said excitedly "Let's color together, for one whole hour."

Paulina felt herself shrink from Eva's remark. She felt like throwing the crayon across the room, saying, leave me alone. It was always this way, the more she gave, the more they wanted. She felt suffocated by her sister's demands; she couldn't wait to graduate high school.

Paulina heard Boris, his usual waking sounds of coughing, choking, as he walked down the stairs to the kitchen. "Too bad," Paulina said. "Looks like he made it through another Saturday night without killing himself. Maybe we're going to have to do it for him. Loosen a couple of boards on the front porch or staircase." She reached across Eva to get a pink crayon and smelled the moth crystals on her sweater. She was reminded of the time she hid in the dark, in the hall closet. A box of moth flakes lay open on the shelf above her head, irritating her throat, lining her nostrils until she panicked. "Maybe we can dissolve some moth powder right into his `vodky," Paulina continued.

Anna glared at her. "Don't talk like that Paulina. Mama will get mad at you again." Paulina covered Eva's ears with her hands. Eva struggled to get free. Now was the time .... "Did he ever touch you, Anna?" she asked.

"Touch me? What do you mean?"

"You know."

Eva freed herself of Paulina's grip and asked, "Who? Daddy?"

Paulina attempted to cover Eva's ears again by embracing her head, pulling her across her lap.

"You know, places he shouldn't touch."

"I don't know what you're saying, Paulina. Cut it out."

"Anna, I heard him, the other night, coming out of your room."

"I don't remember." Anna stood and stomped her foot against the floorboards. "Why do you always want to start trouble?"

"I remember." Eva pulled free. "Daddy was in our room. He was standing by Anna's bed. I was scared. It was so dark."

Paulina felt that awful sinking feeling bear down on her. It started at the back of her neck, and worked its way towards her legs. "What was he doing?" she asked.

"He was standing or kneeling next to Anna's bed." Eva said excitedly, he seemed shorter. I didn't recognize him, so I called out for Mama. He came towards my bed. I remember him fixing the blanket on me, and smelling of his `vodky.' He whispered to me, 'Everything's all right, go back to sleep.' "

After a moment of silence, Eva said, "What was Daddy doing?" she asked, her blue eyes growing larger.

Paulina never forgot the night she found Boris standing over her bed, his hand jammed up tightly against her crotch. She had awakened in a panic, the kind of panic she always associated with bad dreams; but this was different, there was no cold sweat; instead her body was strangely warm. She seemed to be on the brink of a recently discovered pleasure brought on by her own touch. Upon seeing him, she thrashed out with her legs, backing away, the heels of her feet digging into the lumpy mattress, until she freed herself from his grip. Her shoulders slammed up against the headboard; her legs beat against Boris as he tried to reach for her. His gait was uneven and his arms were limp and they flailed about. In the darkness, Paulina didn't know what part of his body she'd struck, but he'd stumbled backwards. His solid weight boomed against the wall, knocking over the table where she kept her oil paints and brushes.

Eva asked, "Was daddy drunk again?" She turned to Paulina, "Maybe we need a lock on our door, too."

"No," Anna shouted. Her face twisted in anger. "I don't want to listen to another night of his banging the walls and shouting. Anyway, he'd said he'd go in your room anytime he wanted. He could break that lock in a second, Paulina, you know that."

Paulina thought of the slide lock she and her mother had unevenly fastened: Her mother's radio blared as the hollow tone of a male crooner singing "Night and Day" drifted down the hallway. They made several attempts to drive screws into the hard oak doorjamb, each time repositioning the screws until the brackets met properly. Afterwards, when the screws finally lined up mother threw up her hands in victory, "This is a lesson for us, Paulina. If we ever have to do this again, we'll know how to do it right the next time."

She touched Paulina's cheek. Her mother's hands were damp from work, a familiar moist heat against her face. "It's only when he's drinking, my little cureczka," she said. "He gets confused; he must've thought your room was ours. You keep this lock on when you go to sleep."

Paulina didn't tell her mother that he had done more than entered her room, that he had touched her. They were all too comfortable in this big old house. She finally had her own room. She couldn't or wouldn't risk change. With less than a year of high school left and waiting for word on a scholarship from The Art Students League in New York, she wasn't going to take any chances.

Although the walls of the house were thick, the high ceilings acted like tunnels, carrying voices through the rooms.

That same night Paulina heard her mother and Boris in their bedroom. "You're raising a wild animal," he said coughing into his moth-colored handkerchief. "She needs to be disciplined. She thinks she's better than other people just because she knows how to draw." He coughed harder and longer. "Some kind of princess, she better find a job, never mind painting." He said other things, things she couldn't make out.

Her mother's voice, unwavering, feinted through the darkness. "I will take my children and move from this house if I must. They are my children, but I want us to be a family. Boris, family, isn't that what you wanted?" Her voice was strong, but tender. So terrible and tender that Paulina could almost see Boris, his head in his hands, his shoulders trembling as he groveled for her forgiveness.

Lying in bed, listening to them, Paulina realized that mother was right; Boris really didn't know what he was doing when he was drunk. Like all those times when he couldn't remember how he got home, or the morning they woke and found a Morningstar Pure White Flour corrugated box at the bottom of the staircase. Inside, three kittens were curled in sleep against a bed of newspapers. He had blamed Paulina and Anna, saying they were trying to trick him. Yet for a moment he had stood over the kittens, seemingly stunned by the thought that he could be capable of doing something he didn't remember doing.

"Did you hear me?" Anna said, "There is no lock that will keep him out if he wants to get in."

Paulina drew a picture in her head of the small blue bottle she had placed under her bed. It had once contained raspberry preserves. She had filled it with turpentine, with the specific purpose of throwing it into Boris's face should he ever again enter her room in the middle of the night.

She walked back to the attic window. The snowflakes rushed fiercely towards the house. They touched the glass, melted and slipped downward. The tombstones looked like rows of plump marshmallows. "Let him try," Paulina said softly, now thinking more about going out for a walk in the snow.

Weeks later, on a Saturday morning, Paulina lounged in the parlor in the new chenille bathrobe she'd gotten for Christmas. She was pasting newspaper clippings of Amelia Earhart into her scrapbook. Anna danced around her in her sock feet. Paulina, annoyed with her bumping against the table she was working on, said "Can't you dance on the other side of the room?"

Anna pretended to be breathless. " You must spread out when you dance, become part of the air."

"I can't stand that smell. Every time you pass I get a whiff of cloves. It's making me sick."

"Did you have to mention it? I'm trying to forget about it." Anna cupped her sore mouth and sank to the floor.

"I'm telling Mama when she gets home," Paulina said. "You're a real dummy. Just get it over with."

"It went away for more than a week, it'll go away again. I know it will."

Eva boomed through the front door. "Did anyone see my ear muffs?" She looked franticly through the milk crate at the bottom of the closet. "Cherylanne and I are playing on the hill." Moments later she was back at the door. "See you," she yelled.

"Don't go too far," Paulina said in a voice she knew could've been more protective, more concerned, but she was busy daydreaming about going to New York.

She turned to the newspaper. "Look, Anna. A new theatre has opened in New York. It's the largest theatre ever. Radio City Music Hall."

"Why do they call it Radio City? Do they have lots of radios inside? Better not let Mama find out," she giggled. "She'll be the first one there. You know how she loves the radio."

"Look at the picture, Anna. It says they're going to have shows with dancers and singers. Maybe you can get a job there, dancing."

"Yuck. That's not the kind of dancing I want. I want to do ballroom dancing." Anna pretended to be dancing with a man. "I want a man to hold me in his arms. To turn me around like this, to bend and lift me."

Paulina stretched her body across the width of the armchair, her head and legs limp in the air. "When I get to New York, the first place I'm going to visit is the Empire State Building, then I'm going to see a show at Radio City Music Hall. And after I sell enough paintings and become famous, I'm going to buy my own airplane. I'll fly back and forth to visit you and your ballroom dancer husband."

Anna giggled again and then pressed her palm into her cheek and began to rock back and forth. "I'll have a husband all right, but a sister who flies an airplane? That would be awful."

"Awful? How could you say that? Look at Amelia." She held her scrapbook so Anna could see the photograph of the pilot.

"You know what they say about her. Even Mama said she's probably one of them lizbeans. It's not ladylike, Paulina. You have to be a lady."

For a long time Paulina had thought about being a lady. She had decided that being a woman was going to be more important. Ladies wore white gloves and sat around in hotel lobbies eating morsels of cucumber sandwiches and drinking tea from thin porcelain china. She wanted her life to have more meaning.

They heard Boris's truck pull up alongside of the house. Paulina adjusted the belt on her robe and sat straight in the chair. "Lesbian. The word is lesbian."

Boris entered the house in good spirits. The mines had been on strike through the holidays, and his negotiations with the union had been going well. He placed a brown paper bag on the kitchen table and removed his overcoat. "Jelly donuts," he announced, "homemade from Mrs. Goranski." Paulina looked to Anna, Anna turned away. She knew all about stopping at Mrs. Goranski's: There was that long kitchen table spread with a mint colored oilcloth. An unlabeled bottle filled with clear liquid set in the center of the table, the bottle surrounded by shot glasses. Paulina remembered the day Mother had sent her and Anna to the Goranski's to find Boris. They found Boris sitting with Mr. Goranski at the long table. He even offered them a shot of his schnapps.

Boris came into the parlor. He was wearing the shirt Marishka made him for Christmas; white rayon with navy polka dots. Paulina had thought it ugly, and remarked when he drew the shirt out of the box, that it suited him perfectly.

"Where's Marishka?" He looked at Paulina.

"Mama's at the Cortlands. Today the bridesmaids are being fitted," Anna said, sounding just like Mother.

"I thought that wedding was over with," he said, tearing open the bag of jelly donuts right on the end table in the parlor. The confectioner sugar flaked over his dark pants and shiny shoes. He offered one to Anna.

"I can't," Anna said, looking like she was about to cry. "I have a toothache. Sugar makes it feel worse."

Paulina couldn't help but notice how unappetizing the powdered jelly donut looked in his bare hand. His fingernails were bitten back severely; brownish-yellow nicotine stains covered his plump swollen fingertips.

He then offered the jelly donut to Paulina, "Why aren't you dressed yet?"

"I'm going now," she said.

Looking for Eva, he shouted, "Where's my baby? She loves jelly donuts. Just like her mama."

Upstairs, in her bedroom, the house seemed especially quiet to Paulina. Mother, who was rarely out on a Saturday, was off doing her dressmaking. Eva, who was always clinging, had found a new friend who just moved into the neighborhood. And Boris, seemingly resigned, was playing a game of backgammon with Anna. There was a new kind of freedom, an oddness Paulina didn't know what to do with.

She took off her bathrobe, and passing the mirror she noticed the fullness of her breasts, ran her hands over them and around her buttocks. Bending over she compared the colors of her hair, and found her pubic hairs to be several shades darker. She had wanted to draw herself naked, but was aware of Boris's presence in the house and decided to get dressed.

After dressing, Paulina sprawled on the floor of her room with her sketchpad and charcoal sticks. She drew her hand over and over, each time becoming more excited by shape and form: The strength of her knuckles, the arch of her fingers, the cave of her palm. She drew until her hand became that sensuous thing, until she felt that specialness wash over her, so intensely pure, she felt herself on the verge of tears.

Downstairs, an occasional shout of victory could be heard from Boris as they continued with their Backgammon game. But moments later her trance was interrupted by what seemed like muffled cries.

Her breath caught in her throat, tightened in her chest. The hallway became that long dark tunnel she had heard the miners speak about, the one her father was killed in. She reached the kitchen where the cries had turned into soft yammering incoherent sounds.

Anna sat in a high back kitchen chair. The chair was against the wall. Boris stood over her, his knee pushed into the center of her body. He had pliers in his hand. "Okay," he slurred, "one more time, and we'll get it."

Anna's face was layered in tears, her cheeks burning hot, and her eyes were larger than Paulina had ever seen. They darted about swiftly, more animal than human.

Paulina shouted at Boris to stop. There was a benevolent dumbfounded look upon his face. She saw the bottle of whiskey next to the backgammon board. "Run, Anna. Run," she shouted.

Anna just stood there.

"It hurts." Her nose clogged with tears. "It hurts worse."

"Daddy Boris will fix it for you." He put the pliers around the tooth and Anna's sobs became deeper, heavier.

Paulina lunged for his back. Her arms around his neck, she struggled to stay on him. His sweaty palms grabbed at her, twisting and pulling, burning the skin on her wrists. He flung her body across the room. Paulina's back hit sharply against the wall. Her legs trembling beneath her, she sank to the floor.

Anna pleaded, "No. Let him, let him do it."

Boris pointed his finger at Paulina. His eyes were on fire. "You stay away, girl. You hear me? You stay."

Paulina opened her mouth to speak to Anna, but nothing seemed to come out. She thought about the bottle of turpentine under her bed, but couldn't seem to move from the corner. Collapsing her head into her drawn up knees, she covered her ears and moved her palms rapidly over them — trying to change the sounds. She was almost glad when she heard the one long wail that came from Anna, grateful she hadn't heard the sound of the tooth being ripped from the gums.

By the time mother arrived home, Paulina had chipped a piece of ice from the block in the icebox. She had never held an ice pick before, but she pretended the block was Boris, and the pieces fell away. She rolled a cloth around them and held it against Anna's cheek. Then she locked the two of them in the bathroom. Anna kept spitting blood into the sink. The pain began to subside, but she complained that her stomach felt sick.

Mother never argued with Boris when he was drinking. She would smile, say yes to everything, and help him to bed. Yet that day, after she made Anna bite hard on the gauze and gently washed the blood from the corners of her mouth, and held her for a while. Then mother took Anna's hand and they walked into the parlor where Boris, now so drunk, couldn't keep his head from wobbling. Mother paced in front of him.

"How? How could you do this?"

"You're all crazy, I never did anything. The whole thing's a lie." He mumbled. "Look at me, Marishka," he said, trying to keep his head straight. "I would never harm these girls, never." His eyes glazed over, he went to touch mother's hand but she pulled away and pushed on.

"We are not cannibals. She could've bled to death. How could you do this? And you, Anna."

She knelt next to Anna on one knee. "You must never allow anyone to do something you don't want."

Anna's face sank down towards mother's hands. "But I didn't want more pain, Mama," she said quietly. "Boris said it wouldn't hurt."

Mother rose to her feet, backing away to gather some comprehensible distance. "And you believed him?"

Still looking down, Anna said, "I think I did."

Boris said, "I've had enough." His moist lips twisted in disgust. Saliva spittled onto his Christmas shirt. "You should all be thrown to the wolves." And he stumbled out of the house.

They heard the back tires of his truck on the gravel driveway, skidding, tossing pebbles as he drove away.

Paulina heard her mother crying that night. When her mother didn't answer her knock, she opened her bedroom door. Her mother was stretched out on her bed. Paulina couldn't remember ever seeing her mother lying in a bed.

"Mama, Anna's going to be all right."

"I need to be by myself for a while," she said, her forearm over her eyes.

Paulina had never noticed that her legs, her shape, was much like her mothers. "He'll be home soon." Paulina said.

"It doesn't matter to me if he ever comes home. Please, Hon, close the door."

That night Paulina felt her mother's unhappiness pressing against her chest, as if it were a slab of concrete. When she closed her eyes to sleep, the vision of Anna's wild eyes kept coming to her. At four in the morning she was still awake or perhaps had slept for an hour or so, when someone banged at the front door.

Paulina tied her robe around her waist and walked into the hallway then paused on the steps to listen to what a man was saying to her mother. "I'm sorry, Marishka, but his truck had gone off a hundred-foot drop. One of the striking miners was coming home from standing watch. He saw Boris traveling at top speed. He went flying, straight off the mountain," he said. "Everything exploded when he hit."

Paulina sat on the steps for a while, digesting what she had just heard and feeling nothing but a sense of relief. When the door closed, she heard her mother go into the kitchen.

When Paulina entered the kitchen, Mother was by the sink pouring water into the teakettle. She looked at Paulina, "You know." She said, not really a question. When Paulina nodded, she said, "It was inevitable. It was the mines, the smoking, black lung, or the drinking. One of them was bound to kill him." She said it calmly, as though it were something she had read in the newspaper about a person she hardly knew.

"Can I do something?" Paulina asked.

"No, just try to get some sleep."

Paulina went to hug her mother. Her mother's embrace was always huge and warm, and now it was even more so. Boris's death thrust upon them, and yet the peculiar silence of their embrace, the sharing of this moment, all of it seemed like an unwrapped gift. It occurred to her that the bond between her and her mother would only be stronger without Boris in the picture.

"I tried," her mother cried softly. "God knows, I tried. Yet, I knew it would end this way."

Paulina felt her days of innocence had long passed, and now embracing her mother she knew they had come to another level. She would always be there for her. "I'm sorry, Mama. I'm really sorry."

In the morning Paulina found her mother and sisters already at the table. Some left over tea biscuits and a bottle of milk was in the center. No one appeared to be eating. Eva's eyes were red and swollen from crying. Anna was looking down into her empty lap. "We were waiting for you, Paulina." Her mother's voice was calm. "I need you to stay with the girls today, while I attend to funeral arrangements."

Paulina smelled Boris as though he were still in the house; the coal-dust, the nicotine, and alcohol. She wondered how long it would take to disappear. She thought about opening the windows after her mother left.

Anna started to cry. "I don't want you to go." Paulina went to hug Anna and that's when Anna began to scream. It wasn't normal crying, it was hysteria, out-of-control screaming. She struck Paulina, her fists beat at her head; Paulina covered her face with her arms. Somehow Mother got between them, yet Paulina still felt Anna kicking and yelling until finally Mother had to slap her. An hour later Anna was calm and Mother was able to leave to make arrangements. Before leaving Mother had prepared hot cocoa for them. Sitting in the kitchen drinking her cocoa, Anna asked Paulina if she wanted a cookie. Paulina said, "Look what you did to me." And she showed Anna the bruise on her arm. Anna looked at her as if dazed. She looked past Paulina, out the window where the snow-covered oak branches tapped the window. "It isn't right that you blame me for everything," said Anna. "Is it my fault there's snow on the ground?"

Paulina looked at Eva, who was sipping her cold glass of milk that was filled with pieces of broken cookies, and Eva shrugged. "Well, who else was hitting me?" Paulina found herself getting angry.

"If you're going to pick a fight with me, I'm going to tell Mama when she comes home."

Paulina realized it wasn't anger she was feeling, it was a level of frustration that only Anna could bring out in her. She was dizzy with Anna. She couldn't keep up with her ups and downs. Anna's dark brown eyes were vacant yet so shiny that Paulina thought if she'd get up from where she sat to the other side of the table where Anna was, she'd be able to see herself in Anna's eyes. Paulina didn't know why but she felt chilled by Anna's look. "How does your tooth feel?"

"Tooth? What tooth?" Anna's mouth twisted to a smile, revealing the space where the tooth was. "Remember? It's gone." She said laughing out loud at her own joke.

Late that evening, after a day of neighbors visiting, bringing food and sweets, and Mother completing the funeral arrangements, Paulina wanted to believe resignation had set upon them. Mother sat in the wing chair, Paulina and Anna sat on the arms of the chair and Eva was on her lap. She couldn't help but feel relief—the bad part had been cut away, she thought. The lines on her mother's face seemed deeper and longer. The radiance in her powder blue eyes was gone, buried deep within her. Guilt and a sense of greediness took hold of Paulina for not feeling the loss her mother felt. Seeing her mother tired and drained she felt an enormous love for her. Leaning towards her mother's ear, she said, "I love you, Mama."

Paulina felt her mother's hand tighten over hers. And then an unexpected cry came from her lips. "Antoni... Antoni. Boris is with you now, poor Boris." She spoke the way Paulina imagined she did when alone in her bedroom, in prayer. The tears rolled down her cheeks; Eva began to cry, and hearing her father's name Paulina moved back in time, to a place she had forgotten or had never recorded as memory until now. She is lying in bed with her mother, a high bed with dark wooden posts. Her mother is sobbing deeply. She cannot see her sister Anna who lies on the other side of her mother because her mother's belly rises in the air like a hill. Paulina thinks her mother is still angry with her for talking so much about the dead dog — for forcing Anna to look at the blood on the tree trunk. But then she hears her mother cry out, "Antoni," and she remembers that her father has died.

Back on the arm of the wing chair, Paulina felt the enormity of her mother's pain; she looked over at Anna, and saw nothing. No tears, no smile, just blankness. She embraced her mother and sobbed from that deep-rooted, unfamiliar place, a place she had only just begun to know.

EMILY
1958
CHAPTER FIVE

There is a stain on my inner thigh. A light walnut color the size of Mother's fist. I question Mother about the circumstances surrounding the birth of this scar. "Oh, Emily," she begins, "I'm sure I've told you before. You were just one of those babies that never listened."

It is the middle of summer. The first day of Grandmother Marishka's annual visit to her friend Mary in Boston. Mysterious Mary is what I call her, since I've never met or spoken to her. Grandmother repeatedly tells me the story of how she and Mary spent thirty days together on the same ship, traveling across the jolting, bone-bruising Atlantic Ocean. They never laid eyes on one another until the final day when they disembarked at Ellis Island. Mary was on the line next to hers, a ship's rope hung between them. She was pushing a wooden crate with her foot. Her arms loaded down with family belongings; She moved the crate ahead. Grandmother noticed her feet were covered with homemade pigskin shoes. The same kind she had worn as a young girl. They had locked eyes at the precise moment when the edge of the crate crossed over into Marishka's lane. She helped Mary get her belongings back on track. They've been friends ever since.

Mother has what she calls a 'steamroller' in her hand. She is trying to straighten my hair. Sitting on the gray, puffy lid of the toilet seat, I feel the frayed threads of the chenille cover tickle the backs of my knees. Occasionally the steam from the straightening iron touches my scalp and makes me jump. Mother says, "See. See what I mean? I told you to keep still."

"Please, tell me how I got the burn." Whenever I question mother, I try to be polite. A few simple words could send her into an outburst of uncontrollable crazies. She begins to tell the story in an agitated tone. By the time she is halfway through, I'm sorry I've' asked her. "Your grandmother asked me to keep an eye on the potatoes while she ran to the grocers for more garlic. Removing the potatoes from the oven, I left the oven door open. Some of the potatoes were burnt on the edges while others were raw inside."

Mother pulls at my hair. Glancing up at the mirror of the medicine cabinet I notice her profile. Her nose curves sharply, not quite an eagle's beak but softer, more rounded. Mother takes a long shuddering breath and says, "Your grandmother always cuts irregular pieces. She's always in a hurry. Not like me. I take the time to make everything as perfect as I can."

She pulls at my hair once more, and when I yell she says, "If you want your hair straight I have to pull it as tight as possible."

"So what happened?" I ask, trying to ignore the hot, irritated feeling on my scalp. Now, for no apparent reason, she seems pleased to go on with her story. "I tried to cut the potatoes as evenly as I could. You had been a bad girl all that day; making noise, playing with the pots and covers and wooden spoons that Grandmother always spoiled you with. Then you started crying for Grandma's return. I hadn't finished cutting the potatoes. God, you always tried to make me angry."

It was somewhere between my tears for grandmother's return and mother's anger that I took my two-year old body over to the oven and climbed on the door and sat down.

"The skin on your thighs was singed, stuck to the door. When I pulled you off, part of your flesh remained there." She says calmly as though she were still cutting the potatoes.

Suddenly the steam iron is closer to my scalp, hotter than before. The room swells with the memory of burns, horrific painful burns. I leap from the seat. Mother drops the steamroller onto her slippered foot and yelps, jumps as if a mouse is circling, trying to run up her leg.

The summer seems long, drawn out monotonous hot days. Within the walls of my room I sense Grandmother's absence. The white sheers crisscross my windows, their double ruffled edges made from Babcia's leftover bridal gown material move in the slight breeze. The bedspread I lay on, different shades of white, more remains of bridal gowns, all quilted together by Grandmother's hand. When I was around eight I had begged her to make me curtains and a bedspread that would look like a bride's room. I loved it then when I was eight and nine but now I've hated it for years.

When Babcia Marishka left she said she'd call every three days or so. On the third day of her absence I sit on the wobbly cane seated chair in the hallway waiting for the telephone to ring. Babcia said she'd have to go down to the street and telephone from an outside booth, since Mary had no telephone, there would be no way for me to reach her. So I wait. Eyes closed, I will, concentrate on the high shrill ring to resound. Finally on day four she calls.

Talking to Grandmother on the telephone is always strange. She speaks loudly, shouts the whole time. I'd heard from others, like Mr. Lerner, my English teacher, and Dr. Barrymore's nurse, that Grandmother has an accent. But I only became aware of it that first time she telephoned me. I didn't recognized her voice but once the conversation began I'd begin to feel comfortable. I hardly listen to what she is saying. I'm gearing up for what I need to say. "I'm making a cooking lesson today." She says. "I'm teaching how to make Pirogue Ruskie."

"I'm bored," I say, "I have nothing to do. I'm not happy." I tell Babcia.

"Happiness is like a ghost you hear about, Emily, but never really see. It passes so quickly through you, that sometimes you don't recognize it until it's gone. You'll see, you're going to have a best time." Her conviction has power. As if she knows something no one else knows. Then she says, as if I'm still five years old, "Very soon my dear, you're going to be as big as your Babcia...." And for that moment seated in the dim hallway I want to be that little girl again. I remember the way Babcia always measured her foot against mine, exhibiting my growth. I think of the snow, the long therapeutic walks on those icy cold days. Babcia's large ungloved hand was always rough and raw. She'd clasp my hand so tightly that I could feel her holding my hand long after she had let it go

"Emily, watch for the buck moon," she shouts through the telephone. "In four days it will be full. When we both see the same moon, we'll know we're not far from one another." Her voice flutters, then cracks. "You're my big girl now, okay?"

I hold the telephone away from my ear as she continues, "But, if you get into any trouble, I want you to call Aunt Eva. Do you hear me?" Yes, I want to say, even the new next-door neighbors can hear you.

A few days later when the new neighbors enter my life, I'm convinced Wanda's arrival is some magical feat performed by Babcia. Even Wanda's mother, who sits on our settee in our living room, says, "I really don't know what's come over me. After my divorce, I could've stayed in the old house, but it was like God was telling me I had to move to the East Coast. So here we are."

She is chewing gum and twirling her long blonde curls around her finger. She rambles on in a loud voice so Mother could hear her while she is in the kitchen preparing tea. "Two women living alone. Right next door to one another with their two little girls. How nice, Anna, how very nice," she says even though Anna is in the next room. Through the crack of the opened kitchen door, I see Mother pour a shot of whiskey into her glass of tea. "Emily darling," she calls to me, "give me a hand with the teacakes."

"Oh, let me help, Anna." Wanda's Mother says, but doesn't move from the couch.

I have always loved Mother's sophistication, yet now in front of Wanda I feel embarrassed carrying out 'teacakes' which turn out to be crumb buns and leftover pound cake cut into bite-size pieces. Mother carries the glasses of tea out on a silver tray. I think I'll die should she mix up the glasses, but when I see, under each glass, the small doilies that Marishka had crocheted, I know that Mother, in her preciseness, has pen-marked her doily.

Wanda is so open and comfortable. She throws her long legs across the armchair in my room and says, "Mumsey got fed up with Daddy's business deals and all his 'bad luck.' She wants to marry a man who has money. I hate her for throwing Daddy out."

There are things, small things, I thought I'd never tell anyone.

"Grandmother told me my father died before I was able to focus my eyes properly. She says she and I are alike, that my mother is not as strong as we are. She says I have to give my mother strength." When I say this I see Mother as something fluid, a delicate soft shadow that moves in and out of the rooms of our house. I remember those nights when she'd read to me and then tuck me under the covers and place a kiss on my mouth. Goosebumps rise on the back of my neck; I think of her astonishing breath, at times calm and sweet, a night perfume. Other times a wet, slobbering whiskey breath, confused, swallowing itself.

Before I know it Wanda and I are both close to tears. Me, never having known my father, and Wanda, angry over her mother's short-lived marriage to "some Filipino bastard."

Wanda and I talk on as though we are old best friends, or better still, I imagine, like sisters bound by delicious family secrets. "I hate moving," Wanda says, still crying. It's as though we're sharing a new adventure, there is a freedom, a sort of squandering of feelings that make me feel I am no longer alone.

Wanda springs from the chair and sits next to me on my bed. She puts her arm around my shoulder as an adult would do, and squeezes me towards her. The old spring under the mattress squeaks. Playfully, Wanda began to bounce on the mattress. She removes her shoes and socks and begins to jump up and down on the bed. Before I know it, I'm removing my shoes. Now we are both laughing. I watch Wanda's golden-red hair fly about her face. Her laugh is open, unafraid. Higher and higher we whirl and twirl, bumping into one another until we collapse, falling across one another's bodies. I am dizzy, totally absorbed with my new friend. Later on, as she polishes my toenails to match hers, I ask if she'll be my sister. When she says yes, I am filled with joy, and at the same time, terrified I will lose her.

Although Wanda is only ten months older than I, she is physically more mature. On those nights when I'm allowed to sleep at her house, we shower together. I set her hair in small tight rollers to curl it, while she tries to iron mine flat. We put on Wanda's mother's makeup. When I first see Wanda apply the soft pink lipstick to her mouth, it strikes me that her breasts turn upwards just like the corners of her mouth. I never tell Wanda this because I think it strange, that sometimes when I look at the corners of her mouth, I see her soft pink breast turning up, pointing at me in the shower.

Before Wanda's mother began working nights at the Paradiso Lounge, we'd sneak into her room and watch her prepare for bed: She'd rub small dabs of Preparation H around her eyes and neck. Later, when she comes into Wanda's room to kiss us goodnight, she has large pink rollers all over her head, and her face looks all wet and greasy. We are under the covers, giggling. Wanda is saying silly things like, "My mother thinks her face is her backside," and with her voice muffled through the blankets, she says, "Goodnight, anus."

Her mother says, "I don't know why you call me 'Amos,' Wanda, but if it makes you girls happy...."

"Okay, anus," we say together, laughing so hard that I once wet my panties. Some nights we are so worked up we can't fall asleep, so we'd take turns tickling each other's back. It always seems that Wanda tickles so much better than I do. She puts me to sleep by tickling the backs of my knees.

One morning treading my way through Wanda's back yard to mine, I'm surprised to find Mother in grandmother's garden. She kneels in freshly turned soil, putting in the last tomato plant. "I promised your babcia I'd take care of the garden." She says, "Come, Emily, come help me. We can do it just as good as she does."

I had never seen mother so exuberant, so open, so unprotected under the hot sun. We plant lettuce, cauliflower, and eggplant. Mother's pale, long thin fingers work expertly at tamping down the earth around the plants. At one point she stops and stares at me. Looking into Mother's face, I have the sense that this is the first time she really sees me. Mother looks like Aunt Eva; her face is fuller yet tighter, as though the skin near her temples has been tucked back. There is a clarity in her face, one that I relish, a clarity that tells me she is sober.

We work for hours. When we are done planting, Mother puts her arm around me and kisses me on the tip of my nose. She says it is the only clean spot on my face. We stand back, admiring the garden. Suddenly I feel an impulse to hug mother, so I place both arms around her small waist. It is the first time I remember feeling this close to Mother. The first time I didn't feel the need for Babcia Marishka.

It is just a week later when Mother stumbles and falls in the garden. She'd tries turning the soil with a potato fork, as Babcia Marishka always does, but instead she turns the plants roots up. The one tomato plant that will go on to bear fruit, will remain unharvested. Next to the plant lay Mother's empty glass. Like the tomatoes, the glass will remain untouched until the thick frost of winter weighs upon its surface, cracking it into small pieces.

Wanda and I have our first initials in big block letters pressed onto the backs of our gray hooded sweatshirts. When we walk down the street, I stay to the left of Wanda, so that the letters form the word WE. Wanda says it is a real eye-catcher, something the boys will notice. Boys. They shout at us through the blaring music from their cars: Wanda loves it. She teasingly blows kisses. There is a lot of yelling and screaming from the boys in the cars.

One Saturday morning we meet Vinnie and Gregg at the roller rink. In the girls room Wanda tells me, "These guys are a real catch. Did you notice the back on that Vinnie? So the following day Wanda makes plans to meet them at the beach.

Summer is waning and the beach is practically empty. The four of us play chicken as the high waves break against us. I feel embarrassed sitting on Gregg's shoulders knowing my crotch is pressing into the back of his neck; that his hands are grasping my ankles, touching different parts of my legs. Wanda moves like she has been on Vinnie's shoulder hundreds of times before. She keeps pushing me off into the chilled waves. Later on, when Wanda disappears with Vinnie, and Gregg becomes even more single-minded: my lips become sore from his salty kisses. When I try to stop him, he only starts again. He keeps pressing against me, pinning me to the sand. I feel strange — almost pleasantly disgusted when he pushes his tongue into my mouth. His tongue slides over mine; I shudder from the taste of his saliva.

Gregg thinks this is what he is supposed to do. "C'mon" he says, "My father says when a girl says no, what she really means is yes."

I struggle to remove his hand from my breast, then from in between my thighs. "No. Stop," I yell at him. Finally, he becomes what appears to be disgusted. He releases me and says, "You're nothing but a cold bitch. I don't have time to waste on girls who like to tease." He then picks up his shirt and sneakers and leaves me alone on the blanket.

Wanda is nowhere in sight. A seagull lands near the blanket and picks up a half-eaten roll. It is getting late. The sand begins to feel cool under my feet. I put on my sweatshirt and decide to stay with the blanket. Feeling cold and sickened by the smell of Gregg's dried saliva, which covers my hands and mouth, I sit there shivering wondering what mother would do if something should happen to me.

By the time Wanda returns with Vinnie, I'm feeling anxious and afraid. We've hardly said a word to one another all day. "We're going to miss the bus," I tell her.

Wanda looks strikingly beautiful as she brushes out her long hair.

"You're acting like an old lady." She says in front of Vinnie, and then sits down on the blanket and begins to remove the sand from in between her toes. All the while laughing, playing around with Vinnie who grabs her hairbrush and says, "It's mine. I'm keeping it."

Wanda chases him and they end up rolling in the sand together. Vinnie is on top of her, pressing her hard into the sand. He bites her on the neck and kisses her swollen lips, and all the while she is laughing and loving it.

Wanda sleeps all the way home on the bus. The fumes from the bus are heavy making me feel ill; the same way I've felt when I'd stay on a swing too long. When I get home, I throw up. That night there is a thunderstorm and Mother asks me to sleep with her. Feeling strange and funny, as if I were still on that swing, I cry myself to sleep. Mother holds me. I turn my back against her breath. She never asks why I am crying she just says with that moist thick tongue, and that breath that seems to swallow itself, "I know, baby. I know."

When school begins, Wanda and I have the same science teacher, Mr. Rodriguez. Wanda says she hates looking at him because he reminds her of that "Filipino bastard."

I sit next to Connor, a boy I had a crush on since last year, but had never spoken to. When I meet Wanda for lunch, she says, "No wonder you like him. He's real cute."

I make a decision to talk to him, but don't know what to say. Wanda says, "I'll help you. Show you how to get his attention." She winks at me.

On Friday, when I arrive home from school, I find Aunt Eva in the kitchen. She greets me with her usual robust hug. "Babcia must stay longer in Boston." She says, washing out a water glass. "Mary has taken ill, and since she has no family, Grandma will have to care for her."

I hadn't heard from grandmother for almost two weeks now. She was supposed to be home by now.

"I want to talk to her." I feel anger, or fear, or is it true that I'm just so spoiled by her?

"Of course, honey. When she calls, I'll be sure to tell her to call you. Actually, when you're at my house, I'll have you speak with her."

When I'm at your house? "Why can't she call here?" I ask Aunt Eva as she brings mother a glass of water.

Mother sits at the kitchen table. Her hand trembles as she brings the glass to her lips. Aunt Eva had apparently brought her some books. Quickly, Aunt Eva arranges the books face down, but I manage to glimpse, ALCOHOLISM IS A DISEASE, THE JOURNEY BACK.

Aunt Eva says, "I have to leave now." She flings her black cape around her shoulders, and hugs Mother for what I think is an unnatural length of time; her black cape around them like a transparent shroud of family secrets. Outside, she touches my face, and says in her most gentle voice, "Don't worry, Emily. You'll see, honey, everything's going to be all right."

Her voice is filled with such sincerity that suddenly it strikes me there is a problem even larger than I imagine. I feel the urge to run after her, to ask her to stay. Aunt Eva shouts from the car window, "You remember what I said, honey."

Weeks later, the buck moon had come and gone and Marishka still hasn't telephoned. Aunt Eva says, "She can't leave Mary alone to make a phone call. But she wrote me a letter and told me to tell you that she loves you, and that she'll talk to you soon."

Not receiving a letter from Babcia is acceptable to me, since I know she prefers to write in Polish, but when I ask to see it, Aunt Eva can't remember where she put it.

Around the same time Wanda catches a cold and stays home from school. On the second day of her absence, I decide to cut my last two classes and visit with her. I remembered how comforting it was when I was small and Babcia would bring me a new coloring book and crayons. The way she'd sit on my bed and color with me. Both of us licking strawberry ice pops to help keep the fever down.

On the way to Wanda's house, I stop at the corner store and used my saved up lunch money to buy a box of crayons and even though I knew it was corny, an Elmer Fudd coloring book.

I entered Wanda's house through the side door. Careful not to wake her, using the key her mother always left under the ivy planter. There is a note on the kitchen table from Wanda's Mother: *There's soup in the refrigerator. I'll be home tonight right after work.* The note is signed, ` Love Mumsey.'

I hear Wanda's stereo blasting away. I call out to her. When I reach the hallway that leads to Wanda's room, the record is ending. I hear the moaning and groaning before I see Wanda sitting naked on Connor, riding up and down on him like we once did on the carousel horses. Wanda's head is thrashing about, hair flying, her soft pink breasts bouncing, and he just lies there with his hands all over her backside. Over her moaning, Connor says, "C'mon baby, that's right. Oh yes. Oh yes."

It is only seconds, but in my mind I am left with what seems like a film in fast forward, a flash of a scene that would remain with me for years. I drop the crayons and book, and began to cry. As I start to run down the hallway, I step and slip over them. Looking down at the broken crayons, I feel repelled by my plainness, by my own naiveté that sticks in my throat like a piece of dry cotton. Wanda came after me, half in her bathrobe. She shouts, "What are you doing here?"

"How could you?" I shout back, "You lied. You said you never did it."

She screams at me to grow up, then laughs at my crayons and kicks the coloring book aside, and that's when I stop crying. "This is what grown-ups do," she says, "my mother does and I'm quite sure your mother does too. Probably with that man. You know, the one from the liquor store."

The sight of Connor entering the kitchen makes my stomach sour. Wanda continues, "You know, the one who delivers her daily bottle." Wanda turns to Connor who is clad only in his jeans, and says, "Did you know her Mother is a lush?"

Like the stirring of Marishka's soul touching the tips of my hair, crawling over my flesh, I feel the strength of her spirit swell within me. I lift my hand high and slap Wanda across the face as hard as I can. She stumbles backwards and falls against the kitchen cabinet. As I open the door to leave, the only sound I hear is the sound of the refrigerator humming.

I run the first few blocks away from home. Out of breath, I slow down, yet walk hard and fast, making each step a purpose, an act in itself. I allow the wind to bite into my face and sting the thin wet skin under my eyes. I walk past the church and Briar's Department Store. I walk for what I think is hours.

When I finally arrive home, Aunt Eva is there. "Sit down, Emily," she says, not giving me a chance to sit.

"Em, Hon, you know your mother hasn't been well lately. There's this place — a treatment center — where she can go and be helped."

Mother sits in the club chair in the living room, suitcases alongside of her.

"Maybe," Mother says, a weak chuckle in her tone.

Aunt Eva's touch is cold. "I've packed some of your things. You'll stay with me until Babcia returns."

I stare at the bookcase across the room. I want to count the books. To put them all in some kind of order. The porcelain clock on the shelf ticks on nonchalantly, the pendulum like an urgent pulse. I fail to hear what Aunt Eva is saying. Mother says something, her voice far away. My body begins to tremble. I want to go to her, but it seems impossible for me to travel the distance between us. Unaware of how I reach her, I kneel before Mother and put my head in her lap, and began to cry. Aunt Eva's hands are on my shoulders, trying to guide me away. "Don't cry, Hon., your mother's going to be all right."

I want to tell them about Wanda, but instead I say, "You've got to help me, Mother."

Limply, mother raises her hands to surround my face. "Help you?" she says, a wide, glowing oddness grips her face, "I can't even help myself."

In Aunt Eva's car, Mother holds my hand all the way to the treatment center. When we arrive, a young blonde woman with a heavy tweed sweater greets us outside the building. She looks a little like Wanda's mother when she wears no makeup and her hair is undone. She takes Mother's suitcase, and escorts her up the steps. I begin to think of life as some sort of mysterious balance, we lose one thing and gain another. As I watch mother enter the building, I tell God, Okay, you can take Wanda away, but please, please bring me back my Mother whole. And as we drive away I realize I can still feel Mother's hand clasping mine.

PAULINA
1945
CHAPTER SIX

The first time Paulina met Francesco Ferruggia she was on Easter break from the Art Student's League. She, Eva and her mother had just returned from seeing a movie and settled into a game of gin rummy when Anna entered the parlor with Francesco pinned to her arm. He was dressed in Navy uniform, his hat rolled in his fist. A potato chip had fallen from Paulina's hand, and as she bent to lift it off the carpet, she noticed the gleam of his black patent leather shoes matched the gleam in his slicked back dark hair. His widow's peak was on full view.

Anna with a sheepish grin introduced him as though he were a newly acquired possession, picking a piece of lint off his shoulder, smoothing her hand along his sailor's collar, down his back. She made some remark to him about her mother and sisters always trying to lose weight, showing him the near empty Easter baskets on the sideboard, pointing out her own untouched basket. "And what's this?" she asked teasingly, looking at the bowl of potato chips on the table. Paulina burrowed the potato chip into her crumbled napkin.

Marishka, who was still holding her cards, put them face down on the table and stood. Lifting the bowl of chips to their guest, she asked, "Would you like something to drink, Francesco? Some schnapps?"

"Frank, his friends call him Frank," Anna said, guiding him to an empty chair on the other side of the long table. On the radio Fiber McGee was saying good night. Eva went to turn the radio off. A sudden quiet filled the room, the air stirred only slightly by Eva's return to her chair.

Anna began talking about a jazz club she'd gone to with Frank. Paulina dulled to Anna's babbling, catching only that Frank was going back to the club for a late-night jam session, and that the following morning he'd return to his ship.

"Frank plays the trumpet, don't you, Frank?" Francesco eased Anna's waving arm into her lap, his hand rested on hers. Anna beamed and sat tall in her chair, the gesture silencing her for a moment.

"Saxophone," he said. "I play the sax."

Paulina watched her mother pour a shot of brandy for their guest. Her mother seemed older, more matronly in her pale pink lace dress. She could tell her mother's arthritis had been acting up all that week. Marishka placed the brandy decanter back on the credenza, pausing to rub her wrist. She flexed her fingers, opened and closed her fist, then lifted the brandy glass and placed it in front of Francesco. "For you," she said.

From across the room, an angle of light from the floor lamp seemed to hypnotize Paulina. That same glow spread against Francesco's thick square jawline and flickered in his moist green eyes. His eyes held the light and more; drawing out a gaze that cut so deeply through Paulina's center, that she had to turn away.

The small talk continued for a while longer before she excused herself. "I'm going up to bed." She said, "Got in late last night, and up early this morning."

"When are you going back to New York?" Eva asked.

"Tomorrow. Tomorrow morning." She said, "The nine o'clock train."

"Do you live in New York?" Francesco asked, not waiting for an answer. "That's where I'd like to settle one day. I hear if you're a musician that's the place to be." His elbows on his knees, he rubbed his palms together. Paulina noticed his wide, thick hands like a cave, or a safety net, she thought.

"I'd never live in New York. Too many people and buildings. So crowded." Anna said with a look of disgust.

"I'm an artist," Paulina said, immediately feeling stupid that she said it. "Well, I'm studying to be an artist."

"Same thing," he said with a generous smile. Although he was across the room, Paulina felt as though he was pressing near her, breathing her in. She sighed deeply, hoping no one had noticed her uneasiness.

"What jazz club?" Paulina asked.

Francesco smiled, "The only one right outside of Philadelphia. Some silly name," He looked at Anna for help but she was rummaging through her purse for something. "Jazzamattasa?"

Paulina laughed. "Said like a true Italian."

Anna corrected him. "Jazzmataze."

Paulina knew the place. She had been there before.

"Well, goodnight all," she said and bent to kiss her mother on the forehead.

"Good luck with your paintings." Francesco said. When Paulina went up to her old bedroom, she closed the door leaning against it, she felt giddy and rude, why hadn't she wished him luck with his music?

The house was still. Paulina couldn't sleep. She got herself dressed and packed her few things, and wrote a note to her mother that she decided to take the earlier train back to New York, and didn't want to wake her. But instead she took the train to just outside Philly and grabbed a taxi to Jazzmataze night club.

The night was chilled and she walked through a few cars looking for one that was heated. She slept for forty-five minutes or so, a light sleep, but it seemed to be enough.

When she arrived at the club there was no one she knew, so she sat at a small table against the wall. Francesco was already playing his saxophone with one fellow on the piano and a baritone sax. Some fellow with too much to drink sat up front kept yelling "Besame Mucho."

When Francesco took a break, Paulina walked over to him. He was out of uniform and had on a navy sweatshirt with jeans. Shocked to see her there. "What did I do to deserve this?" he asked.

"I couldn't sleep, so I thought I'd take an earlier train back to the city. I used to come here all the time." She exaggerated.

"Wow," he said, "this is so great. Sit down." He pulled a chair from the table. "Did you catch any?"

"It was very good." She said.

He pulled his chair close to hers. "Can I get you a drink?"

"Just some white wine, I can't stay too long."

When he returned with her drink she asked, "How long do you know Anna?"

"Not long," he said, distracted by the music, and turning to watch the saxophone player.

Paulina didn't know why she had come. This was Anna's boyfriend. What was she thinking? She felt foolish. What was it about this man?

Was it purely because he belonged to Anna?

"I have to go." She rose from the chair, "I'm sorry."

"No." He immediately stood. "I'm the one who's sorry. I promised Jack I'd listen to his new song."

She felt his hand on her elbow. "Please."

"No, really. Suddenly I'm tired, so I better leave."

"Let me get you a cab," he said.

Francesco went to the bar telephone and made the call. He then walked Paulina outside and waited with her. "To answer your question, I only saw your sister three times and it's probably the last."

"Why?"

"I realized tonight how different we really are. She's a sweet woman, but we just don't fit."

The taxi pulled up. Francesco put his hand on her chin, "Maybe we can try this another time."

Months later, on a rainy July morning, Paulina received a letter from Eva. She wrote that Anna's days had been consumed with nausea. The next letter was from her mother. Written in Polish. Always difficult for Paulina to translate, she would write the words she didn't know on a separate piece of paper and bring her notes to the local Polish baker. With the help of Mrs. Elena, and knowing from Eva's letter that Anna might be pregnant, along with her meager knowledge of the language, she managed to understand her mother's letter. Her mother had written of her fears of Anna being a mother. "How will she care for a child, if I still have to care for her in ways?" She wrote, "I am deeply disappointed with Anna and upset that she must marry a man the family hardly knows." Yet, she did sign the letter, soon-to-be babcia.

Lying in bed that night she read her mother's letter again. She tried to imagine Anna as a mother, but in her mind it wasn't possible. Mother was right; Anna could hardly care for herself. She thought about the doctor visits and the trial medicines when she was only fourteen; how sometimes at the dinner table she'd throw the food across the room or at Paulina. The way cruelty seemed to empower her, making her feel superior. For so long now Paulina knew Anna was emotionally confused, and her drinking made it worse. Anna was filled with anxiety, self absorbed and vain. Yet there was no question that to some, Anna's beauty made up for her lack of personality. Paulina folded the letter back into the envelope and wondered how Francesco would handle this. Marry? She felt sorry for both him and Anna, and swore she wouldn't think about him any more.

In the morning Paulina found a note on the kitchen table. Her roommate wrote: Dear Paulina, Jake proposed to me and we're getting married this weekend. I'm sorry for the short notice, but it looks like you'll have to find a new place to live. See you, Amy.

How was she going to find a place so quickly? She knew Amy had been fragmented and not very trustworthy, but what choice did she have? Before going to work she posted a note in the downstairs vestibule, hoping that someone in the building would know of someone who needed a roommate.

At work that afternoon, at the drugstore soda fountain, Paulina poured a hot cup of coffee for the fireman who showed up regularly each day. "Any plans for the weekend," Kenneth asked.

He had sandy blonde hair with blue eyes and a barely visible razor thin mustache. Paulina couldn't remember seeing a man so clean-cut, always shaven and quite friendly. She knew he lived in the area, because they had spoken of housing before.

"Unexpected plans," she said. "I have to look for a place to stay."

Kenneth looked at her with a blank stare. "A place to stay?"

"Yes, my roommate is getting married, so I have to leave her apartment."

A man and a woman came in and sat on the counter stools. The man tapped his keys on the counter.

Anything else?" Paulina asked Kenneth.

"Yeah. Take care of them, and we'll talk." He nodded towards the couple who just sat.

Paulina served them ice cream sodas, then returned to Kenneth to give him his check.

"This is our lucky day," he said. "I'm looking for a roommate. Know anyone?" he smiled.

Paulina could hardly believe her ears. "Don't tease."

"I'm serious."

"Really?"

She thought for a moment. "Would you mind a woman?"

"Humm. . ." he said, "it depends what she looks like."

"Great," she said, bringing the sugar bowl to the man at the far end of the counter.

"Hey, I was just kidding." Kenneth raised his voice so she could hear him.

"How big is the apartment?" Paulina asked on return.

"It's a one bedroom. I work nights. What's your schedule like?"

Although she was in a real bind, she paused for a moment, uncertain if she should even consider this.

"Hey, think about it," Kenneth said, "I only need about fifteen dollars a month."

"Where is it located?" She asked, "The apartment."

It turned out that Kenneth's place was only four blocks from work. How could she turn it down?

All the next day at school Paulina felt unconnected, disjointed. She had begun to pack her things in boxes she got from the liquor store. She had wanted the chance to go and see the firemen's apartment before she moved in, but she would've had to miss her drawing class. In class she usually found the voice of the instructor, Arturo, calming. The uncomplicated, almost loving way he'd run a finger along the live model's arm; "Look at the way it arches," he'd say. "See the crease here, and the shadow. Make it live, breathe into it." But that day all Paulina saw was the move ahead and an uncertainty about living with a man she didn't know anything about. She rationalized that she didn't know anything about Amy when she moved in with her. Wasn't it the same thing?

Two days later Paulina moved in with her new roommate. The apartment in Greenwich Village was three flights up. Two rooms, with a view of a brick wall from the only window. She had a single sized cot that she got from the Salvation Army and placed it against the wall in the living area. There was a half-wall where Kenneth slept on a mattress on the floor. Not exactly a one-bedroom apartment, she thought. In the corner of the front room Paulina set her studio behind a shoji screen she had also bought at the Salvation Army. There she was able to work in oils, but was restricted in canvas size. She learned to utilize every inch of the apartment. On the first warm day she sat on the opened window ledge. Sketchpad across her lap, she drew bricks in pen and ink.

Kenneth worked the night shift and arrived home around 4 a.m. each day. He'd sleep through the early morning hours into the late afternoon while Paulina was at The Art Student League. As it turned out they spent only a few hours together. Kenneth had his buddies he played pool with after work and Paulina had a few artist friends whom she'd meet at Dante's espresso house. They moved through each other's lives smoothly, effortlessly, until one night when they got together to smoke a reefer. Both of them so high, Paulina woke the next morning in Kenneth's bed.

Paulina sold the cot to one of her classmates and purchased candles. She placed them on a low dresser and lined them along the floor near the bed where they both now slept. They formed a mutual agreement there would be no ties for either one of them.

One night when they had just finished making love, Paulina spoke about her family. Her sisters, younger than her, yet both married. She talked about Anna being married to a man who was so different from her. It might have been the way she spoke about Francesco or the way she looked when she did, because Kenneth immediately didn't like him and nicked named him "gigolo."

There was no telephone in the apartment. Giorgio, the tenant above them, allowed them the use of his telephone for incoming calls.

One evening when they were both home, already in bed, Giorgio, tapped three times on the radiator pipe, indicating there was a telephone call for one of them. Kenneth leaped from bed, and climbed over Paulina. His balls, a light iodine color, reminded her of the pear-shaped weights of the clock she still had packed away. The clock was in her family for years. Marishka gave Paulina the clock when she came to New York. She wanted to refuse it but didn't want to hurt her mother. It was those terrible years with Boris. The time she had been necking in her boyfriend's car and tiptoed into the house and found Boris waiting there in the dark hallway. "You're a bad girl." The scent of homemade wine lifted off his tongue. She moved away from him, and found herself against the wall, the shelf clock above her. "You need a lesson," he said, and when he went to strike her, she ducked, and his hand hit the clock. He let out a yelp, and she escaped to her room. The next day he didn't know how he had broken his pinky finger.

Kenneth slipped his slacks on. "I must be crazy going up to Giorgio's without my underwear on. Do you think he'll smell me?" He said with a mischievous smile.

"You're disgusting," Paulina said, and he laughed.

Even though the weather was still warm, Kenneth reached into the pile of woolen army blankets lying on the floor. "When are you going to return those to the firehouse?" Paulina asked. He threw one of the blankets over his shoulders, draping it higher at one shoulder. In a Napoleonic stance, he said, "I shall return."

Paulina heard his bare feet bound up the stairs to Giorgio's apartment. Moments later he returned and said, "It's your brother in-law, the gigolo. He's coming into the city for the big parade." His voice filled with sarcasm. "He wants to know if you're going. The almighty sailor will still be of service to his country." He stood at salute. "He's Marching in the parade. Jerk."

Paulina drew the white sheet up over her hip, and turned away from Kenneth, her breast resting on his pillow. World War II had ended. Victory was in the air. Celebration loomed over New York City, and yes, Paulina wanted to be a part of it.

"Why are you angry with him? You don't even know him. I hardly know him."

"I guess I just can't stand these men in uniform, anymore. You know

I was in the army."

Paulina sat up in bed, "You were?"

"Yup. I was in for two weeks." He sat back down on the bed. "Some bastard planted marijuana under my bunk. I spent four months in the brig."

"That's awful." Paulina touched his thigh. Suddenly aware of the way their relationship was going, she didn't want to feel sorry for Kenneth, but he seemed to invoke this pity in her.

"Well, in the end, I decided it was better than coming home with my cock in my hand." He said bitterly, as he eased himself off the mattress and walked into the kitchen area.

Paulina felt herself shy away from the bitterness and anger. She wanted happy thoughts and the possibly of seeing Francesco again made her smile.

When Francesco called again, he asked if she could meet him at the corner of Fifty-Second Street and Fifth Avenue.

They met promptly at six a.m. in front of Krause & Barrow Shoe store. Wooden police horses were already in place at the sidewalk's edge. Paulina hardly recognized him in his brown suede vest and his plain wrinkled shirt with sleeves rolled up. Francesco greeted her with a warm hug. She remembered the size of his hands and arms, and now for the first time felt them around her, flooding her with excitement. "I've got about forty minutes" he said, "before I have to join company downtown. Let me run and get some coffee." He placed a garment bag over the horse. "My uniform," he said, be right back."

Paulina had brought along two of the woolen blankets and placed them down on the ground for them to sit on. Francesco returned with hot coffee and Danish. Small scatterings of people were already gathering. Francesco rested the containers of coffee on the police horse in front of them. He swallowed a Danish in two bites, then paused to wipe his hands with a napkin, and began to devour another.

Seeing the people lining up, he said, "Try not to move from this spot. By the time the parade marches uptown, there's going to be a mob here." He took a deep breath, "God, how I hate crowds."

"Me too." Paulina said.

"Well, we're certainly not in the right place." He said.

They both laughed.

Francesco tied a 'God Bless America' banner to the police horse.

"How's the baby?" Paulina asked.

"Emily's doing fine. Cute as a button. Just a month old. All she does is sleep. You know how babies are."

No. She didn't know how babies were and didn't want to know. "Is Anna a good mother?"

"Good? I don't know. She can't nurse. Too nervous or something. Your mother has sort of taken over. Now..." He took another deep breath as if some chore were finally over. Lifting the banner, he allowed the breeze to take it.

"The most intimate landmark on all of Fifth Avenue." He stood a few feet from Paulina, his soft green eyes lit with excitement sent a small chill through her. "I'll have no trouble finding you," he said in a whisper. Everything he said was in whisper. It was as though he had captured his own world and no one else was allowed to enter unless invited. Drawn to his slow, staccato voice, Paulina wanted to accept his invitation into this world, but knew somehow that even one night together could prove disastrous.

She sat on the scratchy wool blanket, only slightly aware of the voices, the fanfare of people slowly towering around them. Francesco lowered his gaze to her mouth. Stripped of all pretenses, she felt his eyes on her breasts. She liked watching him look at her. She felt shameless and the heat rose in her making her nipples taut against the lace of her bra. Shifting from his gaze, she saw a grasshopper work its way along the edge of the blanket and another leaped behind on the concrete. Paulina lifted the grasshopper off the blanket, its threadlike legs moved like a feather across her palm. Placing the insect by the curb, she said, "Hurry, go find shelter before the crowds get worse."

"I like that," Francesco said, smiling. "A woman that's not afraid of creepy, crawly things." His fingers mimicked a crawl, and with that he shuddered ever so slightly.

"Afraid? Look at the size of them compared to us."

"God. I can't believe you and Anna are sisters."

She pretended not to know what he was saying — the differences between her and Anna. She felt annoyed that Anna was somehow back in her life again. Now she recalled the time Anna screamed when she saw a spider settling inside the center motif of the tinned kitchen ceiling. Anna had refused to eat breakfast in the kitchen the next morning for fear that the spider was hiding, waiting to crawl into her hair. Paulina thought of the bee that stung her on the ankle while she and Anna were outside playing. How Anna stayed inside the hot humid house for more than a week, positive she'd be the next one to get stung.

Francesco put two cigarettes into his mouth and lit them. He handed one to Paulina. She never liked when Kenneth lit her cigarette. His mouth was too wet. Sometimes the tip of the cigarette paper stuck to his bottom lip, and then she would take a drag of the cigarette and pieces of tobacco fell onto her lower lip. But now when the slightly moist tip touched her lips, she realized not only did she want Francesco's mouth on hers, but there was something about him that brought out a sensation she had never experienced. It was a surrendering, a do-with-me-what-you-will feeling. A recklessness she hardly flinched at.

"I won't be seeing you after the parade. I'm getting together with a few buddies. But would it be okay if I stop by and have breakfast with you in the morning before I head back to. . .to. . .my own private . . . he stopped himself from saying what he meant to, ". . . Pennsylvania?"

"Of course," Paulina said, feeling a little disappointed but glad for the excitement of the parade and the uncomplicated day. She wrote down her address on a piece of paper he took from his vest pocket.

Moments after Francesco left, the crowds began to grow denser. Paulina rolled up the blankets and stood at the sidewalk's edge. The crowd pushed forward. She stood rigid, her feet planted firmly. Her upper body leaning over the wooden horse, she held onto the tied banner. The war was over and she was in the heart of the celebration. Welcome home signs hung from the buildings. Cheers and shouts rose above the marching bands. The skies were filled with confetti, and Francesco would be marching past shortly. Because of his height, she was able to pick him out of his company. How handsome he looked in his formal uniform. She imagined his enormous frame pressing against her body; finally her long legs wouldn't be too long. She knew she was there, not so much for victory of war, but for him. And it was as if he was marching for her, and she didn't want to think about anything else.

A woman next to her was crying. "I can't believe it's over. I can't believe it's over."

Streamers flowed from the windows of the office buildings above them. She wanted to get stoned, to get drunk. She felt the power of the war, oddly, as if for the first time. The death, desperation, the romance and the glory, all falling onto this one place. She felt the need to touch something human. Her eyes filled with tears, she embraced the strange woman next to her. This started a chain of embraces. The small bald man behind Paulina threw his arms around her waist. His head, in a naive gesture, rested on her chest for a moment. It seemed as if there was no need to leave this place, no reason for men to ever go to war again.

The next day Paulina decided not to go to class, because she didn't know how long Francesco would stay. She also called in sick for work. Francesco arrived early. While Kenneth was still asleep in the back room she made espresso with a dash of cinnamon. She had picked up three croissants at the American Deli the night before and placed them alongside of toast on one of her hand-painted plates, one she had painted years before.

"Ah, European breakfast." Francesco sat opposite her on the bistro-sized table. He looked like he hadn't slept. The whites of his eyes held bursts of pink. He placed a small, wrinkled brown paper bag on the table. "Pumpkin seeds," he said. "It was the one thing I craved when I was overseas."

Paulina had to smile, and she thought about her own craving, to live in Europe. "I'm planning to go to France. To study."

"France is nice to visit, but then you go to Florence — Italy. That's where you should study. That's where the best art exists. Why not learn from the masters?" He smirked proudly, toasting her with his cup of Espresso.

Paulina heard Kenneth stirring, grumbling in his sleep.

"I want to go to Paris. There's an area in Paris called Montparnasse, all the artists live there. Have you ever heard of Picasso or Modigliani?"

"Ah, the Italian Jew, Amedeo." Francesco grinned.

The pads of Paulina's fingers began to tingle, the way they always did when she felt excited. "You've heard of Modigliani?"

Francesco nodded. "When I was in France, I went to see some of his nudes. He was a strange bird."

"I didn't know you were really interested in art." Paulina sipped her coffee.

Francesco tamped a cigarette against his thumb fingernail, a nervous habit. His thick lips parted into a smile, and he moved closer, his elbows on the table, he appeared suddenly massive. "I'm interested in all beautiful things."

She felt a quick flush, and reached behind her to open the window. From the restaurant below came the sound of pots and pans. A siren rose above the roar of city traffic.

"Seriously," he said, breaking off a piece of croissant, "I've always wanted to be a painter myself, but no talent. None whatsoever."

The conversation heated her insides. Beside her painter friends, he was the first person she had ever met who'd heard of Modigliani. "Did you like Modi's paintings?" she asked eagerly.

"Very sensuous. Very human, I thought. I read somewhere that when he had his first important exhibit, the police had to close it down. I guess his nudes shocked some Parisians. Imagine shocking the French."

The window had no curtain or shade, and the sun carved angles off the building next door, slating across the table in a pattern of light Paulina had become both familiar and comfortable with.

She noticed Francesco was restless, crossing and uncrossing his legs, each time kicking the table awkwardly. "Florence is still better." He pushed his chair from the table, leaning back he crossed his legs once more and lit the cigarette. "Who can beat Michelangelo?"

"No one," she said, now feeling that she could be taken at any moment, by the pattern of light, by his smile. Yesterday, she had blamed the passion of celebration. What could she blame today for the way he was affecting her?

Trying to break her hypnotic trance, she took a bite of toast. Hastily swallowing, she felt the dry crumbs against her palate. Reaching for her cup of coffee, she said, "I think you're a little prejudiced."

Her remark had touched just the right cord. He laughed loudly, with a fullness. "Of course. There is nothing better than Italia." His laugh began to settle deep in his belly. "May I?" he asked, sliding the croissants and toast onto a napkin on the table. He held the plate up to the light. "Very interesting."

Paulina laughed, "That means you don't like it."

"Oh no. Really, I do like it."

She took the plate and studied its abstract shapes. "It's okay." She said, "It was five years ago. I've grown since then." Surprised by the truth of this statement, she settled back in her chair with a certain confidence.

"My father was a painter so my mother told me. I don't remember him," he gazed across the room.

"I can barely remember mine." This was true, but why was she telling him when she never mentioned her father to anyone? Her father was sacred ground. She sensed him in her bones and blood. It occurred to her that she never wanted to share him before this moment.

"Your sister doesn't remember him at all. But mine wasn't killed, he just left us." He rested the cigarette in the ashtray. "Lord, I can still hear my mother; You can't trust men, they take everything from you then they leave." He shook his head in disbelief, "What did she think I was growing up to be?" He laughed ironically. Francesco ran his hands through his thick hair. "Forget this — listen, walking over here I noticed some artists setting up along the streets. There's going to be a sidewalk art show. Would you like to walk along with me?"

Her stomach fluttered. "Sure," she said. "Why not."

"Why not what?" asked Kenneth, standing in the archway in his boxer shorts.

Francesco turned towards Kenneth.

"You've met Kenneth?" She asked Francesco, knowing they met briefly at Grand Central Station the first time Francesco passed through New York, and Paulina had sent Kenneth with a gift for the baby.

"Yeah, what do you say, man?" Kenneth asked and shook his hand.

Kenneth appeared so small next to Francesco, especially with no real clothes on. Paulina handed him his slacks. "We're going to walk along and see the Village art exhibit." Paulina said.

"Maybe you'd like to join us?" Francesco tucked his shirt tighter into his belt.

Kenneth rolled his eyes. "Don't you have to go to work?" he asked Paulina. When she didn't answer, he said, "Well someone around here has to work." He looked at Francesco. "And I guess it's me. Come give your daddy a kiss goodbye." Paulina had seen this sarcasm before. She hated this behavior and all she could do was blow him a kiss before closing the door.

The art exhibit had lots of sailboat scenery and flower-filled vases on standard sized canvases. Mostly amateurs, Paulina thought, but then came upon some interesting pen and ink drawings. They wandered along the streets, filing past tables of handmade jewelry and pottery dishes. It was so crowded Francesco grabbed her hand so as not to lose her. She couldn't remember feeling so safe and lighthearted, lively, like a schoolgirl. "Ah," Francesco saw Giacomo's bakery window, "Would you like a biscotti?"

Beaded curtains hung in the store entrance. Francesco strummed them with his fingers, "Jazzy," he smiled. Even though it was still morning they left the bakery eating gelato. Stopping in a jewelry store that sold only silver and turquoise, there was a tray with lavender incense burning. "Jazzy." And yet there was only one painting he saw worthy of being called "jazzy." His overuse of the word and the small gesture he made thrusting his fist whenever he used the word was something Paulina grew fond of, something she would smile at later when alone.

At Dante's, Paulina introduced him to two of her friends, Jack and Damien who were in the midst of an argument over who had done the laundry last. It was there that Francesco scribbled on the inside cover of a matchbook: Sweetwater's, Bleeker and Cornelia Streets, 10 P.M. Wear black.

She decided she couldn't call in sick again. She needed the money.

There would still be time to run home and dress to meet Francesco at Sweetwaters.

When she got home from work she took a quick shower and douche. She couldn't make up her mind whether to wear her black lace or her new chemise dress. What are you doing? She asked herself. She slipped back into the chemise for the second time. The deep square neckline emphasized her large breasts even more. I'm turning into a cow, she thought, as she ran her hands along her hips, smoothing the sheath against her body. She rumbled through her jewelry box, lifting a heavy copper earring to her ear, thinking I hope this neckline isn't, too revealing, and at the same time, maybe I shouldn't go.

She heard Kenneth at the front door.

In a moment he was leaning on the doorjamb of the bathroom. "Why are you home so early?" she asked.

"I have a headache."

"Oh." She turned back to the mirror, and clipped on the earring. Kenneth hadn't been himself since that disaster a couple of months ago where a bomber plane hit the seventy-ninth floor of the Empire State Building. He had been fighting the fire for more than two hours, working the hose, and removing debris. But then on the sixty-sixth floor, he was convinced he heard a woman in the elevator. He had just begun to cut a hole through the elevator wall when flames came shooting out of the shaft. He was overcome with smoke and spent that night in the hospital. As it turned out there was no one in the elevator, but sometimes in his dreams, he still heard that woman call for help. The headaches always followed the dream.

"Where's the aspirin?"

She could tell he wanted to be babied but she didn't have the time. "In the kitchen, where they always are."

She slipped the strap of the black wedge shoe over the heel of her foot.

"Where are you going?" He hadn't moved to get the aspirin.

"Out."

"What the fuck is that supposed to mean?" His face was beet red.

She glanced at the clock. A couple of minutes to ten o'clock. "I've been invited to a jam session."

"Oh, I see, Francesco is still in town. Why don't you tell him to fucking get lost?"

Paulina hastily emptied the contents of her white purse into her black envelope bag.

"Paulina, listen. God, we really have to talk." He was turning soft and this would take more time than she had.

"Okay, hon." she said, without looking at him. "We'll talk when I get home."

She walked up to him and pecked him on the cheek.

He turned his cheek. "Tell him to go home to his wife and baby."

"Remember, Kenneth, we agreed; no ties. We're not married. So please stop acting like we are."

"Sure, no problem. I just may not be here when you get back."

Paulina closed the door behind her. She felt the tips of her still wet hair on her neck and shoulders.

The club was crowded and dimly lit. There was a moment when Paulina thought she'd never find Francesco, but then she felt his hand on her arm. He drew her close to him and kissed her on the mouth. The taste of his lips, hot with Bourbon, flooded her veins. The place was smoky. Men and women, holding drinks, laughing and giddy. Voices and the sound of a live band vibrated across the room. He led her to a table up front. His saxophone rested on the chair. Placing it on the floor, at the corner of the stage, he positioned his chair next to hers. His movements hurried, almost urgent. He put his arm around the back of her chair. She felt his hand touch her hair. He was so close to her. His breath near her ear made her feel like she was floating. It was like the room was wired with opium, as if all her pores, all her senses, were opened for the first time.

"Gin? Bourbon?" He whispered in her ear, over the blaring trumpet.

In the middle of the table there was a small dim lamp, in the shape of a snail.

When her drink came she sipped it slowly, knowing on a night like tonight, it would take her quickly. Francesco played the table with his fingers, occasionally turning to look at her. She saw in his eyes that he was gone, the music working him, owning him. He itched to get up and play. An itch

Paulina was familiar with, like a creature, an animal waiting to be set loose at her canvas. It was Francesco's turn to feel that urge, to quell under and wait.

When the band took a break, the drummer and piano player stopped at their table. The piano player was the oldest in the group; they called him Bopa Joe, instead of Papa Joe. It seemed that Francesco had been to the club many times before. All three laughed at some inside joke, and then they patted him on the back and disappeared into the crowd.

Francesco ordered another round. The mix of alcohol and music always made her heady. But now the voices rose over the noisy jukebox, the hollow, tinny sound brought her back to reality, and she felt relaxed, the way one glass of red wine would make her feel.

Out of nowhere, Francesco said, "Your sister drinks too much, you know."

Paulina felt uncomfortable talking about Anna. Here she wanted it just to be them two, but how could this be, when in reality Anna was there and always would be. Shifting her weight, the wooden chair made loud creaking sounds. "I know. My mother and Eva have written. Anna has other problems, too."

"What do you mean? He asked. "She's always edgy, nervous."

"You call it nerves. Its not nerves, it's — it's more mental." Sorry she had spoken, she didn't want to talk about Anna, not now. For a moment she gave in to the vision of Anna standing in her nightgown, in the middle of the night. Anna had smeared turpentine over a canvas of a nude Paulina had just finished. "Disgusting, sinful," she screamed. Her eyes furious, filled with hatred, she rubbed hard, pushing the easel down on the floor.

Paulina grabbed her arms but was unable to hold her back. Her strength was overwhelming. Her arms thrashed about wildly. Anna raged on, trying to destroy all her canvases, until Paulina and her mother pinned her down long enough to give her a pill to quiet her. For Paulina, Anna had lodged her madness within the walls of her room for months. At night when she'd put her head to her pillow, she saw Anna's crazed eyes, wide and blinkless, more dead than alive, Paulina hated her for destroying her work, but she hated her more for making her feel such fright, for forcing her to learn so young that any dread was possible.

Francesco sat quietly, both hands around the rim of his empty glass. The background noise so far away.

"You said mental, do you think she's mad, crazy?" he finally asked. Not waiting for Paulina to answer, he said, "I just know she's been a lot worse since the baby's been born."

Paulina hesitated, and then took a deep breath. "Didn't Anna ever tell you about the doctor visits when she was young?"

He shrugged and leaned on the two back legs of the chair.

"When she was about sixteen my mother took her to a Psychiatric Clinic for an evaluation. After several visits the doctor diagnosed her as having something called dementia praecox. I had to look it up in the dictionary." She stared across the room, at a man inserting a coin in the jukebox. She felt the length of her gaze reach inward, as though the dictionary was still opened before her eyes. "It said mental deficiency, madness, out of one's mind — that simple."

Francesco looked up from his empty glass. "That can't be true. If that were true, she would've been completely loony by now. There are times when she manages better than I can."

Paulina placed her hand close to the snail light. The edges of her fingers glowed red. "I'll always remember those words. My poor mother had the doctor print it out for her in big letters, on the back of a grocery list she must've had in her purse. I saw the paper whenever I'd sneak into her underwear drawer to use her perfume. It was always there, folded under mother's perfume flask." She saw herself running the crystal stem from the perfume bottle along her mother's neck, along the inside of her own wrist, the way her mother always had. Suddenly Paulina felt the urge to cry.

"She had severe mood swings during the pregnancy, but since Emily's birth she's really gotten worse." He looked over at Paulina. Paulina turned her eyes from his. "Hey, what's this?" With his thumb he wiped the tear from her cheek, then held her hand. "Let's not talk about this anymore. Another time. Let's talk about you. How are things with you and Kenneth?"

She was glad when a friend of Francesco's approached the table. What could she say about her relationship with Kenneth? That she'd moved in with him out of convenience? That she only recently discovered that she's using him? And that she was really fond of him as a friend?

Francesco was happy to see his buddy. They hugged tightly. Francesco said, "This is Artie," and then added, "Mr. Johnny-come-lately." They both laughed.

"We were on the same ship." A petite brunette hung onto Artie's arm. Her arched eyebrows were plucked very thin, and her lips were outlined in bright red lipstick. Her speech was slurred and she could barely stand.

When Francesco introduced Paulina, he said, "This is my friend." He never once called her "sister in-law."

"I'll catch you later, man," Arty said, "I'm in a hurry." He gestured towards the woman who was almost asleep on his shoulder. He reached around and patted the brunette on her backside. Paulina watched as Arty went through a few motions before he could get the woman in a position where he could walk her out of the club.

"Arty and I were on 'the magic carpet run' together." His eyes reflected the excitement of a young boy.

"Magic carpet run?"

The man who had put the coin in the jukebox was now dancing with a woman. Their bodies swayed. Their movements were uninhibited; the man had his hand on the woman's backside as he pushed her into him, their hips were one, moving back and forth, circling and dipping. Paulina watched in amazement.

Francesco turned to see what she was looking at. "Yeah," he said, smiling at the dancing couple. "I'm sorry. Sometimes I forget. A run —" he drew his index finger along the oilcloth on the table, "—from one point to another. Our destroyer was still off the coast of Normandy when we heard the news that the war was over. There was a week layover. We were waiting for fifteen Navy men stationed at Southampton Hospital to return to the states with us. Arty was one of those men." He squeezed her hand, and then relaxed it over hers. His touch, the intensity of his look, the stillness of her hand inside his was like an aphrodisiac.

"Anyway, regulations that week, let me tell you, were pretty low. Someone brought a couple of cases of champagne on board ship. The cook went all out with meals. We began to joke that the ship was turning into a luxury liner. Then someone said the fact that we were going home at all was something magical, that the ship was actually like a magic carpet." He sipped his bourbon. "Wow. It sure caught on. The magic carpet run."

Bopa Joe was leading the band into a new set.

"And was it?"

"Was what?" His voice rose above the music.

"Magic."

"Yeah, it was all right. Coming home. But nothing—" he slipped his hand under her hair, cupped her ear and the side of her face, "— nothing like the magic I feel right now, with you here next to me."

The mix of bourbon and gin was layered in the air around them. The repetitious beat of the music seemed to swallow them. Paulina felt herself move forward, their lips gently kissing, and then more ravenously as they began to take of each other's mouths. Francesco was the first to pull away, his eyes held her like no one else had ever done. He put his lips to her ear. "I need you," he whispered loud against the trumpet's crescendo.

It was around two-thirty in the morning when the club began to empty. The guitarist, Charlie the Counter, called to Francesco, "You ready to jam? Com'on Frankie boy, let's show these peons what jazz is."

Francesco was dressed in street clothes. On stage he looked awkward. His pants had too many pleats at the waist, and she noticed before he rolled up the sleeves of his blue dress shirt that they were too short for his arms. Yet in this awkwardness there was something genuine and youthful.

He played a tenor sax. His tones were cool and clean. A lonely hollow sound pierced the room. He made love to the saxophone the way she knew he would, the notes pouring out from his center till his whole body seemed wracked with a longing, a longing no human seemed capable of surviving. Now bringing the rim of his glass to her lips, finishing his bourbon, Paulina saw herself as an extension of his saxophone, his passion filling her, reaching across one of her canvases, entering her soul, making her limp with desire.

After their jam session, Charlie the Counter gave them a ride uptown. He dropped them off two blocks from the Ballantine Hotel. The lobby was narrow and dark with wood paneling. A scent of bug spray hung in the air. The night clerk was asleep at the desk. Paulina felt buzzed. A searing desire to live for the moment possessed her. She didn't want to think about anything. It would all be over tomorrow, and she'd have the memory to hold onto to.

Francesco signed the register, Mr. and Mrs. F. Ferruggia.

"Shit," Francesco said, as he fumbled with the key in the lock. After several times he managed to unlock the door. Paulina laughed. She had been feeling good, laughing and giggling her way uptown. When the door opened, she called out, "Abracadabra." Inside, she threw herself across the bed. The faded rose chenille bedspread smelled of nicotine and mildew. She turned onto her back. There was a long chain hanging from a light bulb in the ceiling directly over the bed. She imagined herself sitting up, the chain touching the top of her head, her somehow balancing the chain on her head, and she collapsed into laughter.

Francesco sat on the bed. He had removed his shirt and hung it on the opened closet door across the room. The reflections of light from the closet made his hairless chest seem shiny, waxed. Smiling at her giddiness, he offered Paulina a drag on his cigarette. The heated cigarette glowed in the semi-dark. He put the cigarette out and then he lay down next to her, wrapping his arms around her. They stayed that way for a long while until Francesco spoke. "I'm sorry, Paulie girl, I wish things were different. You and me." His lips brushed against her neck. His voice cracked. Then she felt his mouth on her neck and his tongue touched hers. Pulling away for a moment, she saw tears in his eyes, and she wished for the will to get up, to leave before it was too late. But it was already too late and she let him take her. He unzipped the back of her dress and then lifted her off the bed until she stood, the dress slipped onto the floor. Paulina felt his gaze drawing her up inside of him. She heard him moan as he unhooked her stockings from the black garter belt. He was on his knees now. She ran her hands through his hair. He kissed her thighs, spreading them slightly so he could also kiss the insides of them. He undid her bra and as each breast came forward he kissed her nipples. Laying her back down, she had only her panties on now. He lay on top of her and reached for the light chain. "No," Paulina said, her eyes closed. "It's too bright."

"I have to," he said, in a voice that seemed huskier, more breathy. "I want to look at you."

It was the way he sounded that made Paulina open her eyes. Suddenly she felt sober, serious. His neck was thick and the veins at the surface reminded her of a Roman sculpture. His face dropped to a softness. He slipped his hand under her panties, his fingers spread her lips, and touching a warm moist spot, his expression changed. Something turned inward. And when he moved inside her she was thankful for the light he had turned on, for his eyes that held that haunting glaze looking down at her.

They made love through the morning into the afternoon; their nakedness became a natural part of them. In between, they napped and talked. He spoke of the frustration of finding work, knowing it would be years before he could make money in music. "I was offered a job driving a coal truck, and it looks like I have to take it," he said. Paulina felt the weight of his head resting on her belly. She stroked his thick hair. "I'm having a hard time adjusting. This new civilian life —being a father— living with a woman I can't seem to get to know—and now you." He mumbled something she couldn't understand, his lips brushing the flesh of her stomach and quietly he fell to sleep.

As he slept, she thought how they both had said, "I don't want to think about it now." Yet she did think about it. How could she not? Her sister's husband was sexually spent; sound asleep on her bare stomach. Paulina must've dozed off for a few minutes because when she woke she found Francesco asleep beside her, their legs entwined, and his breath smelling like her breath. She thought about her sister and mother and knew in the surrounding silence that she was lost.

When Francesco awoke, he turned on the radio next to the nightstand. "I feel terrific" he said. "Let's dance." They danced naked, swaying back and forth on the same spot of the rug. Paulina felt his limp cock near her groin. The taste of his skin was sweet and salty. She began to think of his skin as a sexual organ. Dropping to her knees, she kissed his groin, her tongue reaching his cock, she tasted him again until he filled her mouth.

Afterwards, they fell asleep for a while. Police and fire truck sirens both near and far, woke her. This is a big fire, she thought, her mind racing towards Kenneth. He would be on one of those trucks. She had to go home, to think. She needed to think. She didn't know why she was doing this. Was it all about sex? Or did she actually feel love for Francesco?

"I have to leave," she said, and reached for her bra.

Francesco let go of a yawn and stretched. "I don't ever want you to leave," he said. And then leaped from bed and gave her a lighthearted love bite on her backside as she was about to slip on her panties. "I mean it," he said, embracing her. His ache seemed to transmit into her body. She felt their sadness walled-in, as if insulated deep in their hearts. She moved to touch him; he swallowed hard and whispered, "Carissima." Her hand ran along the scar above his nipple, their eyes met, and for a moment she felt the power of the hurt they would helplessly impart on each other's lives.

She turned from his gaze.

"Woman, you make me hungry," he said.

Glancing at his wristwatch on the nightstand, Paulina saw it was five o'clock in the evening.

"Let's have some breakfast," she said.

EMILY
1960
CHAPTER SEVEN

At Aunt Eva's house there is a schedule for everything. Six o'clock we have dinner. By six-thirty George Junior and I are in the kitchen doing the dishes. In a way it's nice. Some of the times I pretend he's my brother, but then he always does something to remind me what a complete and utter nerd he is. He constantly asks me questions. Makes believe he's interested in a tenth grader. Then he rubs it in; sophomores know nothing. Especially girls. He says, "Emily you're so lucky to be going to the same school with me," but doesn't ever say why. He washes the platter with a seriousness that should be reserved for his chemistry class. As though he were examining particles of an atom, he focuses his eyes so close to the plate that his thick eyeglasses become pitifully coated with soap bubbles.

Sometimes he thinks it's his duty to educate me, just because I'm a girl. "Roaches dwell exclusively with man." When I tell him I'm not interested, he says, "That's one of your problems, Emily. You're not interested in anything." He removes his glasses, takes the linen dishtowel from my hands and wipes the soap from them. "Did you know that roaches have wings?" Now he is wiping his glasses with a piece of paper torn from a pad he keeps in his pants pocket.

Living with George Junior for the second time around, since Mother's been back in the treatment center, I seem to know more about him than I care to. There is an odor about him, not foul or sweet, a sort of flat dull smell that dominates the air around him. His pockets are always filled with crumpled tissues, because his nose is always runny. When I think that maybe the odor is from the dampened tissues stuffed in his pockets, I want to puke.

"Do you know why they don't fly even though they have wings?"

"No," I say, holding the dishtowel in my hand, waiting for him to get on with the washing.

"House pests. They've lived with man so long that they've lost their need to fly. We did the same thing to the chicken. Chickens can no longer fly either."

My eyes focus on the counter top, on the leftover scraps of dinner. Chicken skin with a glob of yellow fat attached, no doubt mine. Chicken bones mixed with peas and watery mashed potatoes. I avert my eyes. In the kitchen sink there are more scraps, wet, all squished together. Just when I think I really will puke, Aunt Eva enters the kitchen. "What are you kids up to? George Junior, what's taking so long?"

I'm confused about living with Aunt Eva and Uncle George. Sometimes I feel we're a family, which is the part I like, but mostly we go through the motions, like going to the supermarket together, and watching the same television shows week after week.

Most nights it is difficult for me to escape to the bathroom after dinner. There is no privacy. So I've arranged my time to shower after we get done doing the dishes. I worry that too much time has gone by and that I'll start to gain weight.

The best part of being at Aunt Eva's is living with Grandmother Marishka. Since her stroke she can no longer care for herself. She's unable to walk without assistance, and when she tries to speak, a strange moaning sound comes from her. They had lied to me. It wasn't Mary, Grandmother's friend, who was sick, all along it was grandmother who had a stroke. I couldn't understand why she never returned from Mary's house in Boston. Babcia's silence made me feel as though she lost interest, had set herself free from Mother and me. Ultimately, when Aunt Eva had no choice, and Grandmother was going to live with her, I was finally told the truth.

"We didn't want to upset you," Aunt Eva said, her wide-eyed innocent face like the saint she kept in the carved niche by the front door.

The other best part of living here is that Uncle George is always working at his practice. When he's home everyone has to be more of something. Quieter, more conversational, more pleasant and polite, in general more inclined towards a rigid routine of nothingness.

The worst part of living here is going to church all the time. Aunt Eva seems haunted by the possibility of sin. Everytime she enters another room in her house, she kneels before a statue of the Virgin Mother or a statue of a saint she had purposely placed, and says a prayer.

I hate religious instruction. It's embarrassing. I'm too old to be there, but Aunt Eva is very active in the church, and Father John gave her special consideration, being my situation is unusual.

I learn all about sin in religious instruction. Every time I say I hate Religious Instruction, Aunt Eva says I'm committing a sin. Sin, I discover is talking against the church or God, talking back to your parents or teachers, and not obeying. It's a sin to steal something from a store, or to take something from a friend that doesn't belong to you. It's a sin to lie, and to think bad thoughts. Bad thoughts, that takes in a very wide scope. Rosemarie, who sits next to me in my Wednesday night religion class, says her mother told her it's a sin to touch yourself between the legs. "Even if you keep the washcloth there too long, it's a sin," she whispered. The thought of Rosemarie with her thin, wiry arms and legs and stringy brown hair humping a pure white cloth, made me laugh out loud and got me into trouble with Sister Claudia. I had to say one hundred Hail Mary's.

Then of course there are larger sins like murder or having a child out of wedlock. Some sins could send you straight to hell, while others could keep you nervously waiting in purgatory, until such time He makes a decision.

Sometimes you can commit a sin when you don't even know it's a sin. "That's why the Catholics have confession," Aunt Eva says. "Don't take any chances. I go to confession at least once a week."

The first time I went to the confessional, even though I was intimidated, I was a smart aleck. Selective with my sins, I never mentioned stealing or thoughts of sex. When I finished confessing, the voice of Father John came through the dark mesh screen, "God bless you, my child." My wise response to his blessing was, "I didn't sneeze."

By the time I finished my penance that day, my knees were sore, filled with the creases from the worn leather pew.

I think of my sins as secrets.

Those thoughts that cannot be verbalized. Those yet unexplained feelings that exist in the shadow of my heart. My secrets — the ones I record in my diary. My feelings, these are my sins.

Two months ago, for my fifthteenth birthday, Aunt Eva gave me a strand of black and silver rosary beads. I keep them in my room, on the shelf between the statue of Saint Francis and the white votive candle. I light the candle whenever I write in my diary. I do not believe in the church and question whether there is a God. Why would a God condemn innocent people like Babcia? So I think of writing as a religious act. When Aunt Eva opens my bedroom door to say goodnight and sees the lit candle, she smiles with contentment. "Good Emily, you've been praying." Sometimes she'll add, "Don't forget to say a prayer for your mother."

Each evening before I go to sleep, I go into Grandmother's room. I sit on her bed and read to her. This week I've been reading Rilke's poems. At times she seems unconnected, unaware, but her eyes are always present. They seem to transcend any physical abnormalities. I don't understand all of Rilke's poetry, but the words flow off my lips, they surround Grandmother and myself, giving way to the illusion that we are in another place.

> The deep parts of my life pour onward,
>> As if the river shores were opening out.
> It seems that things are more like me now,
>> That I can see farther into paintings.
> I feel closer to what language can't reach . . . .

In school It's as though I'm thirteen years old again and still struggling to get through the pain of losing Wanda. My desk is near the window. I stare out at the buildings across the street. I fail to hear what the teacher is saying. My mind wanders. I'm a misfit. A social misfit. Someone wrote on the wall in the girl's bathroom: `M' is a pinhead and a slut. I'm convinced whoever wrote this meant to write `EM' for Emily, which is the way I introduce myself. George Junior tells me that in the third floor boy's bathroom there is something written on the wall about this `M.' He says it suggests that she, this `M,' loves to do certain things to boys. He says these certain things are written in detail, and just devouring these words on a daily basis seems to be enough for some of the boys.

"I avoid the bathroom as much as I can. It's a sin — disgusting." He shivers.

Mrs. Staver is my English teacher plus my homeroom teacher. She takes a special interest in me. In homeroom I doodle on whatever is available. I make triangles and ice cubes. I learn to put one ice cube into another. One of the meanest girls in the school sits next to me. She is so mean she has more friends than anyone else. I purposely don't look at her. As I draw the ice cubes I think about being mean, and that maybe, I, too, would have lots of friends.

In English, Mrs. Staver is enthusiastic. She reads two essays out loud on what it means to be a teenager. I couldn't write the essay, instead I wrote a poem. Then, to my astonishment, she reads my poem outloud. It is so personal I feel vulnerable even though she doesn't announce the name of the student who wrote it. It is a poem about rain and truth. Obscure, fashioned after Rilke. An odd combination that drew me to its urgency. I feel my whole body flush when she reads the line: O' God, when can we let our garments down, and let these silver drops touch our naked skin.

At this point, the class stirs. There are a number of whoops. Even after she goes on to read two more essays, I still can feel myself secretly basking in the moment.

After class Mrs. Staver asks me to stay. She touches my shoulder, then slides her hand down my arm. Holding my hand she says, "Emily, you really are a very good writer. Think hard about what you want to say." Her voice is soft and filled with clarity; "We are who we are. Don't let it go to waste." It was like being offered a secret message, one I would have to learn to decode.

At night before I go to sleep, I take my poem into Grandmother's bedroom. I sit down on her bed. She is happy to see me. I know this by the way she thumps on my hand with her fingertips. I start to read my poem to her. Keeping my voice low, afraid Aunt Eva or George Junior might hear, I lean into her face. Her breath reaches my nostrils in small puffs. Her breath is bitter, like metal. When I am finished reading, I look into her eyes. There is a film upon one eye. A film I've never seen before. I lay into her bosom, taking her good arm, I place it around my back until she is holding me. It is a hard caress. Now the film appears on both her eyes, and suddenly I know in some small way my words have reached her.

Every six weeks or so, after church on Sundays, we go to visit mother in the treatment center. A neighbor, Mrs. Wilenski's daughter, comes to stay with Babcia while we are gone.

It is the first warm day in May. Puddles left over from last night's rain evaporate quickly. The trees along the highway are beginning to bloom. George Junior sits next to me in the back seat. Wild flowers flourish along the edge of the road. I roll down the window to try to capture fragrant air.

"Em, hon., please close your window. George Junior has a cold. I don't want him to get worse," Aunt Eva in the front seat. I roll the window back up, and look over at George Junior. He has a smirk on his face, the smirk he always has when he gets special attention.

The ride up is boring. Uncle George never seems to have anything to say. Aunt Eva knits until we get there, not missing a stitch. George Junior usually falls asleep, his head back on the seat, with his mouth wide open.

This is a different treatment center. Much larger than the first one mother was in. There are hallways lined with solid wooden doors, then swinging glass partition doors that lead to other sections. Aunt Eva says it is not a hospital, but to me it looks just like one.

When we arrive, I have to stay in the waiting room with George Junior. On my last visit I never got to see mother. She was on new medication that made her sleepy. Aunt Eva thinks I'm upset when I can't see mother, but I'm sitting here hoping I won't be able to see her this time.

The waiting room is filled with chairs covered with brown nugahyde, and wobbly legged Formica tables. Each table has an ashtray filled with cigarette butts. The room smells of stale cigarettes. The magazines on the center table have frayed edges and torn covers.

"Talk to me," I tell George Junior.

"What do you what me to say?" He rearranges the cuffs on his white dress shirt.

"I don't know," I say, at the same time I'm thinking. "That's it, tell me something I don't know."

"Jeez, Emily, we don't have that much time." He laughs and slaps his thigh.

I start to flip through one of the torn magazines. Soon he will be dying to tell me one of his weird stories.

"You want to hear about twins?"

"Twins?" I ask.

"Yeah. You know any?"

"No. I never met any twins."

"It's no wonder. Most of them are killed off. You could've been a twin yourself. Maybe even I was a twin."

"What's that supposed to mean? I know I'm not a twin." I toss the magazine aside.

"You only know what you've been told. You see, in the womb there's always one dominant twin."

I'm surprised he uses a word like, 'womb' and doesn't think it's a sin. "The dominant twin, for some unknown reason, draws all the nourishment from the weak secondary twin. He sort of sucks the life from the other fetus. Before anyone ever knows there are twins, the second twin calcifies and whammo — it slips away into the mother's abdomen — mummified."

He has my interest again. "Where'd you hear about this? Is that true?"

"Read, Emily, read. And I don't mean poetry." He wipes his runny nose with a crumbled tissue he draws from his pants pocket. "I read about it in my science magazine. Proof. There was this woman who had an operation, and during surgery they found remnants of a calcified fetus just floating around in her stomach. It had hair and teeth."

"Oh, you're disgusting!" I say trying to control the level of my voice. "How can you make up such ugly things?"

"Make up?" he chuckles. "It's all true. Once they found one in a spine of a pregnant woman."

I rise from the seat. "Oh, you're a real sick-o, one sick freak. Science?" I say. "'Science fiction' is more like it."

It is this freakiness that draws me to George Junior. A world filled with vivid and unique details, a world sometimes darker than my own.

George is laughing at me and shaking his head no. As his mother and father enter the waiting room, I wonder if being amused by weirdness is committing a sin.

Uncle George says, "C'mon Junior, the girls are going in to see Aunt Anna, so let's wait outside."

Aunt Eva and I walk down a long corridor to get to Mother's room. This is a new part of the building. The last time I saw Mother, she was in a different section of the center. We visited her in a room that was made to look like a living room, except it was filled with strangers.

Mother is sitting up in a hospital bed. There are steel bars on her window. There is a toilet and a sink next to her bed — no door for the toilet. Mother looks as if she has been sleeping for a month and still needs more sleep. Her eyelids keep closing. She wears no makeup and the color of her skin blends with the blandness of the room.

Aunt Eva says, her voice louder than usual, "Anna, look, Emily's come to visit."

Mother has a blank stare. I want to run and leave this awful place. But suddenly, in a delayed reaction, mother throws her arms out and starts to laugh.

"Emily," she cries. "Emily."

Aunt Eva urges me towards her. She laughs and hugs me. This is something I never expected. I try to ask, "How are you Mother?" But her laughter leaves no room for words. She hugs me and sways back and forth, laughing, saying my name. Then she notices Aunt Eva, releases me from her embrace, and throws her arms out to her. "Emily," she says, and squeezes Aunt Eva. She laughs and sways with Aunt Eva, calling, still saying, "Emily."

This is how the visit goes. Mother doesn't stop laughing. There is no conversation. Yet oddly, her calling my name, hugging me, and her beguiling exhaustive laughter leads me into a strange delusory state where I find myself sitting on Mother's bed, laughing just as hard.

Aunt Eva leaves the room and returns with a nurse. "Whoa," the nurse is smiling, "looks like we overdid the happy pills." She pats me on the shoulder. "Did we give you some, too?" I get off the bed and roll out a wad of toilet tissue to wipe my eyes and blow my nose. The nurse is about to give Mother an injection — we leave the room. I walked down the hall feeling spent, exhausted by my mother's illness. Each time I come to visit with her I feel she will never recover. Her sickness has taken us both.

On the way home in the car, Aunt Eva with her knitting needles going a mile a minute, says her usual, "Well, that was a nice visit."

Suddenly I can't hold back. "You lie, how can you say that was a nice visit?" I am shouting, practically jumping off the back seat of the car. "You never say the truth. That isn't a treatment center. She's in a mental hospital. My mother's crazy. She's in a mental hospital."

Aunt Eva turns from her knitting needles. "Now, Em, hon, please don't say that — your mother's not crazy . . . ."

Uncle George pulls along the shoulder and stops the car. "Emily, I want you to apologize to your aunt. You must never shout at your aunt again." For the first time ever in the car, I see his face, not the bald spot on the back of his head. I look at George Junior. He is looking away, out the window. I am silent.

"It's okay, George, really, Emily is just upset," Aunt Eva pleads with him. "She's just had such an awful time of it — let's try to be understanding." She turns to me. "We'll talk about this later at home. You and I will have a nice talk, honey."

All the way home there is silence. George Junior makes believe he is sleeping, but I can tell he's awake because his mouth is closed.

I shut my eyes against my tears. I've finally admitted out loud that my mother is crazy. No one in the family has ever come close to saying it. I'm the only one. I wonder if Babcia were able to talk, would she speak the truth? I feel so frustrated and alone. A flush of guilt and shame comes over me, and I start to wonder what Wanda is doing. I try to recall her face, but I can only see her hands clearly, her long white fingers, nails like oyster shells, no cuticles, and I hold this image as long as I can.

Later, as predicted, there is no talk with Aunt Eva, other than, "I love you, Emmy baby," and, "Yes, Mother has some problems, but they're trying to work things out. It's just a matter of finding the right medicine."

I don't answer her because my throat is hot from throwing up, and I don't want this warm comfortable feeling I feel afterwards to leave so quickly.

At night in bed I think of my mother and my grandmother, and myself. I think maybe we are all calcified fetuses — survivors. But then I recall Grandmother, the many ways she used to be. The moon slips through the edge of my curtain and I remember that day in May years ago:

"Oh, it's so cold," I yell.

"Just run in," Grandmother calls from the sea. I inch my way into the water. I'm already numb to my knees. "You'll get use to it," she shouts.

It's getting dark. I can hardly see her. Ahead of me she is doing her strokes across the inlet.

"But it's icy cold," I continue to yell.

"You'll grow stronger, kykla." Her voice shows signs of tiring. I clutch the towel still wrapped around my shoulders. "I'm up to my thighs," I yell.

"Good," she says, "grandmother's proud of you." Then suddenly she shouts, "Look behind you, Emily." Startled, I turn so fast the water laps around my waist, soaking the edges of the towel. "There's the planting moon." Her voice, like the waves, rises and falls breathlessly. "In two days it will be full, and then we'll go night swimming again."

Now that same moon marks the far wall of my bedroom. I tiptoe into Grandmother's room and lift her shade just enough to allow the moonlight to enter. She is sleeping, or her eyes are just closed — but I want her to see the moon. "Babcia," I whisper, "open your eyes, Grandma." I nudge her good shoulder. Quickly, her eyes pop open, confused. "Look, Babcia, look," I turn her frantic face hard towards the window. "See," I say, as though she is that child I once was, shivering in that dark sea. "See the Planting moon." Her wide brow is creaseless, her eyes seem not to blink, but her face, lit by moon-glow seems almost brilliant, knowing.

PAULINA
1945
CHAPTER EIGHT

Paulina was first to arrive at the Greyhound Bus terminal. Francesco had sent a message to say he was on his way to see her. At first she was angry he'd called, severing their promise to not see one another for at least six months.

She sat on the bench outside the station, waiting for the bus to arrive from Easton. It was an unusually sunny day for November, the air crisp and clear. Her eyes were drawn to the ground, on the varying forms and shadows of people entering and leaving the bus terminal.

Paulina retrieved e.e. Cummings from her handbag and tried reading. But now, after months of pressing silence—of trying to forget, she felt Francesco moving through her veins.

But why was he returning? She'd been telling herself she didn't want the problems that came along with him. Perhaps he was coming to say goodbye, to say he was sorry for their affair, that he and Anna would give it another try.

Paulina imagined Francesco stepping off the bus, changed, transformed into a brother-in-law. Maybe her sister Anna and baby Emily would be with him? She was stung by the thought. No matter what, she was prepared. She told herself, even if it means never seeing him again. Since she last saw him she had tried to turn her thoughts to her work, but she was deaf and dumb to all that was around her, and when she painted she thought of him even more. It seemed what he touched in her was also at the core of her desire to paint. The longing, the pleasure in both mind and body and that glorious fulfillment she felt was at the root.

A man in a tweed overcoat rushed past her, his newspaper slipped from his underarm and flew about. His opened overcoat flared around him as he chased the loose pages. She remembered Francesco just out of uniform. The baggy black overcoat he'd bought at the Salvation Army store the last time they'd been together. He modeled the coat with his arms wide apart. "How do I look?" In the shallow light of the store his skin appeared translucent and his green eyes glowed. Now something familiar rose within her. A vague involuntary feeling washed through her veins. She felt slow - dim witted, jubilant. Although she tingled with the anticipation of seeing him once more, she was uncertain how to behave, what to say.

Drawing a cigarette from her handbag, she saw the tickets for the concert. She checked the location of the seats. Seventh row center. Everyone at Dante's espresso house had been talking about this exciting new singer from France. Her plan, before Francesco called, had been to surprise Kenneth. But now she felt a greediness growing inside her. It was like those times she had to share with her sisters; always the struggle to own something of her own. And now this need seemed boundless. She no longer felt capable of sharing with anyone but Francesco, and yet ironically, having been drawn to the forbidden, she found herself sharing that which is most sacred between sisters.

The bench felt warm through Paulina's gabardine slacks. Each time a bus entered the terminal, her heart raced beneath the lapel of her suit jacket. Busloads of passengers marched towards her, emptying into the doorway to her right. A small elderly woman who walked with a cane asked Paulina for help to the waiting room. She had lost a shoe somewhere between Oklahoma and New York City.

"It simply disappeared!" Her face, although wrinkled, was like a child's, full of surprise and innocence, about to cry. Paulina assisted her to the ticket booth and informed the man of her problem.

"Lost and Found is over on Tenth Avenue."

The woman looked down at her stocking foot. "What am I going to do?" Her eyes filled with tears.

"No. You don't understand," Paulina said to the man behind the counter. "She's lost her shoe. How is she going to get to Tenth Avenue? She just got off the bus. Maybe her shoe is still on the bus. Can't someone search the bus?"

"What bus was she on?"

"The bus from Oklahoma."

He checked through his schedules.

Paulina glanced around the waiting room, wondering if Francesco had arrived as yet.

"Lady, the bus from Oklahoma doesn't get in till nine o'clock tonight."

By now it was obvious the woman was confused. Paulina helped her to a seat. The old woman complained of the cold. "My foot is near frozen," she said. Paulina untied the ankle strap from her platform shoe and removed her sock. The woman's foot was wide, with distorted toes. Paulina had to stretch and pull the top of the anklet over her bunioned large toe. Just as Paulina decided to summon a police officer, a hand touched the back of her neck.

Francesco's' embrace was terrifyingly familiar. She felt weak, radiant with joy. The sun gleamed against the plate glass window and she saw their reflection thrown back to her — he was really there. His beard felt thick, scratchy against her cheek, yet he was wearing a new suit. The smell of the cloth was fresh, and it felt crisp against her fingertips.

The old woman was moaning.

"She's lost her shoe," Paulina said, easing from his arms, trying to avoid looking into his eyes.

"Oh, let's see what's wrong here." He said to the old woman with enormous enthusiasm. He kneeled before her, "Now, wouldn't it be nice if we knew where we lived? That's why I keep my wallet. If I forget, all I have to do is look at the papers in my wallet."

"Oh, she said, "that's a good idea." And she released the strong grip on her handbag and handed it to Francesco.

Within minutes they were in a taxicab on the way to the woman's apartment. In the cab Paulina felt Francesco's eyes on her. He smiled and said, "Tu sei molta bella." Although she didn't know exactly what he'd said, she had a sense he was complimenting her by the softness of his eyes. After that, his voice stilled for her, speaking only to the old lady who sat between them.

The woman was well dressed in a leather-trimmed suit. She wore a deep brown felt hat with three feathers that looked like they'd come from a rare exotic bird in the Amazon. She lived with her son, who was always away on a business trip. She didn't know why she had thought she was in Oklahoma.

"I've forgotten where I've been," she said to Francesco.

He held her hand. "It's all right," he said. "It's where you're going that counts."

The old woman smiled. "Yes, that's what counts. You're right," she said with determination in her voice

The moment gripped Paulina. Her body and mind felt free. She tingled with excitement. She remembered shamelessly with awe the last time they were together. She had never felt this way about any man.

"Your wife is such a nice lady. She gave me her sock."

She lifted her foot to show him.

At the apartment building, Francesco carried the woman up three flights of stairs. Once inside, she seemed to know where everything was. She went to the closet for her slippers. Then like a small bird finding its nest, she settled into her wing chair. "What an exhausting day," she said.

"You rest," Francesco said. "We have to go now."

"Thank you, thank you so much," she said.

Paulina stepped into the darkened hallway. Francesco was about to close the apartment door when the woman called to him. Through the opened door they could still see her sitting in the chair. In a voice that was small and tired, she called out, "I love you."

"I love you too," Francesco said, without surprise, calmly, as though he had known and loved this woman for years.

They walked three blocks to the Automat. They sat at a table by the window. The cafeteria wall was opposite them. Paulina could see the sandwiches and slices of cake encased in glass. Patrons put their nickels and dimes into the brass slot and the door would pop open. Once the door closed another sandwich or cake would appear. Francesco stared at the black and white marble floor. After three cups of coffee, his mood was agitated, less gentle: "I've been trying so hard to do the right thing," he said, "you know, for Anna and the baby." His lips were chapped from the cold wave she'd heard about in Pennsylvania. Outlined in red, they appeared even thicker.

"God, I hate my job." He shuddered, a long deep breath inward. "You can't imagine how awful it is."

Paulina folded her napkin over and over into a small triangle, a nervous habit handed down from her mother. Every so often she looked up and saw his heavy black lashes and those eyes that sparkled even in time of sadness.

"Driving that damn coal truck day after day. The same route week after week. Seeing the same drab hillbilly towns."

His black widow's peak appeared deeper than she had remembered, and his hair was much longer since their last meeting. He had to move his head back, to keep it from falling in his eyes. "Towns?" He corrected himself. "Some of the 'towns' are a block long." He laughed deeply. She felt him look hard at her.

"I'm sorry, Paulina, forgive me." He reached across to touch her hand.

She shrugged as if to say, it's okay. "How is your music coming along?"

"Well, let's see...on Saturday nights I travel thirty miles to play to a roaring crowd of ten or so." He looked embarrassed. "I really am sorry. I don't mean to complain."

Paulina sat in full view of the revolving door to the Automat. It hadn't stopped turning since they'd sat. Men and women coming and going.

"I haven't stop thinking of you." He said.

She had wanted him to say these words so badly — but now that he had, the words seemed part of something more. Alive with a harsh sensibility of what was to come, she couldn't look at him. "I know." She said, surprised by her honesty, by the quick dismissal of her plan to say goodbye to him before it was too late.

"I ache for you, Paulina." His lips touched the inside of her cupped palm. She felt his mouth find the center of her. When Paulina looked away from Francesco she saw a man at a table near them, looking down at her shoes. She excused herself and looked for the restroom.

Inside the Ladies room she removed her sock and tossed it into her handbag. Looking in the mirror she found herself glowing, vulnerable. She whispered to herself. "What are you doing?" The mirror only reflected him it seemed, and the way he saw her.

When she returned to the table, she almost didn't recognize Francesco. His back was towards her and he sat facing the plated-glass window. His legs were crossed, and his elbow rested on the table as he watched people passing. Seeing him from this angle, she realized she'd never known the ordinary in him. They had only shared their passion for art and music and their insatiable desire for one another. Now the question, which had been whirling around in her mind, kept her awake at night loomed larger than reality, if he left Anna would they be capable of a normal life together?

Two women placed their trays of food on the table next to theirs. It was obvious they were sisters. They had the same face. The fatter one made a ritual of placing her food and napkin and silver just so.

"How are Anna and Emily doing?" Paulina asked.

He turned from the window and smiled at her as if it were the first time he'd seen her all that day. "As far as I know the baby is fine. I don't get to see her much. Only when your mother is visiting."

Paulina drank the cold coffee, wishing she had something more substantial, like bourbon. "Why is that?" she asked.

"Anna always has some excuse. Em is sleeping, or there are too many germs in the air — I might bring some into her room. Oh, the latest one is I'm not supposed to see her unless she has a diaper on."

"Why not?" The soap from the metal dispenser in the Ladies room lingered on Paulina's hands. It reminded her of the brown soap her mother used to wash clothes with. Her mind wandered to the washboard in the sink, her mother's red raw hands wringing the wash, until every drop of water was released.

"I don't know," Francesco was saying. "She thinks it's a sin for a father to see his daughter naked." He shook his head in a hopeless gesture. "And lately poor Em never seems to be diapered. Your mother says the best cure for a diaper rash is exposure to the air."

Francesco lit a cigarette and inhaled deeply. The tip of the cigarette glowed red. She followed his eyes to the women at the next table. "You were right. Your sister's getting worse."

"I'm sorry to hear that, but I had a feeling — Mother's letters. She should've never — ever had a baby." Suddenly, Paulina needed to leave the restaurant. This seemed more than she could handle. She felt claustrophobic. She weaved her way through tables and chairs into the revolving doors, Francesco close behind her.

Outside, the air was nippy, circling around Paulina's sockless feet. "I must get back to the apartment," she said.

Francesco checked his watch. "I have to be downtown in an hour. I'm auditioning for a new band that's forming."

They started towards the subway. Francesco turned his collar up against the cold. "When I spoke to the manager on the phone I told him, I'll be there, hell or high waters, I'll be there."

Paulina was surprised. "Here in the city?"

"Not sure. Maybe on the road. I'll take whatever they offer."

His hand touched her shoulder, to slow her pace. He gazed at her with familiar warmth, yet under that warmth his eyes held an intensity she had not seen before. Whatever it was, unsettled her.

"I'm making changes," he said, "important changes."

They agreed to meet in front of the theatre at 7:30 p.m. As they parted Paulina heard Francesco call to her; "Bella, mia." She turned and saw the wind tousling his hair. "Thanks for the invite. I look forward, amore."

That evening Paulina huddled under the marquee of the theatre, waiting for Francesco to arrive. She felt the winds beat against the hem of her coat. She had made herself numb to the past, to the future. It is now that counts, she thought, it is only now that matters. In art school someone had left behind a copy of Goethe's philosophy. It was thrown amongst the failed canvases, an old painter's smock and a black knitted woolen muff. Bleached by the sun, the book had turned purple on the front cover. It was now Paulina's bible. Each night she'd read a small section and tried to memorize it before falling asleep. She vaguely remembered—living in the moment. And so she repeated to herself, it is now that matters.

She spotted Francesco crossing the street. He had a long grey woolen scarf around his neck, the edges flapping in the wind. There wasn't much time to talk, the show would begin shortly. Paulina knew one small word or an exacting touch would set off the desire that festered within her.

And then it happened. In the darkened theatre, moments before the curtain rose, Francesco put his arm around her. His breath was warm against her ear, sending chills down her neck and spine. "Ti amo, carissima, ti amo." His words caught in her throat—like the time she was a young girl, asleep on the grass and was woken by what seemed like a hundred fleeing sparrows — the sound of their wings beat in her throat, taking her breath away.

The applause for the singer when she appeared on stage was exulting and when she started to sing Paulina fell into a hypnotic state. Her voice trembled with what seemed like uncontrollable passion, and when she sang "Non, Je Ne Regrette Rien," Francesco turned to Paulina, the stagelight glimmering like cracked glass in his eyes, he said, "I too regret nothing."

When the concert was over, two people came on stage, and threw a blanket over the small singer that was nicknamed "The Sparrow." They held her still for a moment. She seemed drained, and while the audience stood and roared for more. Paulina saw the poignant sad eyes of a woman, frail and uncertain about whether she had given enough.

"I can't stand her sadness." Paulina said, feeling the passion of the evening enveloping her.

"Dio di Christo, such vibrations from a performer. Brava, Brava," Francesco shouted excitedly. "Damn, that's what I want to do with my music. Touch someone." He moved a hair that fell across Paulina's forehead and drew it gently behind her ear. "That's what you do with your paintings."

For a brief moment in the dim theatre light and the roar of the crowd she believed that's what she did do with her paintings. But when the house lights came on and the audience began to leave, the idea evaporated as quickly as it had formed.

Leaving the theatre, she thought about Kenneth briefly, how he would've loved the concert and how sad they couldn't all be together. She knew her vision of the world was more peripheral, bolder than most; willing to take risks. On some level she felt gifted—not only in art—but in the way she viewed the world. Francesco's arm around her they walked down Forty-eighth Street; "You make me so happy." He said. And Paulina felt such impossible joy.

It wasn't difficult to notice that the desk clerk at the Ballantine Hotel remembered them from the last time they were there. He was a large man with a tremendous belly that hung over his belt line. He looked away from Francesco to her, and said loudly, "Mr. and Mrs. Ferruggia," as though they were being announced.

Francesco took the room key and saluated him casually and said, "Good night, buddy."

Later, lying in each other's arms, Francesco spoke about Italy. Florence, where the statue of David stands. He described the Piazzas' and the cafes. And the glorious fountains. To Paulina it all seemed like a dream.

"So much has been ruined by war." He said, "It will be a while before we know exactly how much art was destroyed."

Paulina couldn't imagine the destruction of art, and then she thought of all the human lives that were taken innocently.

"Oh, I have one good story," Francesco said, moving strands of her hair behind her ear. "Aldous Huxley had written an essay back in 1925 about a Fresco in the small village of Borgo San Sepolcro. It's in the Tuscany area. The essay was titled, 'The Best Picture in the World.' Apparently many years before some idiot had covered the fresco over with thick plaster and it lay hidden for more than a century. The painting is called the Resurrection, and it was done by Piero della Francesa." He lowered his chin to look at Paulina whose head rested on his chest. "Have you ever heard of him?"

She shook her head no.

"Well, apparently the German artillery commander, who destroyed most of the village had read Huxley's article, went to see the fresco and then ordered it not to be touched." Francesco bent and kissed Paulina on the forehead.

"Yes?" she said, feeling like a child again. "Tell me more stories." She remembered her father in something plaid, sitting on the bed reading to her and Anna. Polish fairy tales, she thought. She felt herself flush with tears. She loved hearing stories of men. Their world fraught with so many differences gave her a taste of what freedom would really feel like.

"So, my question to you is . . . " Francesco ran his fingers up and down the length of her arm. "Who really saved the painting? Was it Huxley for having written the essay or was it the German Officer for being sensitive to art?"

"It was the painter, of course." Paulina sat up.

"The painter? How did he save it?"

"Well, if he didn't paint the image on the wall, then the whole building would've been destroyed."

Francesco took a pillow and tossed it at her. "You think the artist is the Savior?" He laughed.

"Yes," She laughed and threw the pillow back at him. Paulina felt empowered; life was upon her and she didn't want to let it go. His hand resting on her breast, she placed her hand on his and said, "For so long now, I've been living on the surface. I don't want to, not anymore." The wallpaper above the headboard was peeling off at the edges. Roses torn in half.

"I know . . . there must be . . . I have to find a way to make things better for all of us." He said. "Anna doesn't want to live in New York. She's never even been here, yet she hates it. I'm glad though." He flicked his cigarette ashes in the ashtray that rested on Paulina's stomach. "This is the greatest city in the world. How can anyone hate it?"

"Maybe because I'm here." Paulina said, realizing she needed Anna to hate her. Also, she wanted to slather Anna with blame for allowing this to happen. Taking the ashtray from Francesco, Paulina put out her cigarette. She remembered the conversations she and Anna had as children. Never agreeing on anything. It was hard to believe they were from the same parents.

"You? She never talks about you at all. She says she has very little memory of you and her growing up. She remembers more of Eva. Then again, she sees Eva on a weekly basis."

"Hide the truth. That's what Anna always did well. She never really got along. We were always different — I never gave her her way — the way the others did, allowing her the delusions."

She removed Francesco's hand from her thigh.

"You see, I always thought she'd get better if we made her face the truth. But none of us, including myself, had the courage to see it through to the end."

Francesco lay quietly. He was somewhere else.

Paulina took a deep breath. She wanted to ask if he ever makes love to Anna. "We have to stop this," she said.

He sat up, folded the pillow against the headboard, and leaned back. "I know we do, I'll figure it out," he said, and lit another cigarette. He paused to get his breath back. He watched the smoke circling above their heads.

"I also don't know how I managed to screw up my life so badly. I guess I was a coward — couldn't say 'no, I don't love you,' not after she found out she was pregnant."

Paulina leaned against his chest. He didn't love her? I must be evil, she thought. When had she turned bad? Touching her chin, he tilted her face upward so she could see him. "God, I felt so sorry for her — and still do."

She didn't want to hear this. Paulina gathered herself. Hugging a pillow to her stomach, she sat Indian style, facing him.

"I didn't want to be like my father. My mother died when I was twelve."

She sensed his past turning in his stomach.

"I had to go and live with my aunt and uncle. My uncle was always cheating on his wife. 'You can't trust men. They take everything from you — then they leave.'" He took another drag on his cigarette. "Over and over, my aunt pounded."

He looked at her with a face she had never seen before, a muscle in his cheek twitched. "Jesus, sometimes I think she jinxed me, played me until I played the part."

Paulina bent to kiss him. He looked about to cry. "So I had to marry Anna — how could I turn out to be one of those men?"

The traffic outside the closed window hummed continuously, and now the sound of a police siren screeching past brought Francesco back to the present.

"If I don't get this job with the band, I'm going to take a job driving over the road — one of the interstate truckers — they're always looking for men." He looked at her. "Maybe it'll help. Getting away from her. I just feel awful for the baby."

Paulina felt his hand stroke her hair. His touch made her feel secure. Strangely, she felt grounded by this almost incestuous love.

"I made an awful mistake — marrying her," he said.

Paulina hesitated. "I'm not married."

"What do you mean?"

"Kenneth and I never got married."

He stared at her. "I only said we did so my mother wouldn't get upset."

Francesco reached for her. He embraced her with a kindness she could only recall feeling when her mother held her. "What does it matter?" he said. "None of it matters."

They made love on the bed, on a sheet thrown on the soiled rug on the floor. They made love in the shower. Their lovemaking grew thick around them, making Paulina swollen, difficult to enter. Francesco knew her body well. "I love every inch," he said, and soothed her hot swollen lips, licking until she had nothing left to give. Later, exhausted and dreamy, Paulina searched her handbag for her eyebrow pencil and came upon her sock.

Francesco took her sock and kissed it.

"Anything can happen in New York." Francesco glowed, excited by the possibilities.

Suddenly this small woman, this Sophie, who they met briefly, was the most important part of their relationship. It was as though she in some way documented them as being a real couple, allowed them into the ordinary world.

"She's really our first friend, the first person who ever spent some time with us. Except for Charlie the Counter, but he doesn't count." Francesco laughed then turned soft. "When she called you my wife, it felt good." His face lit like a young boy's, "Maybe we'll ask her to be a witness at our wedding."

Paulina planted her feet on the floor, picked up her underwear and guided her arms into the straps of her slip. "Why do you say impossible things?"

Stepping into his trousers, and in that calm almost childlike delusional tone Paulina had heard when he spoke of his music, a manner remarkably idealistic, he said, "Anything is possible."

For a moment she wanted to cling to this. Yes, anything is possible, but where would they go, what would they do? All she wanted was to take refuge in his arms, in her paintings, her appetite, her passion couldn't be tamed. Francesco was slipping his arm into his shirt sleeve, and she wanted to paint him sitting on the bed with his trousers on and his shirt half on; but suddenly she wondered if Anna had ironed his shirt.

PAULINA
DECEMBER 1945
CHAPTER NINE

Weeks had passed and Paulina had heard nothing from Francesco. Her feelings ran from euphoria to anxiousness. She kept herself busy with work and art school, but the only thing that made her feel sated was her painting. She had purchased a new handbag at Klein's Department Store, and inside the small zippered pocket of the old purse she found the ticket stubs for the concert she and Francesco had attended. Remembering that night, she pressed them to her lips, then placed them in a small envelope, and slipped it under the paper liner in her underwear drawer.

Paulina was glad that Kenneth was working a double shift. She wanted to paint. She had just begun to remove the shoebox of oil paints from the closet when Francesco appeared at Paulina's door. He held both suitcase and saxophone under arm. An unexpected thunderstorm had drenched the city. The late afternoon skies were lit with sporadic lightning. "I've left her," he said. His face was glistening with raindrops. His eyes held shadows beneath them and were puffy from lack of sleep.

Francesco held onto his suitcase awkwardly, looking for a space in the already cramped apartment to put it down. Paulina felt stunned, surprised by the news. He had spoken of it, but she didn't think it would happen so suddenly. She had tried to not give her opinion about what he should do, she wasn't certain herself.

"Let me make a pot of espresso." She said.

When they sat, Paulina took small deliberate sips of the bitter coffee. "I feel like I'm in mourning." He said. "As if I've been waiting for someone to pass from a long illness—and now that it's over — I feel this tremendous relief."

Paulina coaxed him to remove his wet overcoat.

"I'm a mess," he said. "She threw a bowl of soup at me." He wore a frayed tan wool sweater too tight around his thick neck. And when he turned to put his coat over the chair, she saw the back of his sweater stained from the soup. She went to touch his back and he winced. "Was it hot?" she asked.

He looked thoughtfully at her for a few moments then took her hand in his. "She says if I don't want to be with her, I can't be with Emily."

Paulina had never seen him so tense, so jittery. He couldn't stop tapping his foot on the floor. "I can't believe how mean she is."

She remembered Anna throwing things. Anna destroying her paints, diluting them with the household bleach mother kept under the kitchen sink. Anna siding with Boris, squealing on Paulina whenever she'd sneak off to meet a boy; that time Anna and Boris showed up at the movie theater embarrassing her in front of the boy. But the worst was when Paulina and her friend Carson cut school early to go to their first live radio show. Mother had said it was all right. "Let's keep it between us," she said knowingly.

Paulina never told Anna, but Carson, quizzed by Anna on almost a daily basis, innocently told her. Ten minutes into the radio show, Boris staggered down the studio steps, Anna behind him. "So here's the princess." Boris's voice still vibrated inside her head. "Who do you think you are?" He grabbed her by the hair and pulled her up the stairs, past the rows of surprised onlookers. After that time, Carson ignored Paulina and never really spoke to her again.

What hurt the most was that Anna didn't seem to possess any love for her. She had a self-righteous holier than thou attitude. When Paulina cried, she gloated and smugly said, "You deserve it."

Paulina knew early on that something hard was growing in Anna's body, something mean and unsympathetic. Yet now she wondered if Anna were home alone and worried about the baby. "Was my mother there?"

"I went to her house to tell her I was leaving. She was on her way."

This was the first time Paulina felt sorry for her mother and for the child Anna had borne. All along it had been easy — not meeting Emily. She was just a name, not anything real, until recently when her mother sent along a photograph of her holding Emily in her arms. The background in the photograph was strange. A heavily carved piece of furniture Paulina had forgotten about was behind her mother and Emily. The baby possessed a typical peaches and cream complexion with large round hazel eyes. Her bone structure, so much her father. Paulina was glad she'd never met Emily. As long as Anna was alive, she felt she could never have a real relationship with her niece.

Paulina had agonized for so long. Felt guilty over Anna. Now remembering Anna's vicious behavior towards her, she somehow felt justified. She willed herself to hold onto those "Anna" incidents, for when she did she felt herself somewhat excusable.

After three or four shots of bourbon, Paulina found herself in bed with Francesco. The candles that banded the head of the bed were lit. They were drinking heavily all afternoon and Francesco complimented her on the aroma of turpentine that filled the apartment. "It layers the air...food for the soul," he said.

"I should've called work," Paulina thought out loud.

Looking towards the shoji screen, he said, "Let me see what you're working on." Francesco moved to get off the mattress.

"No." She laughed, pulling him back onto the bed. "Not until I'm finished. Never," she giggled, "till I'm finished."

On the radio someone sang, "Get out of here and get me some money too..." Francesco turned the volume up, and naked, they sang along.

Unaware of the figure standing in the front room, watching them, they sang with exaggerated booming voices. When the song was over, Paulina, laughing, went to lower the radio. She rolled over Francesco's body, kissed him on the neck. Then, as she reached for the knob on the radio, she caught a shadow out of the corner of her eye.

Kenneth stood there, his face hanging in a way Paulina had never seen. "You bitch." His voice was phlegmy from holding back tears. The words soured in his mouth, gasping, "You rotten bitch. Your sister's husband!"

Paulina grabbed the crumpled white sheet and tried to wrap it around herself. Francesco already with his briefs in hand.

"We have to talk," Francesco said. "Let's stay calm and talk."

"You go to hell, and get the hell out of my apartment."

"Leave," Paulina said to Francesco sharply, "please."

The wind blew the rain noisily against the window. Francesco fumbled with his trousers, as Kenneth looked on. Paulina felt the residue of their sins hang in the gaping silence, disabling Francesco, taking him longer to dress.

At the door Francesco hesitated. He seemed lost, standing there hugging his saxophone to his chest. "I'm sorry," he said to Kenneth. "We never meant this to happen."

Kenneth sat at the table, his head in his hands. Paulina knew he was crying. Without looking up, he said, "Save it for your wife — asshole."

Paulina eyed Francesco to leave. He was gone only seconds when she noticed his suitcase up against the icebox. She thought to run after him, but felt sick inside. Nausea gripped her.

Kenneth began to kick the suitcase. He kicked it against the wall flinging it across the room. "I knew it," he said repeatedly, "I knew it."

Chills ran through Paulina's body. She pulled the chenille bathrobe tight against her body. The suitcase knocked over the burning candles. Kenneth pried the suitcase open, raised the window, and began to throw Francesco's clothes out into the alleyway. "You guinea bastard, you goddamn wop bastard!" The rain whipped into the apartment, against Kenneth's dress-white firefighter's shirt. How reckless of her, how could she have forgotten the firefighter's funeral, that he'd be home early? His expression was contorted, an ugly prune-face against the rain. He continued to curse Francesco. The small Tiffany light hung by a chain over the kitchen table, seesawed against the wind. Paulina felt her stomach roll out of control and reach her throat. She ran to the bathroom to vomit.

When she returned, her books that were lying near the bed were on fire. She screamed to Kenneth, but he sat on the opened window ledge, holding one handle of Francesco's empty luggage, glaring down into the alleyway. He looked exhausted. His shirt was soaked against his skin. Paulina grabbed the rumpled army blanket, and tamped the fire out. She collapsed onto the mattress on the floor and began to cry. She held the book, Goethe — Wisdom and Experience, in her lap. The burnt edges of the paper flaked onto her bathrobe. As she peeled away the charred corner of the pages, she realized she could salvage most of the book, but what of herself? Paint, she thought. This was all she had to do. All she wanted to do — paint. It was the one thing she had that no one could take from her. The only refuge she had.

She would spend the rest of her life working — nothing else. Her tears were no longer for Kenneth or Francesco or Anna, but for herself.

For her life that seemed destined to ungodliness. Somehow along the way, without her knowing, without her wanting, she'd become impure, and now she felt bruised and angry.

Kenneth closed the window and began to take deep long breaths, the way he did after escaping a fire. Wiping his neck and face with the soiled kitchen towel, he spoke. "Well, it's over. That's the last we'll see of that bastard."

Paulina was stunned. This was it? He was going to let this go so easily? Still clutching Goethe to her stomach, she looked up at him and said, "What do you want to do?"

"Do? The only thing to do is for you to stop seeing him." He was calm. A puppy-dog look began to emerge, evoking sympathy.

Paulina swallowed hard. "Do you really think after this we can go on the way we were?"

"As long as he's out of the picture, I'm willing."

Her breath grew rapid. "And what if he's not?"

He knelt beside her. "Paulina, this is your sister's husband. You have no choice."

"He's left her."

"For how long?"

"It's not like that, Kenneth."

"Bullshit. Married guys like him — they all say the same thing."

He walked to the sink for a glass of water, took a quick gulp then turned to her. "You're not seriously thinking about being with him?" His eyelid twitched nervously.

Since her affair with Francesco had begun it seemed she'd lost all reasoning. "I don't know," she said. "I don't know anything. I need time to think."

She sensed the fear inside Kenneth, but he stuffed it away; the way he always did. He touched her arm, her hand, and in a voice weak with pain, he said, "Okay. I'll give you time."

"No, Kenneth. It...it won't work." She inhaled deeply, in need of air. Somberness grew over her. She couldn't undo what was done. There was no turning back. No where else to go. "I'd like you to leave."

"Leave?" His skin looked white as his shirt. "So you made a mistake, we can work this thing out. I'll give you the time you need, but don't ask me to leave...don't." He moved to touch her, but she pulled away.

"Just give me a week or two and I'll find my own place. Please."

She began to feel sick once again. She got up and went to the window. Now the rain, still heavy, was falling straight, bouncing off the pavement below. Francesco's clothes were splayed on top of the garbage pails in the alleyway, between the buildings. She recognized one of Francesco's shirts. One she had perhaps unbuttoned. One she might have put her cheek against. "It was never right with us, Kenneth. You've got to know that much."

"You're serious? You're really thinking of being with that creep."

"No. I don't know. I only know that we — we don't work anymore."

She wanted to say we never did, but the pain was so deep now, that truth no longer mattered.

Kenneth went to the table. He sat down and began to toy with the espresso cups, spinning them on their saucers. "I can't make it...not without you."

"I'm sorry Kenneth, you can stay at the firehouse for a couple of weeks. Please." The chill that covered her skin was now in her bones as though she'd been out in the rain for hours. "We should have done this a long time ago. We've just been fooling ourselves." Now she needed to touch him, to hold him in some way, but she knew he would misinterpret her caring.

He picked up one of the espresso cups. "Is this the cup he drank from?" He threw it into the sink. It shattered into pieces. "Maybe this is the one?" The other cup went crashing.

"Please...Kenneth, please. If you don't leave... I will."

Although she was still facing the window, she felt his eyes on her for a long while. She heard him move from the table.

"I curse the day I met you. What's your sister going to say? Huh, Paulina?" He removed the duffel bag from the bottom of the closet and began to pack some clothes. Paulina tried to help him.

"Don't you dare —" he pushed her away. "Huh, Paulina, answer me, what's your sister going to say?" He was moving quickly, shoes mixed with underwear.

"My sister's not going to know."

He turned to her. "Your sister's not going to know?" His eyes were small and hateful. "When I get down to the firehouse, she'll be the first telephone call I make." His fingers wrapped around the cord of the duffel bag. Pulling it and knotting it, he began to laugh a forced ironic laugh. "You honestly think she's not gonna know? Boy, you and that guinea bastard really deserve each other. I can't wait to tell her."

She didn't believe him. She wasn't going to beg him. She remembered what her mother always said when she found herself no longer in control of a situation. So, in fractured Polish, and with her heart beating wildly, she said, "We do what we have to do."

Emily lies in her crib. Her visual life takes shape in shadows. She is fortunate to be small and fragile — this way she does not understand her mother's agony. Her mother screams and cries. Emily hears the echo of the dead fly still buzzing at her window. Emily's mother mouths wet words over her bassinet, "Your father is dead." Then for many days her mother's shape does not appear. Only the large warm shape of her grandmother is visible. Her breath is sweet, warm like the milk she draws from the brown rubber nipple. Emily's grandmother's cheeks are wet. When her grandmother holds her, she feels moisture against her own cheeks. She is nourished by her grandmother's tears.

Two days after Kenneth's telephone call to Anna, Paulina roused by a heavy knocking at the door. When she opened the door to the apartment, Giorgio, their upstairs neighbor, was holding a round loaf of bread in his opened hands. "For strength," he said, "health and strength." Giorgio was thin and blond and handsome. Fast moving, he didn't waste time. "Get dressed, Paulina. Get off your ass, woman. Your life is not over just because that gorgeous bum walked out on you. Besides, you've got that hunk, Francesco, calling twice, three times a day. I can't keep telling him you're not home." Handing her the bread, he then shook her by the elbows. "Take it from me. I've been through the worst of them. Screw all men." Paulina wondered what he'd say he if knew what she had done.

"Here's your mail." Giorgio handed her a letter. "Okay, love. Now if you need me, six taps on the radiator pipe. Bye . . . ." His back towards her, he waved his fingers at her as he walked down the hall.

The letter was from her mother. Paulina rested it against the ball clock on the kitchen shelf. She wanted to get back in bed, but had been in bed for days. When Francesco went home to get the rest of his clothes, he heard about the shame they had both brought to the family. Her mother had told him how disappointed she was in her daughter, how they had both hurt the family. When Francesco called her from the transient hotel across town, where he was waiting for word of a job, she'd told him, "I need time to think. Since we've met, our lives are in turmoil."

Francesco didn't like it, but he understood. He said, "Know that I love you, Cara Mia."

They had been possessed with rapture, passion, and all the things that one might read about in a torrid novel. There were moments she missed the simple life she had with Kenneth; his clean, uncomplicated presence.

She prepared a cup of espresso and poured some bourbon in it. She sipped the brew, staring at the envelope. She knew what it would say.

Secretly Paulina was glad for Kenneth's vengeful telephone call. It made her feel less guilty about hurting him. A small redemption, she thought.

Paulina opened the letter. She foolishly hoped it would be in English, but how could it be? Would her mother really confide such a delicate family matter to her English speaking Polish friend? She poured more bourbon in her cup. Her mother's handwriting was larger than usual, pressed hard against the note-paper.

It was not a good letter. She hadn't expected one, but this letter seemed untidy, almost chaotic. She saw her anger without knowing what all the words said. She struggled to understand. The lines at the end, she needed to know exactly what they meant, but how could she take it to the baker's wife? How could she ask a stranger to translate, to tell her what her fate was to be with her mother?

Along with the Polish dictionary, she took the letter to bed. She became irritated by the tediousness of trying to translate. When she could no longer bear it, she got dressed and wrote those words she didn't understand on a separate piece of paper. Then crumpling the paper so it appeared worn, she slipped it into her pocket.

At the bakery, the baker's wife was packing an order of rolls for a man dressed in an officer's uniform. "Be right by, Paulina," she called loudly in her broken English.

Paulina waited until the man left the store. She stood before the baker's wife and lied. "I found this. It was written in the back of one of my Art books in school. Can you tell me what it says?"

"You look funny." Mrs. Gongolski said. "You not feel good?"

Paulina pretended to be getting over some bug.

Mrs. Gongolski had trouble translating. At first, Paulina thought in her haste that she might have copied some of the words incorrectly. "Maybe you should send this to your mother," she paused, turning the kerchief that tied loosely around her neck until the tip of the scarf became available to wipe the perspiration from her chin. "This person has no school. Some words not even Polish maybe." But Paulina knew her mother's articulateness. The many hours she spent reading both the Polish and English dictionary surpassed any language Mrs. Gongolski possessed.

Walking home from the bakery, she felt a weighted sensation — resembling relief. She thought about washing her hair. It seemed so long since she'd been out of the house, and now she let the city take her. She melded to its power — its distracting noises. Out of context, her mother's words seemed remote, as though they really had been written in that Art book. Although her mother wrote that she had "committed the worst of all sins," and used the words "hurt" and "anger," Paulina knew her mother's strengths and weaknesses. Her mother had written that her heart felt a "heaviness," that she had "stripped the family of their pride," but at the end she had also written: "You are still my daughter and will always be." Yes, her mother's love was relentless, as steady and powerful as the city that Paulina now yielded to. Yes, it was relief she felt — her mother's reaction was the final stage of her crime — or so she thought.

Her monthly periods were always regular, never a problem.

It came so suddenly — her legs just out of the stirrups. "I need to have an abortion." Paulina spoke to this strange doctor. It was the part she forced herself to play — going the distance. Not allowing a moment to feel, or to think of consequences. It was right. There was no other way. What about her career? Besides, Francesco didn't want to be tied down any longer. And did either of them really desire to have a good family life?

The small man in the white doctor's coat removed his rubber gloves carefully and slowly. "I can't help you," he said, his black eyes like ice.

Paulina felt herself shrink inward, her real self-moving away. "You know no one?" It was more of a statement than a question.

"No," he said, turning to leave the examination room. "And don't use that word in my office again. Don't try to get me in trouble."

Francesco had gotten a name from Charlie the Counter. Several nights later Paulina and Francesco crossed a bridge into Brooklyn in a borrowed car from a musician friend. They walked three flights up the dirty tenement building. The hallways reeked of piss and a mixture of ethnic cooking smells. On the third floor landing, a few doors from apartment 310, someone wrote on the wall in huge black letters, FUCK TILL YOUR BRAINS FALL OUT.

They waited for someone to open the metal door. Sounds carried from the floors below and above. Babies cried and children screamed while radios blasted.

A man opened the door. A Negro woman stood behind him. They seemed pleasant enough, but Francesco wasn't allowed in the apartment. He had to wait outside, but was instructed not to wait in front of the building. "Go for a nice ride," the man told him in a strange accent. "Return in twenty minutes." Then he held his hand out for the money.

As Paulina lay on the kitchen table that was prepared with a vinyl cloth, she thought, only twenty minutes, just twenty minutes. Then the woman pushed a block of wood into her mouth and said, "Bite down, sweetie, this gonna hurt a little." The wood was dry and tasted like a piece of old canvas. She couldn't stop trembling. The nurse grabbed her knees and steadied them.

On the opposite wall from where the woman stood, there was an Oriental painting, shiny, on tin. It was old, bruised in many places. Pieces of metal showed through the gold. She wished for her mother to be there, to hold her hand, to comfort her. Paulina heard her mother's voice, "We make our own misery." She felt herself grow giddy with all the misery she had managed to make. Her mother's words now turned inward — pushing out, through the piece of wood in her mouth, through the sharp steel poking and scraping at her insides. Her whole body began to scream — she could no longer separate the pain from her body. A long fierce howl rose through the block of wood and intertwined with the sounds of the tenement halls.

Hours later, at home, Paulina got into bed and wrapped herself in the woolen army blanket. Francesco elevated her legs with a cushion from the loveseat. He wanted to make her a bowl of soup. He put a cold compress against her stomach, and then she asked him to leave, to go back to his hotel room. She needed to be alone. There was an anger and bitterness welling inside her. Besides, it seemed she felt she had nothing left to say to him.

"I'll find us a place." Francesco said. He was helpless and it glowered on his face. "Ti amo, carissimo." He whispered trying to hide his own fear.

The clots of blood continued to slip from her like small round pieces of liver. The cramps came and went, but that terrible frightening wetness remained between her legs. The room was black. She had come this far. Broken so many rules. But why? She began to shake from the cold. She pulled the cover up; the rough, itchy edge of the blanket touched her chin.

And then, somewhere in that insulated part of her, that part that nothing could touch, she was back in Pennsylvania, in the coal-mining town, the shadowy image of her father carried her out into the cold dark night. He swaddled her and Anna in the warm army blanket. Her mother pointed the way to the car with a flashlight. Paulina saw her father's eyes, glowing, welcoming. The cool night air touched the base of his neck. She pressed her forehead there, and without knowing it transferred her warmth to him. A scent of mint and almonds clung to his skin, and she could smell it now. She could almost feel him there with her, in her bed, swaddling her in the blanket. Her breathing grew rapid with the desire to have him hold her once more. And for a moment he was there, but then the chill that covered her body brought her back.

She crawled off the mattress onto the floor and groped her way in the dark to the pile of blankets Kenneth had left behind. Lying on the floor, she arranged the blankets over her body, one by one, until her arms could no longer reach. She lay still, waiting for the chills to dissipate. The weight of the blankets surrounded her. They seemed to ground her to the earth, to give her some solid purpose. The cramps began to ease, and the blood clots seemed to lessen.

She didn't move. The blankets, their weight, their warmth, had now become her world. She could feel herself sinking into sleep.

PAULINA
1948
CHAPTER TEN

Fall was in the air and the trees in Washington Square Park had already begun to change color. Students from New York University propagated along the benches and grass.

Paulina and Francesco walked passed a group of young men and women with their school bags and books spread out on the ground. The excitement of a new semester was in the air. Paulina thought of her days at the Art Student League and reflected on how simple her life was then. She was beginning to feel older. A past ripe with remorse made one older.

Headed down Broome Street Francesco inhaled deeply, purposely taking in the crisp night air. "September." He said.

Paulina felt his arm warm her shoulder. Leaning closer he added, "My favorite month in New York. Actually, no matter where you live, September is always the most beautiful."

Paulina sensed he was especially vulnerable tonight. His hair longer than usual curled onto his forehead. He seemed courageous and yet heartbreakingly defeated. So much had changed between them but still there remained his ability to hold her captive.

"Umm." Paulina agreed.

Heartbreaking. She thought. This was the unspoken essence of their liaison. Still drawn to him, but in that place inside her she sensed their secret eating away what was left of their love. Their love seemed frail and froth with loneliness.

"Remember my mother is coming to visit tomorrow night. I'm really looking forward to it. I miss her." Paulina said.

Francesco nodded, however she could tell he didn't want to show any anger. "Si. Si. I know all about missing." He said impatiently.

She recoiled when he'd say how he missed seeing Emily. She always felt like he was blaming her for not being able to see his daughter.

"I told you. You must get a lawyer. You have your rights." She said.

"I don't want to talk about it now." He said, letting go of her hand to adjust the gray wool sweater wrapped around his shoulders.

"I'll stay with Charlie for the week, while your mother is here." He said. "Besides I've got a gig in Jersey so I'll be busy a few nights."

Paulina thought of her paintings back to back against the wall of their apartment. "I'm excited to show her my work." She had grown so much since her mother had last seen her work. At least that's what Francesco had been telling her.

The streets were crowded. A homeless man came towards them pulling a rusted wagon filled with his belongings. He pushed his way to pass between them, and the air became permeated with a foul odor.

Francesco guided Paulina by the elbow and stepped away from the man.

"Did you ask her to bring a photograph of Emily?"

"Yes. But who knows if she will." Paulina said.

They were walking into a storm of people crossing the street. "I don't know how anyone drives in Manhattan. It's always packed." Paulina said.

"You want to see packed? Go to Tokyo." Francesco said. "What's going on here?" He asked, as they turned the corner onto Mulberry Street. "What in earth are all these people doing here?"

"Oh look." Paulina pointed to the multiple rows of colored lights that were strung across the street from the building tops. As they walked closer they heard music playing.

"This must be the San Gennaro Feast." Francesco's eyes brightened. "I read about it the newspaper but forgot all about it." He looked thoughtfully at her for a moment. "Would it be Okay?"

Paulina remembered the year she went to the feast with Kenneth and some of his buddies from the firehouse. The guys had made fun of the Italians, and Paulina, even though she felt foolish, had laughed along.

"Hot sausage! Peppers, onions." Francesco stood looking down at the filled trays, and smiled at Paulina. Paulina hadn't seen him this happy for a long time. There were women frying dough in huge vats of oil and sprinkling powered sugar over the round fried balls. When Francesco's mouth wasn't filled with food, he sang along with the music. Different Neapolitan songs were playing in individual game tents. Paulina attempted to throw a basketball and lost a nickel, but then Francesco won a prize.

The woman behind the booth handed him a Panda bear. Paulina sensed Francesco's discomfort as he held the stuffed toy. He Looked at Paulina for a moment then handed the Panda back to the women and said something to her in Italian. Paulina registered his mood immediately, and knew not to say anything. It was about Emily. About guilt and no longer liking who you are. About learning to live with your own kind of destruction.

They stopped a few tents down and ate Gelato spilling over in cups. They watched as a man struggled to get through the crowd with an accordion. Surrounded by loud chatter and music, Francesco motioned to Paulina for them to follow him. They passed more concessions of food and drink and games. In the middle of one of the streets, at a makeshift stage, the man with the accordion and another with a violin stood up on the wooden planks and began to play. The crowd circled around them. Paulina leaned against Francesco. He bent slightly, embracing her around her waist. Then he sang and hummed along with the music, his breath on her neck. Francesco said something, but Paulina couldn't hear him. Now he spoke directly in her ear. "I sometimes feel I don't belong here. Here in America." She detected a tremor in his voice. They had spoken of his going back to Italy one day, but it seemed to be just something they talked about. She wasn't sure if he wanted her to be part of this, to join him, and was afraid to ask.

Paulina looked up at the tenement buildings, strings of colored lights, and banners attached to light poles; the sky wasn't visible. Man has taken away the stars. Paulina felt herself taking deeper, shorter breaths until she couldn't breathe at all and rushed from Francesco, pushed through the crowd, into a clearing of parked cars and taxicabs coming towards her. Francesco was steps behind her. "I'm sorry," she said, leaning against a car.

"It's okay." He said, "You did pretty well. It was really crowded."

The cold sweat began to leave her body. It had been a while since she had one of these attacks. Each time she felt an attack come on, it was like tasting that piece of wood in her mouth all over again. Her mother, the abortion, Anna, Emily, Kenneth, all of it made her feel like she was drowning in remorse.

"I'll wait here for you." She said, "Go on back."

"I've had it. Done." He said, stroking his belly in a soothing manner and they began to walk back to the apartment.

The next morning, while Francesco went out for the Sunday newspaper and croissants, Paulina prepared the coffee and then sat before her easel. The room was cool and still dark. She pulled the shade up and the sharp morning sun lit the room.

Her work had slowed especially since she'd been promoted to manager at Walgreen's cafeteria. It took her months to finish a painting. At this rate she'd never have enough paintings to show a gallery. Time was the enemy. Sometimes she'd stare at a blank canvas for an hour or more, and by then she'd have to leave for work or prepare something for dinner. Living with a man also took more time from her, but she didn't mind. It just seemed somewhat unfair to her that women were expected to do for others, before themselves, so she was glad for those nights when Francesco had to work.

Paulina heard the front door close. "I don't smell any paint yet, but I do smell coffee!" Francesco spoke from the kitchen. "I was lucky. I got Il Giornali at the news stand and the Times for you."

They had fallen into this Sunday morning ritual. Having a long leisurely breakfast and reading the newspaper. Paulina hated when he read the Italian newspaper. Afterwards, he'd be filled with melancholy wanting to go back to Rome. To the bars where people would stand five deep waiting for a turn to get their espresso and the low-ceiling, smoky jazz clubs. He missed the Tuscan hills and the tall cypress trees and the rows of grapevines, especially this time of the year.

Paulina covered the canvas with a cloth and entered the kitchen. Francesco was at the table already unaware of her presence. He tucked a lock of his hair behind his ear as he read. Without looking he reached for his cup of coffee and brought it to his lips. His skin was sun tanned, darker after the summer months of his supplementing their income by working in construction. She had watched him night after night scrubbing away at his hands, trying to get the black from out under his nails. She had mistakenly told him that it was honest, clean dirt. He snapped at her, "People see my fingers when I play the Sax. It's a sign of a loser." It was the first time she saw this snobbishness in him.

"Why are you standing there?" Francesco said looking up from the paper, and taking a drag on his cigarette.

Paulina placed a kiss on his wrinkled brow. "No reason," she said, and sat down next to him.

"De Sica has made a new film. They say it's a Masterpiece."

"What's it called?" Paulina asked.

"Bicycle thieves. It says here, it's a 'realist' approach to telling a story. One of his critics says it's more like a documentary." He laughed.

"Well maybe they'll show it here, eventually."

"Maybe." He said putting the newspaper down on the table and folding it. "I might as well take the paper over to Charlie's. I better go pack some things."

Paulina was glad he was leaving early. She'd have the whole day to clean up the place and put away any signs of his living there. Marishka knew they were together but they had never really spoke of it and Paulina didn't want to parade it in front of her.

Hours later, her chores done, Paulina decided to bake something for her mother. For some reason, her mother had insisted on taking a taxicab from the bus station. She was dusting fine sugar over the still warm chrusciki when the doorbell rang. Marishka stood in the doorway. It was the first time she had seen her mother since before the news of her affair with Francesco. Her hair was whiter and loosely pulled back in a bun. Short ringlets escaped and framed her face. If it weren't for the lines in her face, she would appear younger than her fifty-four years. She wore a thin brown raincoat that Paulina had recognized. Overwhelmed with joy, Paulina went to hug her but Marishka put a halting hand out and closed the door behind her. She then placed her suitcase on the floor and slapped Paulina with such force that she stumbled backwards against the wall. "I've waited for three years to do that." Her mother said, choking on her tears. Then she held her arms out for an embrace. Paulina, stunned by the slap, but not really surprised, began to cry. There in her mother's arms she felt like a young girl again. Forgiven, safe and secure, and loved.

There would be much to discuss but for now it all seemed to be unimportant. She prided herself at sensing her mother's needs. Her mother sat and slipped off her shoes. She opened her suitcase and put on her house slippers the way she would at home. The next move would be to put on some hot water for tea.

"Tea?" Paulina asked, wiping her eyes with her handkerchief.

"That would be nice." Marishka said, putting her shoes into the bag where her slippers just were and about to place them in the suitcase.

"No, Mother. Here let me take that in the bedroom. I hope you don't mind sleeping with me. I promise I don't kick anymore."

"Oh, so I guess he's not here." Her mother rose from the parlor chair.

Paulina was wrong. There would be discussion sooner rather than later.

"I made some Angel Wings. Let me put up the water."

In the kitchen Marishka broke off a piece of the chrusciki and tasted it. "Hum . . . I haven't made these in years. Your sister is always dieting and doesn't like little Emily to have any sweets, so whatever I do, I have to do behind her back."

It wasn't going to be easy talking about Anna and Emily and their life together.

"Milk or lemon today?" She asked knowing her mother switched between the two.

"Lemon." She said, picking up a piece of the pastry and holding it in her hand, "Your father once bought me a box of these from the bakery. Funny, because I always made them. He was very superstitious and believed a woman would have good luck if she had a box of angel wings on Friday the 13th. So whenever the thirteenth fell on a Friday he came home with a box." She smiled. "He said if I made them it wasn't the same."

Paulina poured tea into her mother's cup and then her own.

"I wonder what he would've said about what you did to your sister." She looked down at the floor. Pressing her lips together; contemplating, forming words that Paulina knew would strike at her any moment. "First you live with a man that you tell me you married, and then this thing with Anna's husband." Marishka stood and went to the sink and began to look for a drink of water. Paulina rushed to the cabinet and handed her a glass.

She drank the water quickly. "And now you've also made a liar out of me."

"Liar?"

"Yes, a liar. I told your sister that I was going to visit my friend Mary in Boston."

"Mary? Who's Mary?"

"I don't expect you to remember her. Mary was the woman I met when I first came to this country. We were on the ship together. We've lost contact. About sixteen years ago. And does it really matter who she is?" She walked back to the table and sat before her teacup. "If your sister knew I was here with you she'd probably go crazy." She sighed heavily, then speaking softly, "More crazy."

She began to cry once more. Paulina thought of begging for her mother's forgiveness.

"I'm sorry, Mother. Really. What can I do to make it better? Do you want me to get down on my knees and beg you for forgiveness?"

Marishka's fist hit the table hard. "Do you really think that will make a difference, now?"

Paulina shivered from the truth and mumbled, "I'm sorry." She could no longer cry. This remorse she felt was oddly not for Anna, but for her mother's heartbreak. "I never meant to bring you pain, Mother."

"All I ever wanted was for my daughters to be happy, to get along. To be friends." She began folding the napkin until it became a small square and then unfolded it and started all over again. "Your sister has great depression. She likes to drink also."

"I heard."

Her mother looked up at her. "Umm."

"How is the baby?"

Mariskha brightened, "Oh, she's my angel. Such a lovely child. So much like . . . ." She stopped herself. "She's curious and happy. And no one can tell her what to do." She laughed. "I've got my hands full." She looked up, "Like I had when you were little."

Her mother had a way of making her feel loved, no matter what. Paulina rose from her chair and embraced her. "I know things will get better. I know it." Still in her arms, her mother shook her head, yes.

Paulina had an uneven night of sleep. Aware of her mother lying next to her she hardly moved for fear of disturbing her. Marishka woke refreshed and was eager to go and see the city. "Can we go to Radio City Music Hall?" She asked.

"Oh," Paulina chuckled, "you remembered?"

"I don't forget anything." She said with a little smile.

That evening before going to see the show at Radio City Paulina showed her mother her paintings. They stood in the dim hallway, her mother backed away from the canvases lined up against the wall, squinted, then moved in closer. "They're wonderful. Just wonderful." She said.

"Do you really think so?"

"Of course. How can you doubt it?"

Contemplating one of the East River and the high buildings along the shoreline with a burnt orange sun in the sky, she said, "You're more like me than I thought." Her mother lifted two of the paintings and brought them closer to the light of the window.

Paulina felt herself swallow hard. She wanted to embrace her, to fill her with kisses and hugs.

"One day I'll show you some of my old paintings. Ones that I started when I first came to this country."

"How well I remember you painting. I always wanted your paint and brushes." Paulina laughed. "I'd love to see them again."

One of the paintings her mother held was a portrait of Francesco. Last year there had been a cold spell and they had to wear sweaters and jackets in the apartment. Francesco sat in the deep parlor chair with his black overcoat open and his shirt unbuttoned. The smoke from his lit cigarette swirled profusely against the dark maroon background. He had the beginnings of a beard then. The image was fearless and spirited. Whenever Paulina looked at the painting she felt a seduction of her own making, and now prayed her mother didn't see it.

"I like your style." Marishka said and put the painting of Francesco down facing the wall. "It's sort of . . . brave."

She could only manage a weak "thank you" without tearing up. "Mother, why don't you paint any more?"

"Well, one way you're not like me is that you're a dreamer. You took that from your father. Where do I have the time?"

She was right. She looked into her mother's face. There she saw the ageing she was trying hard not to see. Her eyelids drooped slightly and the lines around her mouth. Her mother not only had her daughter, but now a granddaughter to care for. She had betrayed her family and now it seemed they all paid the price.

The next day Paulina took her mother to the Metropolitan Museum of Art. There was a film crew in the great hall when they arrived. They were able to watch for a while and got a glimpse of Jennifer Jones. Her mother beamed, her blue eyes aglow, "No wonder you love New York."

Paulina was always excited when visiting The Metropolitan Museum of Art, but now with her mother her excitement brimmed over. The French, Italian, Dutch painters; Greek and Roman sculptures, the Spanish, the American artists. Her mother was overwhelmed with paintings she had longed to see for many years. Paulina had to laugh when she insisted on looking for the painting of Whistler's Mother. And finally upon seeing it she asked, "What is all the fuss about?"

By evening they were exhausted and stopped for dinner at a Polish restaurant. They shared a meal of pork and sauerkraut, and had many small plates of appetizers and a bottle of white wine. A rare drinker, her mother was easily affected by alcohol. She'd flush and relax and feel the need to chatter. At one point, she took Paulina's elbow in hand and said, "Thank you for today. I'll never forget those glorious paintings." And then she laughed, "And Jennifer Jones. I saw my first movie star."

"The next time you come we can go again. You only saw a quarter of the museum"

Her mother looked off in the distance to a table where four people were dining.

"I hope I'll be able to come again, without too much fuss."

She wanted to ask, what fuss? But feared the response would somehow have to do with Anna and Emily, and in the end would come back to her, be her fault.

"Let me know if there's something I can help with."

"Help? Its too late for that, Paulina."

The next morning Paulina asked her mother to walk with her to work. They walked along Eighth Avenue. Paulina was amazed her mother still had that vigorous pace and had to rush to keep up with her.

"The telephone is right next to the luncheon counter, so you can call Anna after we have breakfast."

Marishka nodded a yes.

At Walgreens, Paulina's co-worker prepared eggs and bacon and toast. Her mother wanted tea with milk and honey. She was beginning to understand that her choice of milk or lemon had to do with her mother's mood. Milk being the favorable one.

After breakfast she began work and started recording the earnings of the prior nights sales. From the corner of her eye, she watched her mother on the telephone. Apparently distressed. Asking questions, showing great concern.

When her mother returned to the counter she called Paulina to the corner. "I have to go." She whispered.

"Why? What happened?"

"That was your sister Eva on the phone. She was at the house. Anna apparently left the oven door open and Emily sat on it. Eva was just taking them to the doctor."

Her mother was pale. Her whole being taken by the news.

"How bad is it? Do you know?

"No. I'll go back to the apartment, get my things and take a taxi to the Bus Authority. That poor baby, all she did was scream."

Paulina had no time to think. "Why don't we wait and call Eva in a few hours?"

"No. I must go."

They embraced for a long moment. Paulina wanted to cry, "Come back soon, Mother."

"I will. I'll try." She said and held her for a moment longer.

When Paulina arrived home she found a blank envelope on the table.

Inside was a photo of Emily. She was an adorable three-year old with black curls tumbling around her head and the hem of her dress gathered into her hand shyly covering her mouth. She looked so much like Francesco. The picture was taken outside where there were low-lying bushes and there seemed to be an open field in the background. Paulina held the photograph for a long time then put it back in the envelope. She wanted to just crawl into bed and coddle herself. Coddle her self for days. She didn't call Francesco and ask him to come home or to tell him that her mother had left and that Emily had been hurt. Her mother's visit had filled her with uncertainty, misgivings about the present and her future. She didn't know what she wanted. What she should do with the rest of her life.

At the end of the week when Francesco walked into the apartment he was different. He handed Paulina three long-stemmed roses. "I've missed you." He said and they embraced. His color was high and he was radiant, glowing like someone who had just discovered love. "We're going to have to get used to missing each other."

Paulina moved from his embrace. "What do you mean?"

"I mean I got a permanent gig. Paolo, my friend in Roma. I told you he bought an old river boat and has fixed it up."

This was the first she was hearing of it.

"He sent me a telegram at Charlie's saying he wants to go ahead with river cruises. It's going to be jazz boat." He unzipped his duffle bag. "He said the tourist are starting to slowly come back, and that a lot of rebuilding of Roma is in the works." He laid his trousers and shirt over the back of the chair. "Can you imagine cruising the Tiber night after night, doing what you love to do and getting money for it?"

Paulina's felt her knees shaking, her world sinking. She had seen it coming but refused to recognize it. A sensation of suffocating came over her and she went to sit on the sofa.

"Bella," Francesco kneeled before her. "It's going to be okay. I'll be just a year or so. Once I get set up you can come and join me. You always said you wanted to go to Italy."

He was still there before her touching her arm his voice trumpeting but she saw him on the river nodding his head to the whistles and shouts from the audience, his generous smile lighting up the room, and her heart began to sink. She swore she could taste that dry wood in her mouth. Francesco hugged her tightly and she saw the reflecting white of the envelope with the picture of Emily on the table. He never asked about her mother or the photograph and she wasn't going to tell.

EMILY
1965
CHAPTER ELEVEN

The first thing I notice as I leave the taxicab, are thin veiny oak leaves gathered in the corners of the brick steps of the house. The air is spiked with a chill. Dropping my duffel bag on the stoop, I search for the house key. Slipping my backpack off my shoulder it thumps onto the damp pavement.

When the front door opens, I remember the letter from Aunt Eva. It was delivered to the wrong dorm, and someone slid it under my door two weeks later. Aunt Eva had written: "Your Mother finally has good home care. Greta is from the old stock, thick-skinned and tough."

I am not surprised by the appearance of Greta. She is a large woman, tall, with broad shoulders, and a huge back side; so abundant that when she turns and shuffles down the hallway with my duffel bag in tow, her housedress creeps up, revealing a hanging layer of fat at the back of her thighs. The popping sound of her slippers slapping the heels of her feet feels like an intrusion —I don't want her here — this stranger.

"So, I finally get to meet little Em-ly. Anna," she calls, her voice booming in a thick Polish accent. "Em-ly is home from college. Let's see if we can fatten her up." Even though Mother is nowhere in sight, Greta seems comfortable walking through the rooms of the house, talking to herself.

I kick off my clogs, and they bounce against the oak-paneled wall. When grandmother lived here the house smelled of yeast and potting soil. Now, an odor of medicine, or disinfectant, fills the darkened hallway.

I catch a glimpse of myself in the mirror. The reflection from the amber lampshade makes my eyes appear more yellow than they really are. Eddie says they're "Tiger eyes." Suddenly I don't know why I'm home. I should've gone to Eddie's for Thanksgiving dinner, and spent the rest of the time hanging out in the dorm, smoking dope, getting it on with him, and maybe go dancing. Instead, I'm here in the hallway putting off seeing Mother. Afraid of what she may look like, or how she feels.

I have a vision of Mother sitting in the small parlor on her worn Martha Washington chair, even before I see her.

"Mother!" I call as I enter the parlor.

"Oh," she says, hardly moving in her chair.

Her perfectly ironed magenta dress reeks of the forties. She sits tall, with her straight back and long legs, knees pressed together effortlessly, from years of sitting this way. She is queenly, elbows resting on the chair's blue doilies, and her hands gently crossed in her lap. Her posture, an inkling of deception, fills me with wonder.

"You seem well," I say, and quickly press my lips to her cheek.

"Maybe, maybe," she says. I know it will take her a couple of hours, perhaps days, to warm to me. Either she has just woken from a nap, or she is on another medication that makes her eyes huge and glassy. She gazes past my shoulder at nothing in particular.

Greta enters with two glasses of tea and one of grandmother's blue and cream dishes filled with the usual dull array of store-bought cookies. It is obvious that Mother likes Greta. She beams and looks over at me to see if I am aware of her new prized possession. Greta rushes back to the kitchen for milk.

"It's so nice to have a servant who knows what she is doing," Mother says with her aristocratic air.

I can never resist the truth. "Mother, she's not your maid — she's your nurse."

"Greeeeta," she calls.

Greta appears with a pitcher of milk in hand. "Yes, Anna. No need to scream."

"Are you my maid?" she asks anxiously, as though her life depends on Greta's answer.

"Yes, Madam," she says, and she winks at me.

I realized a long time ago that Mother possessed this absurd power to have people lie for her. She practiced it with Grandmother and her sister Eva and any other person who got to know her well. They fed into her fantasies to keep her calm. Now Greta has become part of this mold and I remain the only outsider.

Mother takes a glass of tea and points to a napkin. Greta shuffles her bottom along the loveseat, reaches out, and hands one to mother.

Greta motions for me to take a glass. "I don't drink tea," I say.

She quickly grabs her tea, scoops up several teaspoons of sugar, and deposits them in her glass.

I want to say, Servants don't take tea with their mistresses, but nothing comes from me.

"Where did you get that raggedy skirt?" Mother asks.

I already know this visit will be a difficult one.

"It feels cold in here," I say to Greta.

"Oh yes, oh yes." Greta says. She shuffles her way off the couch and goes to check the thermostat.

Mother sips her tea. We both sit there. Her breathing is in sync with her chest, rising and falling. When Greta returns she says, "I think there is a problem with the boiler. It's not making noise." She looks at me. "Go put socks on — you'll feel warmer."

I plan to ignore her — to let her know I don't need another critical mother, but Mother speaks too quickly and the moment passes. "You look like one of those Bohemians — doesn't she, Greta?"

Greta says nothing.

I stand. "Oh, Mother, I thought you'd love it," I say, twirling, to show my long floral skirt at its best.

Mother replies, "When I was young Greta —"

"Here we go again," I mumble under my breath, knowing what's coming.

"— I used to dress like a movie star. Impeccable, not a hair out of place. Take a look at my daughter. She must take after her father."

Now she has my attention. I want her to talk about father, to tell me something about him — anything, but she babbles on almost deliriously about her good taste and manners.

I talk over her. "Greta, did you know my father?"

Mother looks at me; some kind of dread consumes her expression.

Greta smiles sympathetically. "Of course not, Kykla. I never knew your mother when your father was alive."

"Did Mother ever show you a photograph of him?"

"No," she says, and looks at Mother who is tearing paper napkins into thin strips. "Isn't that right, Anna?" Greta says, and collects the torn pieces of napkin from the hollow of her lap.

Mother looks up at Greta. Her eyes loom large like a frightened child. "Why?" she asks, "problems, always problems. Everyone wants to start trouble, always problems." She moans, until the sound becomes a soft aching whimper.

I feel such anger towards Mother. Everything is about her. Always her.

Upstairs, my room is even colder. Greta is calling Diamond Fuel Oil. She says a man who once proposed marriage to her works for them and she knows she'll get preferential treatment. I hear her shouting his name on the phone.

I sit on my bed and wrap myself in the Navajo blanket that lies at the foot of my mattress. On my dresser there is a portrait, a black and white photograph of Babcia. Her face glows — radiates like a full moon. Next to grandmother's picture is a color photograph, a studio pose of Aunt Eva, Uncle George, and George Junior. These seem to be the only remaining pictures in the house. I've searched the attic on several occasions for Grandmother's album, but I fear Mother may have burned it, as she did the others. All of a sudden I can smell the Vicks that Babcia Marishka rubbed into my chest that night, a heady menthol aroma. A substance setting me up, cueing me. I feel Mother twisting inside me, forcing memories, making it all come out wrong. I begin to rock back and forth, and all at once I'm thrown into the past. I see Mother, reckless, on her knees, hanging over the edge of the bathtub. A hurricane lamp crashes in the bathtub; Flames shoot up in surprise. Mother laughs her madness laugh. It cuts through my small body, I see myself by the opened bathroom door, barefooted in my nightgown, my arms out as if mother is going to embrace me, but I am numb, frozen in position until grandmother swoops me into her arms.

Now, I am under the blankets. Trying to read about the birth of spiral galaxies when Greta knocks at the door. She doesn't wait for me to answer. She pokes her head through the opened door. "We have to bundle up. Roger can't get here till tomorrow night. Isn't that nice, even on Thanksgiving Day? I knew he . . . ."

"Greta," I interrupt. "When you knock, please wait until I ask you to enter." She tells Mother she's her maid, so I decide to treat her like one.

Greta's face is red. I can't tell if she's angry or embarrassed.

"Oh," she says, and quietly closes the door.

I burrow even deeper under the covers. I hate myself for speaking to Greta that way. I do the sign of the cross and say a Hail Mary, and repeat the same prayer I say each night. Dear mother of God, please help my grandmother to recover — give her back the strength she once had. It is quick and simple, more out of habit than belief.

I open the book again and lay it across my chest. Sometimes, I think I really hate Mother. She stirs up a meanness in me when I'm near her. I force myself to read, and begin to feel my body relaxing. Tomorrow I'll be nicer to Greta. I'll eat everything on her Thanksgiving table, then I'll come upstairs and get rid of it.

The aroma of turkey cooking wakes me. I know I'm not in my dorm. The homey smell and the cold air do not blend. At first I'm confused, but then I remember there's no heat. I go downstairs unshowered, in yesterday's clothes and with socks on my feet.

I find Greta in the kitchen. She has on the same pink housedress, and gray pilly cardigan. "Good morning," I say.

"Morning," she says.

"Well, it seems warmer in here. With the oven on."

She doesn't respond.

Mother is still in bed. It's ten o'clock in the morning. I boil some water for instant coffee. There is no coffeepot in the house.

Greta says, "I'm going up to get your mother dressed and down."

"Can I do anything?"

She turns to me, "I manage on my own," her accent sharper than last nights.

The sunlight is broad across the walnut table. I haven't seen the sun for days. I walk to the window. Closing my eyes, I bathe myself in the floating particles.

Mother complains all through dinner and won't eat because she's freezing. "Feel my hands," she says. Reaching out for mine. She touches my neck. I jump at her touch and agree, it is cold.

Greta takes an old pair of Mother's gloves and puts them on her. "There, eat now," she says. The gloves are turquoise wool, with three magenta bows lined up on the top of each hand. I remember playing with them and getting in trouble for wearing them.

Mother eats. Greta has on a navy woolen sailor cap. She says that all the heat from the body escapes through the head. So she's holding on to her body heat.

Seeing mother's gloves moving up and down, Greta's hat, and the Navajo blanket wrapped tightly around my body, one shoulder available so I can maneuver the fork from mouth to plate with my right hand, I think we all look mad, insane. I can't tell if it's the company or the temperature in the room, or both, but all at once I start to laugh. Mother looks at me, shakes her head disapprovingly just as Greta is about to laugh. Greta can't hold herself back. She points to my Mother's gloves. We laugh harder. I point to her hat and we crack up. Mother takes off her gloves. She doesn't know what we're laughing at. I wipe the tears from my eyes with my cranberry stained napkin. "Mother," I say, "it's good to laugh."

"No," she says, and she begins to suck in her cheeks until her face becomes a mask. Motionless, almost dead. She wills herself into this paralyzed state, I think.

"C'mon, Mother. We're just playing."

Greta tries, "Anna, we're having some fun, that's all."

Mother doesn't budge. If only I knew what she was thinking. What was inside her head.

"This fun is over," Greta says as she rises from her chair, and begins to pick up the dishes. "Homemade mincemeat pie?"

Feeling as though I will burst, I say, "Sure, why not."

"Good, Em-ly. You're all bones."

Although Mother is sitting next to me, deep in her trance, I say, my voice edged with a small chuckle, "You better not say that in front of Mother."

Greta lifts the plate of leftover turkey and walks towards the kitchen. "Well, your mother is too skinny, too."

Mother's eyes begin to close. Greta is talking to herself in the kitchen. Before I know it, Mother's chin rests against her chest. I've gotten used to distance, of feeling alone. I tell myself I will no longer cry for Mother, but as soon as I think this, I well up with tears. What flashes through my mind is that summer when Wanda betrayed me, and no one told me Babcia Marishka had a stroke. That's when I started bingeing. I ate whenever I could. When Mother began to notice, she took away whatever I was devouring. Soon, I began to steal food from the cupboard and bring it up to my room. As Mother began to sleep more and more, it was effortless. One day when she was feeling more herself, she pinched the skin of my upper arm, and marched me into her bedroom. Pushing me in front of her cheval mirror she said, "Look at yourself. You're so fat. Aren't you ashamed of yourself?"

Ashamed? I thought, what did I do?

"I don't want a fat daughter. Do you hear me? No fatsos in my house." Her face was twisted up in cruelity. I felt myself cringe. My body crawled with chills catching the hairs at the nape of my neck. She kept saying she was nauseous. When she stopped shaking me, she looked straight at me, her eyes that whitish-blue, and said, "You are a monster. Look what you've made me do."

I saw my reflection in her mirror, a bulbous shape, oyster white skin filled with red blotches, I began to cry. I had always thought my looks were acceptable. Babcia used to tell me I was beautiful. Classic, she'd say. I liked my thick black curly hair, my widow's peak, and the color of my eyes. And my clear complexion. Everyone in school had pimples on their faces. Yet that day, when I saw myself in the mirror, I saw an ugly teenager. My hair was straggly, unevenly wild — and the whites of my eyes were pink. I also thought there were pimples on my face.

Greta interrupts my thoughts. "What's wrong Em-ly? Your mother be okay. Here, eat the pie." She reminds me of both Aunt Eva, who also fantasizes about Mother, and of babcia who always tried to feed me when I felt sad.

Mother sounds like a cat purring.

Greta takes a huge piece in her mouth. "Happy Thanksgiving," she says mumbling through the pie.

It's not so bad having Greta here. At least there's plenty of food, and someone to talk to. "How often does Aunt Eva visit?"

"Oh, such a nice lady. She comes always."

"Have you met George Junior?"

She finishes another bite of the pie and clears her throat. "Oh, he's going to be a big dentist. Just like his father. He's very busy."

I wonder about George Junior, if he's still Mister Weirdo, if his nose is still runny, and if he still has that foul odor about him. I can't imagine him leaning over looking into my mouth.

After my third piece of mincemeat pie, I go upstairs to the bathroom.

I hate the gagging part, but it comes quicker now, then the rest is easy. At first, I feel aroused, excited. I've even grown fond of the irritating scratch in my throat because I know right after that a feeling of serenity will wash over me. When I'm done vomiting, and that sensation moves through me, I imagine Mother feeling this way when she goes into her trance.

The whole evening it rains, making the house seem even colder. I put on Eddie's sweat pants and layer myself in sweaters. I prop myself up with pillows, begin reading and taking notes on electromagnetic waves and the speed at which they travel. I have a hard time concentrating. There are noises in the hall. Greta is helping Mother to bed. "I need a pill to sleep. Is Thanksgiving over?" Greta appeases her, yet she repeats her request for her sleeping pill over and over.

"Drug addict," I say under my breath.

An hour and a half later, the door bell rings. I hear Greta's voice, but can't make out what she's saying. There is a man in the house. It must be Roger to fix the boiler. I think about going down to see what this man, who once wooed Greta, looks like, but I decide I would rather stay in bed. Knowing the heat will be on soon, I close my eyes.

It is still dark out when the doorbell wakes me again. In my sleep ridden mind I quickly calculate that Roger had to leave to get a part to fix the boiler. Even though I've kicked the covers off-hours ago, I don't make the connection. There is a harsh knock at my door. "Em-ly, get up. You've got company. 5:30 in the morning, terrible," Greta says, "disgraceful, waking people from their sleep." The floorboards creak from her heavy steps, then her bedroom door closes.

I jump out of bed. I'm afraid to see who it is. Who would have the nerve to visit this time of night? A moment later my question is answered.

"Eddie. What the hell are you doing here? Are you crazy?" I whisper.

"Hey, I missed you, babe. What kind of welcome is this?" He lunges to hug me, but I move aside and he stumbles against the wall. He has been drinking or is high on pot, or both. I guide him to the couch where he falls.

"How did you get here?" I ask.

"Six fucking hours, I drove. Boy, you sure live far away." He stretches across the sofa and tries to rest his head on the armrest.

"You can't sleep here," I say.

"Hum . . . " he murmurs. He is already falling asleep. I sit on the chair next to him. I hate the way his cheap leather jacket smells. He looks like he slept in the street last night. I thought he was staying home for Thanksgiving. His stepmother was supposed to be cooking. I feel trapped. My ears begin to sting, and my heart races. Mother, and now Eddie, who is so out of place here. The fact explodes inside my head. I take a few deep breaths and tell myself I'll deal with this in the morning. As I tiptoe up the steps, I'm relieved there isn't a sound from Mother's room.

I can't go back to sleep, so I lay there amongst the wrinkled sheets like an embedded fossil, waiting for the house to stir.

Hours later, I hear Greta and Mother in the bathroom. I am alarmed that Mother needs help in the bathroom. I think Greta's mothering is making her worse.

I want to stay in bed. Put the covers over my head, and block out the world. Either that, or drive back to college. Eddie, I remember. Mother will have one of her hysterical fits when she sees him sleeping on her couch. I think of going down to try to get him to leave.

I must've fallen back to sleep, because Mother's screaming wakes me.

I walk down the stairs very slowly, not wanting to deal with this.

"Where is Greta?" I ask Mother.

"Emily, call the police—get this man out of our house. He comes here to fix the boiler and falls asleep on my couch? Oh God, what is happening? What?"

Eddie is sitting up on the couch. His heavy beard already showing. He rubs his bloodshot eyes and looks bewildered. When he sees me he says, "Oh man, now I know what you mean —" he sneers, "—Jesus, she's completely off."

What have I said to Eddie? I tingle with disloyalty towards Mother, towards my family, it lodges in my throat.

"Be quiet, Eddie," I say through my teeth, "not now."

"Emily, don't you dare speak to that man. Call the police. I'll watch him."

Where is Greta? "Greta," I shout.

Greta appears from the basement door. "Greta is trying to do laundry," she says, her rough red hands on her wide hips.

Mother attacks her, "Greta, get this man out of my house. You took advantage of me — you — your boyfriend, how could you?"

Greta starts to laugh. "Anna," she says, "this is Emily's friend, not mine. Here, sit down, the house is nice and warm now."

"Emily?" Bewildered, she sits across from Eddie, who is slapping the pockets of his jacket, looking for his cigarettes.

"Emily would never have a friend like that." Pointing at him. Seemingly uncertain as what to say or do, she settles on a shiver, "Oh . . . he's. . . he's so shabby."

"Thanks, lady," Eddie says, and goes to light a cigarette.

I signal Eddie by widening my eyes to put it away. He does reluctantly.

Mother still carries on with Greta. She threatens to fire her.

"Mother, Greta is telling the truth. This is my friend, Eddie. He goes to college with me." I wave my hand at Eddie, to stand up. The teakettle is whistling away. Mother puts her hands over her ears.

Eddie says, "Yeah, college, sure. I should be that lucky."

Greta must have removed the teakettle because the whistling stops.

"This person — never even saw a college." Mother says in a nearly calm tone.

Sometimes Mother's intuition is amazing. Her vision is clear, like an astronaut, like grandmothers. I would throw Eddie out this very second if Mother would stay this way.

Greta calls from the kitchen, "Breakfast is getting cold."

"Okay, he can eat with us, but then he has to go." Mother says.

Stunned, I show Eddie where the bathroom is so he can wash up. When I ask him to take off his earring, he says, "No way, Jose."

At the kitchen table Greta says, "It's so nice to have company. Isn't it, Anna?"

Mother replies with a groan that we assume means yes.

Eddie sits next to me. I pray he'll keep on his jacket: I think Mother will die if she sees the dragon on his forearm, but then I realize the irony: I see Eddie to spite Mother, to get even, yet I don't want her to really see him.

Eddie looks around at the oak-paneled walls and ceiling. "Nice," he says, "real nice. Reminds me of home." His sarcastic laugh sounds like a bark. Eddie lives in a trailer park.

"This was Grandmother's house," I say, almost defensively.

"Was? What do you mean was, it still is," Mother says.

Greta hands Eddie a plate of fried eggs and toast.

Mother continues to eat her corn flakes and half of banana. The same breakfast she eats every morning.

The silence is once again awkward. I don't know what to say. It's so strange, Eddie and Mother sitting at the same table.

I tell Eddie about not having any heat, how we looked at the thanksgiving table, and that I haven't showered since I arrived.

"Well, man," he says, "you've heard the slogan: SAVE WATER, SHOWER WITH A FRIEND."

Mother's spoon falls into the cornflake bowl. "What is that supposed to mean?" she says.

"Hey lady—get with it —"

I kick Eddie under the table and explain to Mother about the draught—the campaign to save water that's going on in most of the eastern United States.

Eddie pushes his toast into the last of his egg yolk. He has impacted grease under his fingernails from working on cars and yellow nicotine stains on his fingers. Mother, Greta, and I watch the glistening yolk slide off the bread, onto his finger. A chill runs through my body. Eddie licks his finger. Mother looks at me. I turn away from her gaze. He doesn't notice when she shakes her head, disapprovingly.

I've had enough. I stand, "Eddie, can I talk to you a minute?"

He looks up, "Sure, babe, why not."

Mother echoes the word babe.

We walk into the hallway.

"Emily, you know what I expect. Leave the hall door open," Mother says. And then in a lower voice she says to Greta, "That man can only be trusted as far as you can see him."

In the hall, near the front door, Eddie says, "Hey, what's with that old lady of yours—she's got a real—"

"Eddie," I say before I lose my nerve, "you have to go."

"Go? Com'on I just got here."

"I'm sorry Eddie, but we have to go visit my grandmother."

"So I'll drive you. We can . . . ."

"No," I push, "this is family time. My Mother . . . ."

"Your Mother? All of a sudden — what happened to," he mimics what he thinks is me, "I hate my Mother. She's a crazy bitch."

I've never told him that. Never.

"— that crazy bitch."

He's saying all the wrong things. I open the front door. "Get out," I tell him, "get the hell out. No one asked you here."

At first he seems shocked, then hurt. "Well, fuck you, Miss Emily. You snobby little bitch." He backs out the door pointing at me, "Don't you come looking for me at the station, 'cause I'll spit in your face."

I slam the door shut and rest against it a moment. My pulse beats in that sore spot of my throat, my whole body trembles. Eddie leans on the horn for a long minute before he drives away.

Mother enters the hallway. I try to get my breath back. "Are you all right?" she asks. I can't remember the last time she showed concern for me. I think about Eddie. Is this the reason he came into my life? So I could have this moment with Mother?

Her voice is soft and even. "He wasn't really your friend, was he, Emily?"

Maybe this is why the others lie to her — to have this tiny moment of intimacy.

"No, Mother." I say. My lie ends there. "He's just a local boy who lives near the college. He fixed Nora's car once, that's how I met him."

"Who's Nora?"

She's forgotten. "You know, my roommate."

"Oh," she says. "Well, maybe this Nora should be the one to visit. Greta," She shouts, "I'm going up for a nap." She looks at me, her voice still soft, clear. "I didn't sleep very well last night. You did the right thing, Emily."

My eyes meet hers for an instant. They are proud. She turns and ascends the stairway, a magnet drawing me, a quarry of feelings. Her French twist in place. Her body moves with a dancer's grace, a flawless line of brown crepe, dignity abounds, until the undone hem at the back of her calf.

"Mother," I say, my voice trembling, "can I take you up?"

"No." she stops and turns slightly to see me. "Daughters aren't supposed to take care of mothers, but thank you anyway, dear."

I am in this narrow, dimly lit hallway. My clogs are still on the floor, where I kicked them, and she is a magnet, pulling me. I think, mothers are Gods. They can make you or break you. Contrary to the happiness I feel, I begin to weep. At first slow, hesitant tears, that stumble, cut short, choking me, but then they flow easily. I have come to this place many times, but never with this sense of joy, with this relief. My tears fill my being with hope, with the knowledge that somehow, one day, I may rid myself of old childhood ghosts.

When Greta comes down from settling Mother in I tell her I haven't seen my mother so close too normal for years. She says that Mother's new medication does give her moments when she's aware and lucid. It's been so long since I've felt this good. I want to hug Greta, to snuggle against her chest. I want to say I love you Greta, but before I can allude to my affections, she says, "It won't last long. Your Mother steals a shot of Vodky here and there, whenever she has a chance, and that messes up the medicines." She takes the dishtowel and wipes her arms up to her elbows. "Makes her real drowsy. The doctor says it's all experimental. Your poor mother is like a guinea pig."

By afternoon I finish my paper on the galaxies. I'm nervous to see Mother again, but I take a couple of deep breaths and go downstairs.

Both Greta and Mother pray in front of a small homemade altar in the living room. A statue of Mary draped in a light blue garment, a lit votive candle, and a bronzed Jesus on a black crucifix are arranged on the credenza. I'm surprised to see that Mother still prays.

I go in the kitchen and make myself a cup of instant coffee. On the table there is a bowl of baking powder biscuits with raisins, half covered with a dishtowel. I forgot to have supper last night, and I realize I'm hungry. My throat feels better than yesterday. It crosses my mind to pray each time before I eat, to ask God to help me stop bingeing. I say a prayer under my breath. I think it works because I cut the tea biscuit in half.

Mother and Greta enter the kitchen. Greta talks about praying and how good it makes them feel. Mother doesn't disagree. Aunt Eva is right. Greta is a godsend.

I announce that I've finally finished my report. No one seems impressed. I wait for a response from Mother, but she just sits, rocking in her chair.

Later on, Mother seems to be in better mood. She asks me to brush her hair. I jump at the opportunity. Mother's hair is all one length, not like mine, which bears a resemblance to restlessness and youth. The brush glides smoothly, all the way to her waist. Her hair is almost all gray, premature for a woman in her late forties. I wonder if I will take after her.

When I see Greta with the laundry basket, I think she really is a maid after all. "Anna sure looks spiffy," she says, passing through the kitchen.

Mother is humming a tune I never heard. "Mother," I say, "can we talk?"

"Oh," she says, her voice rising in question.

"I am going to see grandmother tomorrow. I'd like you to come with me. It's been so long since you've seen her, and I thought —"

"You thought? Emily, I can't go to Boston. I'm too tired."

I know I am pressing, but I take a chance. "Mother, you know Grandmother's not in Boston. She's only a short way from here." I stop brushing, and kneel before her. "Do you remember where the old movie theater used to be on . . . ."

"Nonsense, Emily," she cuts me off. All of a sudden she has this look of fire in her eyes. "I don't know where you get these wild ideas from." She calls for Greta, her protector. I feel as if I've failed her once again. Suddenly, I'm the one that feels crazed. I hate the doctors, and their roller coaster of false hope, their fucking pills, teasing and hurting.

I've sparked something in Mother, and I will never know what. What does she believe? Why is her truth more painful than mine? I have a sudden vision of myself at seven, trying to cope with Mother's meanness; her throwing my supper in the garbage because I held the fork the wrong way. It was always there — this madness. If father had lived, would it have changed anything? Now, with Grandmother held in her silent vacuum, unable to speak, there is no one left to speak of truth.

Greta rubs Mother's forehead and cheeks repeatedly, rocking her in the chair, "So'kay," she repeats over and over, "so'kay." Mother responds to her in a mournful wail.

I feel as if I'm invading their privacy, as if I've just entered into the middle of an intimate moment between strangers. As I back out of the kitchen, Mother turns slightly from Greta's hand, and says to me, "You never feel sorry for me. Not an ounce of sympathy in you," and then she finds her way back to Greta's palm.

The bus lets me off right in front of the nursing home. I've crossed this threshold many times, but I still feel fearful of what I might find. Outside Babcia's room, the nun tells me that Marishka is not doing well — it's only a matter of time. The Sister must see in my eyes what this moment means to me. She pats my arm, and tries to look concerned. My fear takes on an actual shape. It seems to occupy the middle of my stomach. I should call Aunt Eva—wait for her to come, but then I plant the thought that this is not my real grandmother. When I see her lying gaunt and frail in a bed that looks like a modified crib, I feel affirmed by this thought. In search of breath, my chest begins to expand, as I approach her bed.

Babcia is smaller every time I see her. Blue veins branch out from her hands into thicker more cord-like veins along her arms, yet the skin on her face still looks radiant, penetrated with that delicate light she always possessed. I touch her icy hand. Her eyes open. The nurse enters and lowers the rail of her bed, so I can reach her. When I tell the nurse she's opened her eyes, she says it's just a reflex — a nerve response.

When the nurse leaves, I move the chair close to the bed. I tell her all the things I know she wants to hear; about my astronomy class, and how much she would have loved it, about the poetry I've written, about the heat going off in the house, and how ridiculous we all looked at the Thanksgiving table. I tell her that Greta is a good woman. She takes good care of Mother. And then I tell her that she's missed the beaver moon this month. It's starting to wane. I begin to think of all the moons she has missed, for so many years now. I open my mouth, as though to cry out, but I can't. I feel stunned by my family life, by the things I cannot undo. Babcia's eyes are still open, but they are dead eyes. I lean over, place the side of my face against her bony shoulder, and my arm across her chest. Her chest is strangely warm, hot, like the core of an abscess. I stay there as long as I can, trying to take in her warmth. I cry over her as though she is already dead. Absorbing her heat I remember a line from one of Rilke's poems; —and it is possible a great energy is moving near me. I repeat this to myself several times, and then outloud, and all at once I feel the weight of my grief lifting. It's okay to die, I think, when you're ready, it's easy. The heat from her body, not the memories that pull at me, is the thread that connects us. I kiss her cheek, and put my lips to her ear.

"Babcia," I whisper, "it's time to go. You're ready, Babcia." I look into her eyes, and I think she has met my gaze. "Your spirit . . . ." My voice weakens, I feel pressure on my bones, on my lungs. Inhaling, I take in the cloth from her hospital gown. I try again. "Your spirit will be with me—always. I will never stop loving you." I lay my head against her chest and feel the hot spot once more. I try to imagine her the way she once was. The past seeps into my bones. I see her vibrant, running towards me, as she had so many times before, her arms out to embrace me. Feeling a deep sense of drama, a line from one of my poems comes to me, "— go, Grandmother, go where the moonlight will bathe you," I say. "It's time Babcia. It's time." We lie there quietly, her heart faintly pulsing in my ear.

The nurse enters the room and changes the bag on her intravenous. Grandmother's gown is wet from my tears. I go to the nightstand for tissues and see an opened greeting card on the table.

The card is hand-painted with a huge saguaro cactus and a purple tinted moon illuminating the desert. Inside, someone wrote; I love you Mother. Will visit next week. The card was signed, your Paulina. I hand the card to the nurse and tell her it doesn't belong to my grandmother.

The nurse is new on the floor. "Oh, how pretty." She says. "It only arrived this morning."

"It's not my grandmother's, I say again."

"Oh, I'm sure it is. It was addressed to her." She looks at me, "We'll have to check this out."

EMILY
1965
CHAPTER TWELVE

Three weeks after Thanksgiving I receive a telephone call from Aunt Eva, "You must come home, something — something important has happened." Her voice is benign, but flattened with trouble. After I arrange with my professors to take work home and to schedule one make-up examination I hadn't studied for, I feel resigned, almost peaceful. I find myself telling Nora, who has enough of her own troubles, that my grandmother has died. Nora looks up from her purple spiked hair, her round generous eyes softened with pot. "Ooh, oh, I'm sorry." She cries, and tries unsuccessfully to get off the bed without knocking off the books and papers around her. She throws her arms around me. Nora never wears a bra, but unlike me, her breasts are large. Yet oddly I feel them like feathers against me. "So sorry . . . " she murmurs, more sympathetically now.

I swallow hard, "It's okay," I tell her, "she was sick for a long time."

Nora unfolds her body from mine, "I can dig that . . . ." she says dully, as she begins to make her way back to bed, over her fallen papers.

When I arrive at the station, the bus motor is running. There is no one on the bus; its interior a receptacle of diesel fumes, I take a seat in the middle, next to the emergency window.

Crouching low in my seat, I hear others getting on. Moments later a beefy bus driver stands in the shadow of his half-shell cubicle, and announces that the ride to Portland will take almost seven hours. I stretch to see him over the high-back seat in front of me.

"We're heading straight into a snow storm I'm told." He smirks, indicating doubt in the one who told him, then he raises his hand in a salute. "But no fear, Fred is here," and his whole body shudders with laughter.

I picture Aunt Eva, Uncle George, George Junior, and even Greta, all waiting in their own breathless way; having tea around the maple coffee table in the living room. Aunt Eva's bone knitting needles clicking away in the silence, while Uncle George and George Junior, turn pages of magazines they brought from their office. I picture Greta holding a cloth, pretending to dust, and slipping into the kitchen to have her shot of whiskey or a bite of cookie. Mother would be no where in sight-hidden away, while they decide the best way to tell me that Grandmother has died.

The bus is practically empty; the lights from the oncoming cars flash on the redheaded man seated a couple of rows in front of me. The rocking movement lulls me into a trance, and I slip into a semiconscious state. A voice stirs within me, far inside, it says, your mother is dead, and my body jolts back to the dark interior of the bus. I feel stunned by the possibility of Mother's death. A reality that never occurred to me, until now. Trapped by Mother's illness for so long, I told Howard, my new therapist-counselor, I think of Mother's illness as a small discolored spot on my brain, the part most sensitive to disorder — to madness. I've willed myself to other channels: this is the way she is, this is the way she'll always be. Now the thought of Mother dying turns inside my head, runs sleepily through my body. Shivering, I bring my knees to my chest, and curl against the window. It couldn't be Mother. There comes a time when we must let go of the past. Searching— -is the way towards happiness — the possibilities are infinite, Howard said. Happiness? I thought, "So why —" I asked him, "— do I feel like nothing? Why do I always feel like nothing?"

I think of when I last saw Grandmother in the nursing home, I knew then it was the last time I'd see her. Returning to campus, I felt empty — void of all feelings. I couldn't eat, so I no longer forced myself to vomit. I was transfixed by emptiness. Loneliness seduced me, sweet and familiar, tricking me, until I thought of it as something sacred. Each morning I thought my face thinner, more emaciated. I was taking on mother's sharp nose, and Nora teasingly called me "Twiggy."

I dreamt of Wanda. She was buoyant, alight at the top of Wizard Mountain, where we used to sled. I was below and she repeatedly called me to come to her. I tried to walk, run, but my legs were in dream State. She was laughing at me, at my inability to walk. Her laughter pounded, echoed into a chorus of voices, waking me in a sweat.

After days of living the martyr, enduring my suffering, falling short of my grades; one night while Nora was lying in her bed, earplugs attached, going through her gyrating movements, the pulsating metal bass reached across to my bed and pressed against my chest. I couldn't breath. I began to think of suffocating, of being in an iron lung, and I thought my hands and arms weren't my own. Panicked, and gasping for air, I ripped the earphones off Nora and tried to tell her I couldn't breathe. I was losing any stability I had. I was sinking fast, and worse, I was becoming Mother. At first Nora seemed dumbfounded, but then she quickly identified the problem. Nora had been there; she had pills for it, for all kinds of things. Unprescribed medicine to make you feel better. The pill made me calm and visionary. I was not of this world; wrapped in a cocoon of radiant energy, I floated off to sleep. I dreamt Grandmother's long white hair was clipped, cut unevenly. She seemed angry, but I couldn't see her. An invisible creature chased me, and she did nothing to stop it. Then Grandmother appeared. "You must get well," she commanded, and instantly I was transformed into something happy. Grandmother's hair was undone from her bun, no longer chopped. She touched my hand and we were suspended, floating, hovering low over the turquoise ocean like enormous water birds gliding in long whooping strokes; the thick flanks of our hair fanned out around us like wings. I woke, the flapping of wings in my ears. It was four in the morning. Lightheaded; Grandmother's fleshy hand was still in mine. An involuntary sigh came from me. I lay still, allowing her touch to dissipate slowly, and then I felt the pounding in my temples. Unable to lift my head from the pillow, I waited for daybreak.

Although my head ached the whole next day, the dream remained vivid; it stayed with me for days. I took it as an obvious sign from Grandmother and called the counseling center.

Howard is a small man, boy-like, with red hair cut short. His clothes are too large for him. The sleeves of his pink shirt billow with his movements. He said that my affair with Eddie was a primitive call, a way to harm myself. He swayed back and forth in a maroon leather rocker that was older than he was. "Emily, you have to know — no," he corrected himself, "learn to recognize and understand, that hurting yourself cannot change the past." He stopped swaying in the rocker to write something on the yellow pad on his lap.

"My family," I told him, "their lives," feeling myself stumbling, taking wild leaps, saying things I never knew I felt, "especially my mother's, would be better without me. They would wake at dawn and move through their day without a blemish." Howard's face, except for creases on his forehead, remained expressionless. "If I threw myself in front of a car, and died instantly, Aunt Eva would cry for a day or two — maybe Greta, now . . . . Mother would probably insist I was still in college." I laughed my nervous laugh and tucked my hair behind my ears.

The huge mahogany framed window in his office was opened. I felt chilled, but Howard was hot, pale skinned and at the same time red-faced. I tried to pull myself out of the self-pity mode, but I was so accustomed to comforting myself in this manner, the words came easily, "She never minded my father being dead — she probably wants me out of her life too — if she even knows I'm in it to begin with," I said.

The quiet drone of the heat from the bus reminds me of Marishka kneading dough, like a hush opening and closing. The snow swirls, melts at the warmth of the window. We pass farmland. Holstein cows look frozen in the fields. Their black mottled skin striking against the snow.

Reaching into my backpack I remove my Astronomy book and open to chapter ten, When Stars Collide. Professor Bowden's practice quiz falls between my knees. A couple of paragraphs into rotating neutron stars, and I begin to feel calm again, tranquil, the need to sleep.

I dream a black and white cow repeatedly jumps over a stark hunter's moon. Grandmother straddles the cow as if it were a racehorse. The dream is soundless, but I see her mouth opening and closing, rolling with muted laughter. Molecules and dust particles circulate around her in wisps and streamers, darting here and there throughout a midnight blue solar system. Dust and atoms collide. Amid all this turmoil, Grandmother appears whimsical. She ignores the chaos and apparently loves the cow and how cleverly it performs. Gravitational forces propel Grandmother and the cow onto Saturn. A faintly luminous gold surrounds them. They are centered in this brilliant light. Thermal pressure begins to build and moves randomly towards Grandmother. I sense danger and wake myself. A toddler in the back of the bus is whining. Strangely, my first thought is, I never dream of mother.

At home, the scene is exactly what I expect. Mother is taking a nap. Everyone is relieved that I arrived safely. Greta, in her neediness, pretends to know me better than she does, and scolds me for not wearing winter boots. Aunt Eva's eyes are almost swollen closed, they look painful. She rests her knitting needles on the couch and walks towards me with her arms open, ready to receive me. "Dear child . . . " her sympathy voice at its height, her eyes fill once again.

"No," I say, and push my palm out to keep her at a distance. They all look at me with a genuine sincerity, with great understanding. Somewhere in the core of Aunt Eva's soul she knows. She knows that Marishka was like my real mother— my only mother. Touched by this unspoken knowledge tears well up inside me, but I gulp deeply, take a trembling breath, and wrap my arms around Aunt Eva while she cries.

Upstairs, they have already begun to clear out Marishka's room. All these years the room was unoccupied, unchanged. Yet now the ritual of clearing away the dead seems so important, so necessary. Empty corrugated boxes line the hallway. The bed has been stripped, leaving a lumpy stained mattress. I had forgotten about the wallpaper in Grandmother's room. The off-white background has yellowed, and the brown trees have grayed over the repeated pattern of cape-cod houses. Despite my grief, I smile when I remember the imaginary families that lived in these houses, the adventurous walks they took down the winding paths to their neighbors homes, carrying food and flowers. My finger traces one of these paths and I picture Grandmother sitting upright on her bed, There's Mister and Mrs. Goranski's house. Their daughter Paulina and their son Antoni are playing up in the attic. Mrs. Goranski is making crushiki. Doesn't it smell wonderful? She'd say. Then moments later, she'd unfold her apron and there, centered in her lap was freshly made chrusciki that Mrs. Goranski seemingly brought to our house, when my back was turned. Once, Mother poked her head in the doorway and said we were disgusting to be eating in the bedroom. Even after I accepted the wallpaper people and their homes as sheer imagination, Grandmother and I, on occasion, still talked about the Goranski's as if they were real neighbors of ours. She always said, "They are the best neighbors anyone could have. They never disappoint us."

I prepare to take what I want from Grandmother's room. I bring one of the corrugated boxes from the hallway into the room, and begin to look through her things: I'm surprised to see the enormous pickle jar of quarters still on the floor next to her night table. A quarter deposited for each time we used the washing machine, so there would be money to purchase a new one once it wore out. Under Grandmother's cotton full slips, there is a piece of ginger, hard and shiny, for good luck. In her blanket chest I find her bible, wool stockings, and a Polish poetry book. On the front page of the book there is an inscription in Polish, and in the middle, flowers were pressed with great care so that the leaves appear perfectly symmetrical. In the bottom drawer of Grandmother's dresser I find her silver and blue glass perfume bottle, the one she used for special occasions, wrapped in its blue satin drawstring purse. It is where I imagine she placed it last. Carefully I lift the bottle, and in anticipation, smell the purse. It smells of mold. I draw open the strings and remove the filigree silver stop from the bottle. The perfume has dissipated barely a hint of Evening in Paris.

I continue to place items in the carton. Grandmother's candles which she lit each evening before prayer. When I take the votives down from the shelf, I find dried insects, flies, mosquitoes, and curled balls of spiders in the sunken wax. I remember Grandmother telling me that some insects sleep with their eyes open. I want to keep them exactly as I found them, so mindfully, I place them at the bottom of the carton.

Downstairs there is activity, doors opening and closing. Voices, sounds of years ago, when Grandmother was head of the house.

Greta is fussing with Mother in the hallway, trying to convince her of the benefits of eating at the kitchen table. My ear to the closed door, I listen. When Greta feels Mother's resistance, she changes the subject. "Anna, I have a surprise for you." They are at the top of the staircase now and Greta continues in her cheerful tone, "You'll never guess who's come to see you. Em-ly, Em-ly is home." They begin their descent down the stairs. I press closer to the door and wait, but there is no response from mother. As though the sound of my name commands her to be mute, draws her into her self-indulgent world. The jagged shame of Mother's illness swells inside me. I want to break down the door and scream at her, "Dummy, schizo. Your mother is dead." But as soon as I think it, I feel guilty. Then I remember Howard, his spiritual guidance—like Grandmother's, so I chant the Hail Mary in Polish three times, the way Marishka taught me.

In the blanket chest I find a jar of cream Marishka used to rub into her elbows and feet each evening before retiring. The texture is now watery, but it still smells like almonds. I rub it onto my elbows, up and down my arms. I stroke my neck and the part of my chest where my blouse doesn't cover, and the aroma takes me. Despite mother, I know I exist. I cannot be nothing because I feel the memories pressing down into the soles of my feet, grounding me. Selected memories, bleached, preserved, accounted for so many times — too many times.

Grandmother's spirit seems to embody me, and I feel my spine begin to lengthen. A spiritual growth; I must get on with living. If Babcia were to witness her own death, she would have held her head high, walked tall. I hear her voice: Death is part of life — she moves through me — this is my life, Emily, not yours — leave mine be —you must go and make your own.

And there, under her bed, her spirit guides me to my lingerie box. For years I hadn't seen it. I thought it was lost, or Mother had thrown it away. I dust the lid with the edge of my skirt. The first thing my eye catches are three pieces of hard candy. Mysterious gypsy candy I had to hide from mother, and promise Grandmother I would never eat. "They could be laced with gypsy poison," she had whispered in my ear, arranging the sheet and blanket in neat folds under my chin. Under a greeting card made from construction paper, I find my doll's bathrobe made from Mother's old checkered blouse, and the diary from Uncle Felix. The key is not in the box. I jiggle the lock and pull on it, but it has rusted closed. At the bottom of the box I find unmailed letters, I've forgotten I'd written, all of them to Wanda. I open one after the other and recognize my youthful, careful penmanship. The letters swell with hurt, but I am taken back by the honesty, by the feelings I had so long ago. If I were to meet Wanda again, what would I tell her about myself? Would I lie and fabricate a juicy story or would I say in my learned poetic voice that despite her disloyalty to me, the fragments of our relationship still circulate within my life? Would I tell her I've missed her and have never had an important friend again? An uncomfortable sinking feeling takes hold. It appalls me to think I might accept Wanda as a friend again. That I would open myself to her once more — so I crumble the letters in my lap.

At the funeral parlor, Grandmother is laid out in her rose-colored lace dress. I wear a ribbed black cotton turtleneck sweater with black bell-bottom trousers, and a black embossed velvet vest I stole from the new boutique on College Road. I circled my eyes in black kohl pencil, and purposely applied face powder, with only a light mocha lipstick. I've combed my wet hair severely off my face. I feel dramatic and hurt. I want everyone to see me this way. Even though aunt Eva tries to coax me to sit next to her in one of the two plush wing back chairs directly in front of the coffin, I plant myself firmly in a folding chair in the back row. I am merely an observer from here. The smell of carnations is overpowering and sickening. Uncle George stands by the interior French doors, greeting mourners as though they were entering his home for a celebration. George Junior stands next to where his mother sits. His back to the coffin, he appears to be speaking into an empty chair. His skin tone is still mackerel colored. As he makes his way towards me, I notice his pegged pants. Poor George, he wants to be groovy, but I'm positive he's never been with a girl, and once again, the thought of his pockets filled with moist balls of tissues turns my stomach.

"So I hear you're still star gazing." George says.

His social inadequencies appeal to my sympathy. "Yes, I am."

I try for a smile.

He avoids looking at me. "How much money do you think astronomers make?" It's as if he's asking me how much my bus ticket from Maryland cost.

The room fills quickly. People I've never met. Everyone seems to be a patient or friend of Uncle George and Aunt Eva. They stop to tell George Junior how sorry they are. George doesn't know the right thing to do; he never introduces me or tells anyone how important I was in our Grandmother's life. I feel myself sinking deeper into my own drama: Marishka lives between the empty spaces of my body. She is inside my head, on my tongue. We belonged to each other. Once more, I pity George. He never held this dimension — not even for a moment. His life, I tell myself, has no substance.

The sun reflects off the snow, dazzles through the high colonial windows of the funeral parlor; the kind of sunrays that prohibits one from seeing clearly across the room. Aunt Eva appears to be out of her chair, embracing another woman. The outline of the woman is tall, buxom, on the heavy side, but attractive with long straight blond hair. Their lives have apparently touched. They hold one another without reserve, crying. I strain against the sun. They seem to kiss each other on the mouth.

While George Junior is collecting his condolences, I move to a seat out of the sun. When I look up again, sunspots in my eyes, I see Aunt Eva at the French doors with this same woman. Their arms draped around one other, they both look to where I am seated. A man who has been kneeling at Marishka's coffin approaches them and disrupts their stare. He has black curly hair. His suit is a deep shade of blue and he wears dark sunglasses. I'm not sure if the glasses are because he is crying or because his eyes are sensitive to the sun-rays. He is so large that when he embraces the two women at the same time, they almost fold comfortably into his chest. The man looks my way. I can't tell if he's looking at me, or at the high arched window above me. I am curious, I want to see his eyes. Now Aunt Eva pulls away from him, and is moving her head 'no.' It goes on for a while, then she says loudly, "No. Not now."

The next day, the first day Christmas break begins, we bury Grandmother. After the burial we go back to the house. Someone has draped the mirrors with purple satin cloths. Aunt Eva has a friend who caters all sorts of affairs. In the parlor, where the Christmas tree would have been, food is spread informally on a buffet table. Mother is having a hard time. She avoids eye contact, and keeps insisting someone is screaming. She is talking nonsense and blames Greta for not having a birthday cake ready so everyone can go home. I haven't seen her this bad for a long time. I get a twinge that maybe, on another level, she does know something, and that sympathy she has always drawn from me throbs inside my chest once more.

When Aunt Eva sees mother seated sideways, tilted in her chair, she tells Greta she is better off in her own room, and as they begin their parade back up the stairs to Mother's bedroom, all I can think is, I am stuck home for eight more days.

The main topic of conversation is why I am so thin, and where was I the night of the blackout. It takes a lot of effort trying to avoid George Junior. Although I promised Howard that I would try not to vomit, I stuff myself with potato sun-rays, then sneak upstairs to the bathroom. Afterwards, I stay in my room, and begin reading, You Can't Go Home Again, for my American Literature class. The irony of the title comforts me, makes me feel a strange infinity towards Thomas Wolfe.

Almost an hour goes by before Aunt Eva calls me down to say goodbye to an old friend of Grandmothers. The broadness of Mrs. Wilenski's hands, the cooking scars, reminds me of Grandmother. I want to tell her that Marishka used to say her own hands were like a map of Russia, but I'm afraid she'll take it the wrong way. We talk about Grandmother easily. With a thick accent, Mrs. Wilenski says she remembers when I was little, the way Babcia spoiled me. She says I look like her. She says this to make me feel good or has forgotten what Marishka looked like. Aunt Eva asks me to walk Mrs. Wilenski to her son's vehicle. The day is almost gone. Outside the dimness is like candlelight. I hold Mrs. Wilenski by the arm and help her into the backseat of the car. She asks me to wait until she is situated comfortably and her son arrives. She removes a paper from her hard glossy handbag. The clasp makes a loud popping sound when it closes. "Here sweetheart," she says, "in case you didn't see this. A nice story about your babcia."

I unfold the newspaper article and see Grandmother's name in large print, under the word obituaries. Surprised and pleased, I thank Mrs. Wilenski, and go to shake her hand goodbye. She has tremendous strength for a small woman. She pulls me towards her, kisses me on both cheeks. Her breath smells like a soured washcloth. Her teeth are perfect, too large for her mouth. After she kisses me, they make a sucking sound.

In my mind, I put things off. I recoil to safety. It's intuitive, like poetry. A gift from Grandmother. I did not rush into my room, or lock myself in the bathroom to read the obituary; I simply slipped it into my vest pocket. Now, two in the morning, I wake to pee, and remember the newspaper article. Climbing back into bed, my intuition is cloudy, unfocused, yet my hands tremble as I start to read.

Marishka Natalya Plonka Mikulski

Marishka Mikulski came to the United States as a Russian Polish refugee in 1911 and raised three daughters in a coal-mining town in Pennsylvania, with her husband, Antoni Mikulski. After losing her first and second husband to coal mining accidents, she moved here to Portland and helped to raise her only granddaughter. She was a fine seamstress who made her living designing and sewing wedding dresses. "She was a wonderful artist who chose to devote her life to family — as so many women of her time did," said Paulina Mikulski, her oldest daughter who lives in Tucson. "She was strong and spiritual, and lives on in those who truly knew her."

Baffled, I continue to read:

She died in St. Catherine's Home for the Aged after a series of strokes, which left her incapacitated since 1960. She is survived by her three daughters, Paulina Mikulski, Anna Mikulski, and Eva Hoffman: Her Granddaughter, Emily Mikulski, her grandson, George Hoffman, Jr., and a brother, Felix Plonka, a retired concert violinist living in Kracow.

What? What is this? This is a mistake. Studded with confusion, my thoughts scatter like released molecules. I read the obituary countless times. How could they keep such a secret? Why? Then I realize the name Paulina is not as strange to me as it should be. Deep inside, I have always sensed secrets. Small dark seedlings that now seem about to erupt. Yet in that same space, I feel a kindling of warmth, of something intangible. Paulina, Eva, Anna. Anna, Eva and Paulina. Then I remember Babcia's poetry book and rush to the closet, to the corrugated box of her belongings. I open the book to the inscription page. And there it is: Love, Paulina. Clearly written. My thoughts flee to the greeting card on Grandmother's nightstand in the hospital— the same name. I can see my mother and Aunt Eva keeping a secret from me, but why, why would Babcia lie to me? I am hurt and angry. My bare feet on the hard oak floors sends me back to grandmother's room. I look at the wallpaper once more, and remember Mrs. Goranski's daughter, Paulina. I feel excited and curious and afraid — all these things. "Paulina," I say out loud. And again, why?

Sleep comes with great difficulty. Nerve endings tingle through my body. In my dream I smell incense or candles burning. Grandmother sits in an upholstered chair that rocks back and forth. She is smoking a cigarette. She calls out a name I don't recognize. Mother appears in the way she appeared in my youth, glowing complexion, and a glass tinkling with ice in her hand. Tears roll down her face. I don't want to see mother. I am hiding under Grandmother's rocking chair. It frightens me because I won't be able to stay there too long. I am growing very quickly, and my head keeps hitting the under side of the seat. A faceless man appears. He has small feet and is wearing purple socks and black shiny shoes with large silver taps nailed to the soles. I see his feet, and Mother's, inches apart. They waltz around the perimeter of the rocking chair. I am fearful they will see me, so I curl my body, hug my knees until I become an embryo. I feel my back pinned to the moving seat, which is now caned with hand-tied knots, poking into the flesh on my back, and all I can think is; I must learn to keep time, to be in sync with the rocking motion of the chair, or they will find me.

PAULINA

JANUARY 1966

CHAPTER THIRTEEN

That cool evening on New Year's Day when Paulina wrapped herself in her Navajo shawl and walked out onto the desert behind her house toward the apricot ribbed sky, she felt the heaviness of too much whiskey from the night before, and a deep sense of mourning she hadn't known. It was years since her mother's first stroke. Foolishly, she'd thought she was ready for her death. Yet now preparing a cup of coffee seemed to be an effort. Since her return from Portland, from the funeral, she was unable to work. Her lack of concentration was so unusual she found it intolerable. Restless with thought, in her night garden, she began to pull at the weeds that were still visible by lean daylight. Having glimpsed Emily for the first time at the funeral had brought on a new awareness; Paulina, surprised at her own reaction, was overcome with the need to embrace her niece, to hold her until their touching was normal, without incident, evenly paced and ordinary. How strange. How strong this tie to family, to love someone you've never known simply because they are blood. Was it because she is Francesco's child? Francesco, whom she once loved dearly? A simple comforting thought, but it passed quickly.

Perhaps this was her mother's black magic at work. Yet oddly, for her sister Anna, the one who gave Emily life, there were no feelings of love. Only a deep compassion, or was it merely the childhood memories, those which commit to heart, or did this feeling stem from a loyalty Mother had bred into her daughters?

A steady soft north wind blew off the Sonoran desert. Paulina drew the shawl close to her body. She heard the screech of the aluminum patio door opening, and felt irritated knowing that Lourdes would soon be at her heels. She pulled at the base of what she thought was a young weed, and caught the scent of rosemary. More than ever, Paulina felt engrossed in the past; her mother, Francesco, Anna, and now, Emily. Although she hadn't spoken to Emily that day in the funeral home, from all the years of listening to Mother speak of her, in her heart Paulina knew that the child was her grandmother's soul mate. This thought, this thin thread of hope, caused an excitement, an exhilaration that momentarily lifted her sorrow, turning it bittersweet.

Lourdes called from the patio, "C'mon in, it's getting chilly out there." Paulina heard the scraping of lawn chairs being moved on the patio, the centering of the plant on the table. "The tarantulas are waking soon," Lourdes warned.

Why do I put up with that exasperating woman? Paulina stooped to remove more weeds that came into view by the sudden glow of the patio light. The perfumed scent of the blossoms added to her insistent hangover, making it more difficult to bend.

The moon was beginning to light the night. The flowers on the moon vine glowed like soft fluorescent milky lights over the black iron fencing. The tall stems of the yucca plants had sprouted snowy flowers days before, and now they moved in the breeze like wings of newborn angels. She looked at the sky at the Yule Moon and remembered her mother saying that the January moon was like the July sun, bold and generous. "Yes," she said out loud, "yes, Mother, it is your witchcraft at work."

In the distance she heard a bird squawk, then a long curdled "meow" coiled through the night air. "Cat Claw, not again. Come . . . ." Paulina watched as Cat Claw quickly scooted around to the front porch.

The sound of Paulina's voice prompted Lourdes to call for her once again. "You staying out there isn't bringing our Marishka back," she said in a nagging, but somber tone.

"She's a menace, that woman. After nine years she still hasn't learned," Paulina whispered. Sometimes she felt like packing her up, giving her severance pay so she could retire peacefully in the Mexico village where she was born. She continued to pull at the weeds. But what would she do without her annoyances? Paulina's thought shifted. No one will ever love me the way Mother did; and now she's gone. Gone. The word washed over her, the finality of death circled through her bloodstream. There was an emptiness too encompassing to ever fill. It was easier when she was able to cry. The sadness impaled her spirit and her soul, and there was nothing she could do, even a couple shots of bourbon didn't help. All of a sudden, her mother's remarkable voice, padded with that renewed sense of hope she magically possessed after a crisis, was there in the garden with her, "When one door closes, another opens." Her tone was light and dismissive. Paulina heard the flap of wings nearby and glimpsed a hawk or a fruit bat out of the corner of her eye. Her mother's words ran through her head, One door closes, another opens, and a flash of joy rushed through her. Suddenly she basked in the illusion of having Emily kneeling there along side her in the garden. She then saw her in the kitchen, standing in front of the opened refrigerator, pouring herself a glass of peach nectar. She saw her eyes, intense, yellow, like Cat Claw's, and she rehearsed the words she would speak to her, as she had for so many years now, over and over in her mind.

But why was Emily taking so long to contact her? Three weeks had passed since she saw her at the funeral parlor, since she placed the obituary in the newspaper. What if I am wrong? What if she is not her grandmother's soul mate after all? What if she hates me and doesn't want to see me? She had called Eva several times, and still she hadn't returned her call.

Inside the house, patio door still ajar, Vivaldi blasted. Violins buzzed in the evening air like insects gathering for a feast. "Yes, yes, Lourdes," Paulina cried, "I'll be there in a moment. And lower that music." Her voice rose to a level that made her words vibrate and crack.

Moments later, the violins hummed more softly, a hollow sound, as though contained in the empty clay pots on the patio. Francesco had shipped the four-foot urns from Rome and then when he visited he placed them like bookends at both sides of the sliding glass doors. Paulina loved them even though she knew they were too much for her modest home.

Lourdes was back on the patio. "I only worry about your arthritis, Senorita," her voice now trying to gain sympathy.

"I know, Lourdes. I'll be right there."

How many times had she told her there was never any arthritis, only bursitis that occasionally flared in her shoulder? For some Godforsaken reason Lourdes had to be plagued with misery, or she would become even more miserable.

Lourdes came to Paulina through a writer friend who moved to Europe. She was warned of her free spirit and opinions; but Paulina seemed to enjoy the chaos she brought, besides she was an excellent cook and a fanatic at cleaning. And more importantly, a caring companion.

When Paulina entered the living room Lourdes had already changed into her hound's tooth nightshirt and set up the Monopoly game on the low table in front of the fireplace. She sat on the ottoman, her bare wide feet swinging, hardly reached the floor. "Do you want me to build a fire?" She had lowered the music even more.

"No, Lourdes, not tonight. Just a quick game," she said, knowing in monopoly there was no "quick" play, that she'd have to relinquish the game before it was over. "I want to go to bed early."

Paulina reached for her pack of cigarettes and put one in her mouth without lighting it. She sat on the large brown velvet pillow Lourdes had placed on the floor, kicked off her flats, and stretched her legs out under the coffee table, until her feet butted against the ottoman. Her eyes were automatically drawn to the photograph of her mother and Emily on the fireplace mantel. The miniature roses she had threaded through the filigree brass frame had long since dried. The picture was taken the summer of 1958, when Emily was thirteen; two, three weeks before Paulina's mother had her first stroke. It was the first or the second week of her mother's annual month long visit to Paulina. Mother sat on the old crème-colored sofa, holding the photograph she had brought to Paulina. She was laughing at something Emily had said right before Eva took the picture. Paulina had turned away to pour a glass of ice tea, then she heard her mother's gasp, soft and muffled, like a woman rising in pleasure. The photograph fell from her mother's hand onto the floor. The blue, exquisite iris of her eyes rolled under her top lids, revealing just a crescent of color. Her cheeks puffed with air, and her temples swelled with scarlet veins. Lourdes rushed to Paulina's cries but there was nothing anyone could do. In the seconds that followed, her mother's face twisted, froze into that pitiable expression she was to have the rest of her life.

Lourdes was eating pistachio nuts and offered the bowl to Paulina.

They had fallen into this comfortable life together. Paulina had her work. Most every day she was in her studio. The painting of her coyote, which was reproduced on greeting cards and coffee mugs, and now baseball caps for the National Coyote Foundation had brought in enough money for her to live well and to leave time for her fine art. She was lucky, and she knew it. It was difficult for artists to earn a good living, but somehow she had managed. Lourdes had her baking. Corn breads and muffins and cakes, sometimes daily, which had begun to show on Paulina years before. She also had her chores: Proud of her shiny pots and orderly cupboards, she would occasionally make a point of pointing them out to Paulina. Lourdes beamed with a pride and a purpose Paulina thought inappropriate for simple mundane housework, yet Paulina was thankful to reap the benefits of Lourdes' exaggerations.

"Do you still have your headache? Let me rub it." Lourdes slid her body off the leather ottoman.

"No. It's okay. Really." She usually hated when Lourdes doted on her, but now her thumbs on her temples, at the base of her neck, felt like a blessing.

Cat Claw worked his way up Paulina's legs, and gathered himself into her lap.

Lourdes removed the tortoise shell barrette from Paulina's head, and allowed her hair to fall straight to her elbows.

"I pulled two more stingers from his chest. He's never gonna learn," Lourdes said and as her hands moved thoughtfully along Paulina's crown, Paulina felt her eyes close.

The next morning, after a coughing spell and clearing the phlegm from her throat and chest, Paulina lit the first of three cigarettes she allowed herself. In the kitchen she filled her mug with coffee and walked outside past the garden to the beginning of what she called the desert wall. The sun was a blanket of white heat and Paulina dug into her dress pocket for her sunglasses. The light wind blew her thinning hair about. She gathered it from the ends and twisted it into a roll, then tucked it in back of her collar-less dress. She passed the thorny bushes and the large yuccas that had seeded themselves there years before. The desert haunted Paulina;

the wind and the sun, and the errie strange light set images in her mind, made her paintings alive. Obsessed by its many moods she had to push it from her mind, the way she'd push Cat Claw from rubbing against her leg while she worked.   She remembered the last time Francesco visited: They stood where she was standing now, the spiny fingers of the young saguaro cactus cast its shadow across his square jawbone. "Beauty is most certainly in the eye of the beholder," he said more seriously than Paulina expected. "A desert is a desert. It means deserto — niente."

Yes, she agreed it was a deceptively simple landscape; uncluttered, seemingly unexplorable, yet she knew of the invisible life and the concealed beauty that only showed with the shifting of light. Living in Italy, Francesco had become more "Italian." Not only in his language but in his dress. She had noticed his widow's peak then, the hair near his temples grayer than when she last saw him. He had also gotten thinner through the years. Less bulk with age. The way his shoulders slumped in his unconstructed jacket, had she met him for the first time she would've thought him a beaten man, yet he was more substantial, surer of himself than ever.

Paulina's thoughts were interrupted by a dry churring sound of a bird. She waited to hear its call again and followed the sound to a nearby cholla cactus.   On the ground, near the base of the tree was a fallen bird. As she approached, a repeated pattern of small trilling sounds came from its throat. Paulina put her coffee cup down on the dry pebbled surface, it tilted over, spilling the coffee. Checking the ground for snakes, she bellied down on the desert floor, careful to avoid the spreading branches of the jumping cactus. She never forgot Lourdes' story about her cousin Maria, how she became attached to the spine of the cactus, and how each time she moved, another prickly branch attached itself to her skin. It took four uncles to remove her from the cactus. And two days for her aunts and mother to remove the spiny barbed needles from her body, one even had to be pulled from the lips of her vulva, Lourdes said. It was just a few weeks after that that Lourdes's mother was killed in some strange man's car that rolled into Scorpion Canyon. Lourdes says it was the worst day of her life, the day she became an orphan.

As Paulina reached for the bird, she felt her arm tremble, resisting the slow pace. His body was round like a golf ball. He seemed a mature bird, heavily feathered, with streaks of gold underbelly and layers of brown and white tipped feathers along his crown and back. Making a cradle of the hem of her dress, she carried him back to her studio. The studio was set twenty-five feet from the house. She reached for the key in the hanging planter above the window, and struggled with her free hand to open the door. The studio was formerly a shed. Paulina had glass panels installed on the North side of the roof and last summer she finally had an air cooling system installed, so she no longer had to move her paintings to the house when the heat became stifling. There was a sink and one day she planned to have a toilet installed. Paulina found a piece of canvas cloth spotted with dried oil paint. She laid the cloth on her worktable, then placed the bird on it. His eyes held a blank stare.

The vacuum cleaner boomed through the house. Paulina followed the sound to her bedroom and gestured to Lourdes to turn off the machine. Lourdes looked at her impatiently and switched it off.

"It looks like Cat Claw did get a bird last night," Paulina said as she reached for an empty shoebox on the top shelf of her closet. "Another Cactus Wren. It's a good thing Cat Claw got stung, or the poor thing would be dead."

"I don't mind if he eat bird — he just wants to kill them. He thinks it some game," Lourdes said as she moved her hands over the white chenille bedspread to smooth the creases.

"Don't let him out for a couple of hours," Paulina said, almost out of breath. "I'll let you know when it's safe. And we're going to have to get some ground worms."

"Let him out? You know that cat sleeps all day, then looks for trouble at night." Lourdes then took a small throw pillow from Paulina's bed and tossed it at Cat Claw who was already curled in sleep at the foot. The cat didn't move, his ears just twitched slightly, as though annoyed. Paulina's eyes met Lourdes', they both laughed. Leaving the room, Paulina heard Lourdes talking to the cat. "We gonna rename you — Mr. Troublemaker, or Coma Cat," she said. "Either that, or we gonna throw you to the coyote," Paulina thought of her mother who spoke to all living creatures, including the occasional summer insect that made its way under the floorboards in their old house in Pennsylvania. Her mother could have been talking to one her daughters. "Looking for a cool spot to rest?" she'd ask, as the tail end of a body would slip out of sight. Paulina wondered how she never noticed until now the small, subtle similarities between her mother and Lourdes; they were able to take a basic knowledge, reduce it even further, and still hold on to some humor.

The bird's wing appeared broken. It hung limply. Just how bad it was, was difficult to know. Paulina lined the shoe-box with a clean dishtowel she had pulled from the unfolded laundry, and placed the bird inside. She sat on her stool for a long time, watching the bird, deciding on the best way to treat him. The bird lie on his side, his hurt wing oddly exposed like an opened accordion pleat. She had helped a number of birds survive minor injuries. Resting the wing was most important.

Back in the house, Paulina removed two of Lourdes' ice pops from the freezer. With a paring knife, she separated the ices from the sticks, and put the pieces into a ceramic bowl, and placed the bowl in the freezer. She then washed the sticks in warm water, and dried them by heating them in the toaster oven for a few minutes. In the medicine chest she found a roll of gauze she had used a few months before when the steam from the new pressure cooker burned her forearm. Splinting and wrapping the bandage around the tiny bird without pinning both wings to his body was difficult. After the third try she was successful. The bird, although frantic, was able to walk the perimeter of the shoe-box.

There was a knock on her studio door, then Lourdes walked in holding two wiggly worms between her thumb and forefinger. "Look at these cute little guys I have. Just for you." She said, holding them at arm's length over the bird's beak.

The air conditioning came on, and Paulina shuddered from a sudden blast of air. The familiar sensuous heady aroma of oil paints and turpentine that seemed to inhabit the air conditioning ducts infiltrated the room. She stepped down off the stool and walked to where the thermostat was and adjusted the temperature. The large canvas she had worked on for months was on the easel, covered with an old tablecloth Lourdes had bought for her at a garage sale. The smell of paint was like a shot of adrenaline. She hadn't looked at the painting since her mother's death. In her mind she saw the canvas; the back of a woman with nothing on but a man's sheer dress shirt. She was large, imposing; peering through a suspended six-paned window that seemed to float in the clouds. Her light brown hair and shirt lifted by the wind. Her flesh, buttocks, and thighs voluminous, polished like pink marble. Did she paint the woman waving, or just now think it? Suddenly Paulina was blessed by a whim; an unguarded belief flowed gracefully through her. She could, after all, feel safe in her studio. It was here in this haven, removed from the outside world, where she really lived, felt the strength of who she was. A calm lingering breath washed over her, and she drew it inwards. "Lourdes, I'm going to work for a while," she announced.

"Good, it's about time," Lourdes said, picking up the pieces of wasted bandage off the floor. "I'll make something nice for dinner," and without turning to look at her, Lourdes closed the door.

She slipped the cloth off the canvas and a child's hand emerged from a narrow wall of bricks reaching out for the woman. In the upper right hand corner of the painting, there was another, much smaller window frame suspended. Inside the frame was a black and white portrait of a young Marishka. The painting grew from a dream she had. Now so far from the dream, it would take days before she remembered or could feel the flow of what she was trying to do. She scrambled through the worktable drawer for notes of her dream, then thought they might be in the house. Tossing papers aside, she startled the bird. It began to squawk and run nervously along the cardboard sides of the box. Approaching with a whisper of a voice she said, "You will soon be free, little one." Her voice was so quiet that the bird stilled, appearing to cock his head, as though leaning closer to hear her words more clearly.

Lourdes had not seen her note pad. Had no idea where it was, and had never seen it, all in her 'I told you so,' voice. "If you don't put things in the same place all the time, how do you expect to find them?"

Paulina was in the living room searching under the sofa, having this intense vision of Lourdes' mouth being taped with the gauze she had just used on the bird, when she heard the telephone ring. Seconds later Lourdes tiptoed into the living room, as if the caller might hear her, "It's her," she said, faintly.

Paulina felt her heart jump in her chest.

"Who?" she said getting up off her knees.

"Eva," she whispered. "Your sister."

Feeling let down that it wasn't Emily she walked to her bedroom and picked up the telephone.

"What's wrong?" Eva said.

"Wrong?"

"George Junior said you called three times."

"I wanted to know about Emily."

"What about her?"

Eva wasn't going to make this easy for her.

"You know — have you seen her?"

"I've seen her," she hesitated, "—and she knows about you."

God, Paulina thought, please, please make it right. "You told her?"

"No," she said, her voice harsh. "What I told her was that you did something to the family that wasn't very nice."

Paulina felt relieved. Looking back, she thought of Eva's sweetness and shallowness. Why should Emily learn about her from a woman whose moral courage was never tested. From a woman who placed St. Francis of Assisi and St. Theresa, God knows who else above herself. Eva thought the saints protected her, but it was more like she allowed them to cast a spell over her spirit.

"Does she know how to get in touch with me?"

"That wasn't nice what you did. You purposely put that obituary in the newspaper so Emily would find out about you. Now she's angry at all of us, including our poor dead mother."

"Angry?" She hadn't meant it to be a question.

"Mother and I were the closest to Em, you know. And now she feels we betrayed her — poor thing — as if she didn't have enough troubles, her mother with those problems, and now this — did you have to hurt her again?"

Months before, Paulina read that when a parent dies, no matter how old the child, that adult child finally becomes their real self. It was suddenly clear that Eva had never forgiven her. All that sweetness, the honey pot Eva dipped into whenever Mother was nearby; the words that coined her 'the angel' in the family. Why was Paulina surprised? Eva had always possessed a puritanical view.

"I have to prepare for my church supper, Paulina. I must hang up."

"Eva, you and Emily are the only family I have now." She felt herself sinking.

"Whose fault is that?" Paulina heard her take a deep breath. "— and Anna isn't dead yet, and you happen to be related to George Junior also, or have you forgotten?"

"I would love to get to know George Junior." She had to lie. Eva could make the difference.

"Why can't you leave everything as it is?" She made a small grunting sound.

The smell of fried onions and peppers snaked down the hallway into Paulina's bedroom.

"I can't," Paulina surprised herself. "I'm not going to. Eva, it's been twenty years — enough."

"Well, you won't be getting anywhere with Emily. I told her it's best to leave things as they are, and you don't know this, Paulina, but Emily is just like Mother, strong-headed. And I think that's exactly what she's going to do — leave things alone, the same way Mother and I would."

When she hung up the telephone, Paulina felt strangely and enormously gratified at the thought that Eva had never really known their mother. Paulina had always felt the specialness of her relationship with her mother, and now she felt certain she was her mother's favorite. Even after what she had done, her mother had gone out of her way to visit her and to write and telephone. There were no pretenses between them, no lies. Their relationship had grown rich and profound, without her sisters' interference. Now she would just wait, give Emily the time she needed to meditate on the little she knew. She would get back to work and try to wait.

EMILY
APRIL 1966
CHAPTER FOURTEEN

Sitting across from Howard I sometimes find him appealing. Strange how the way one speaks, uses words, tilts his head, or flashes a smile, can make one attractive; meanwhile a still photo of that same person can cause them to be strikingly homely. Howard's smile forms a charming slight curve, like a small comma on one side of his mouth. His reddish locks of hair are longer than usual and are tied in a short ponytail at the nape of his neck. Seeing him in a tee shirt, I think of our last session when I told him about Michael, who I had just met. When I said that Michael was charming and sexy, Howard's fair skin betrayed him, flushing a deep strawberry over his cheekbones and forehead as though he had too many hours in the sun or had downed a beer or two. "You need to concentrate on your own growth, Emily." His professional voice turned up so high, if seemed unwarranted, as though he was about to boil over. "I would advise you against having any serious relationships at this time. You must get to know yourself better."

His tone had unnerved me, made me feel spiteful, causing my tongue to slip. "Why do you wear such baggy clothes?" And an even deeper beet-colored blush appeared on his skin as he regarded the billowing shirtsleeves of his light pink dress shirt. "I guess it is kind of big!" He said, bowing his head in resignation, as he fumbled with the cuffs pushing them up, and then down along his freckled forearms. Surprised, I realized I had hit a chord and suddenly knew I was able to undo him easily, not on a pyschological level, but on a social plane and yet his kindness, etched with such naviety made me feel so cross with myself that I wanted to confess this to him. *One day*, I thought.

Today, he wears a navy blue tee shirt: *London's National Jazz and Blues Festival '64.*

"Were you there?" I ask, genuinely interested and also trying to makeup for the last time.

"Where?"

"Your shirt."

He looks down at his chest. "Oh yeah, I sure was. A couple of years ago — one of the best times." He had the habit of searching for my gaze when he talked to me, as though the locking of our eyes were some testament of truth. "We're not going to talk about my clothes again today, are we?" He said, totally in control, his pallor colorless, almost opal in tone.

"I don't feel like talking about *Emily* today." I tell him, pushing back the cuticles of my left hand with my right. "I rather think of her in third person."

"Oh, oh." Howard chuckles. "What's going on?"

The high shadeless windows in his office brings in plenty of light, making it difficult to hide. Yet, if one were inclined, even more might be exposed in the dust and clutter of the achieved volumns cross-barred on the shelved walls behind him. Shelves I've learned to lean on when not wanting to face Howard.

"Nothing. I'm perfectly good. Great, as a matter of fact." Since grandmother's death I'd been slowly feeling family ties unraveling. No longer did I feel the need to want to know the how and the why. At least that's what I've been telling myself.

"How long were you in London?"

Howard takes a moment to answer me. "I was in a study-abroad program." He slouches, now relaxing into the deep windowsill where he often sits when restless. "But let's not talk about me today. I haven't seen you since your grandmother died. Tell me how you're doing?"

Even if Howard weren't intelligent, that familiar gentil, comforting gaze alone would one day make him a successful therapist. He doesn't allow the silence to last long. "Have you written anything on the R.O.T slip while you were away?"

Howard refers to the slip of paper he hands me each week with the words: Revelations-Observations-Truths.

The sheet is crumbled between books and other notes in my backpack. I struggle to release it from my bag and hand it to him. "It's too much work. Always thinking. Sometimes I just hate it."

He ignores my whining, irons out the wrinkles with his firm hands, and reads out loud. *"Without mother knowing, she taught me you can't force someone to love you. All you can do is be lovable, then hope for the best."*

His expression is one of pleasure, and stepping out of the strained counsler mode he works so hard to contain, he says, "You're really working it Emily. Crap. . . . I must be honest. This makes me feel so good about myself. I'm really doing the job I should be doing."

Then he chuckles, "Not too professional of me, eh?" And we both laugh. This isn't the first time I feel at ease with Howard. "It's okay to be my friend, too." I say, pushing the boundaries further that he unsuccessfully tries to keep.

"Yeah. I know it's hard. It's work." He says, ignoring my remark. His gaze meets mine once again, then quickly, he turns away and taps a tune with the end of his pencil on the rim of the desk.

In the solace of these moments, the comfortable secure way I feel when near Howard, I still feel the desire to want to cozy up with Michael. Help him practice his lines for drama, I tell myself. But I know it's also the sex and my need to not want to be alone. When I had returned from Portland, I met Michael in the Espresso Café. He was reading Rilke, sneaking a joint, and drinking Cappuccino. I had my portable Rilke in my backpack and was planning to finish a drab Elizabethan novel for class, but I liked the surprise of a sexy man in steel-rimmed eyeglasses. His deep brown straight hair fell over his right eye and I loved the natural way he tucked it back behind his ear, so I made just enough eye-contact as I pulled Rilke from my bag.

"Michael, it turns out, is the perfect solution to keep me from thinking of my family." I tell Howard, not looking at him. "I need a long vacation from them. I no longer want to deal with their melodramatic chaos. Aunt Eva keeps writing me these dumb letters, like she's on a campaign to keep me away from Paulina. She says I'm a smart, good girl. Can you believe how far her manipulation goes?"

Howard sits quietly, waiting for me to unscramble more thoughts.

I don't tell him that when I read her last letter I was in bed with Michael. We had just finished making love and his head was resting on my stomach. At the same time I began to read the letter, Michael grew hard once more. He teased me with the light feathery touch of his fingers, and moaned when he felt the moistness between my legs. His moaning made me dizzy with power. His face tender, smooth with lust, I never finished reading Aunt Eva's letter.

"Your family," Howard says, "is becoming more interesting by the second." He chuckles.

I don't find this funny.

"Em, you must admit, an entire family keeping a secret," he says, "that's highly unusual. Someone evenutally slips, or even worse, wants to get even for with a family member."

"Yeah," I say, thinking of this Paulina. "She's probably another walking loony. Wacky, just like mother.

No one ever talks to her, and from what I gather they didn't for years."

I imagine this mute woman, a combination of Mother and Aunt Eva, confused, unsure of herself, filled with remorse and wood alcohol, living in a makeshift tent under a pissy smelling highway somewhere in the city of Tucson. "She's probably a bag lady, I say, feeling Howard's eyes on me.

"Well, she must be an educated bag lady." With a certainty and gleam in his eye.

"Why do you say that?" I say, pulling on the frayed threads at the hem of my bell-bottoms.

"Well, for one," he says, holding up the photocopy of the newspaper I showed him. "She wrote quite a good obituary." He sways in the leather rocker, left then right, appearing boyish, yet at the same time, pleased.

Michael waits for me in my room. "Hurry, I don't want to be late," he says. He is dressed like a European from the forties; baggy pleated slacks with a white tight fitting ribbed athletic shirt. He has a felt hat cocked to the side where his hair usually hangs, and is wearing crocodile shoes with a matching belt. One of his fraternity brothers has written a one-act play, and Michael is playing the part of the antagonist. To me, he looks too soft, too sexy to be threatening.

"Do you have a neckerchief?" he asks nervously. "Shit, I'm going to be late."

I have never seen him like this. His anxiousness is contagious.

I pull a black and white checkered scarf from the bottom of a drawer.

"Perfect," he says, ignoring the red chess Bishop in the center. He stoops to see in the small mirror over my dresser. His slender hands tie it around his neck with the confidence of a practiced actor.

Much to my surprise the theater fills quickly. Even though the first row is available, I sit in the second row. Soon Michael's football buddies, huge and loud, neatly dressed, but smelling of marijuana and over-cooked Chinese food, fill the first row. My seat shimmies with their antics. Their rumbling gestures reverberate back to the last row.

When the lights lower, it takes a few minutes before some thin wiriy student from the drama department appears from behind the curtain. She introduces Michael's friend as Mark Mastrianno, even though everyone knows his real name is Mark Masters. He is short and thin and quirky. Unexpectedly, Nora climbs over me and pops down in the seat next to me. She leans in and touches my arm. She smells of musk, like the heated ferrets I saw months before in the pet shop. "If he were colored he'd look like Sammy Davis, Junior," she giggles softly into my ear.

Seeing Nora reminds me how happy I am to have a private room. Nora hadn't planned to come back this semester. By the time she decided to return to school, I'd already been assigned a single room. Howard is right, things always happen for a reason. Those nights of Michael sleeping over, love making, pizza in bed, just getting to know each other, all were possible because I had my own room.

Unlike my own life, Michael's childhood seemed to hold all the elements of perfection. A New Yorker, raised with two brothers. He brags how he and his friends would take a private school bus each morning. The bus picked them up at their homes in Westchester county and deposited them at the front door of their school in Manhattan.

"Some mornings," Michael boasted, "we'd be so hungover on the bus, and some nights, buzzed and all, we never went to sleep. We'd tell our parents we were sleeping over a friend's house. Wow, we really had big balls," he said. "We even got the bus driver to keep our bagged clean uniforms under the seats in case we didn't have time to change."

Tired or jealous of his illustrious claims, his bull shit burning inside me, I said, "You and your buddies are spoiled brats." He just laughed and managed, "It's all about the money, babe, don't let anyone tell you otherwise. Even the bus driver liked to get his."

I felt sickened by his attitude, still I let it ride because I too liked when he spent the money: The fancy gourmet dinners. The silver sea shell earrings and matching charm bracelet. The four star restaurants he managed to summon for delivery to the dorm: Weired foods; smoked salmon with asparagus flan and pumpkin ice cream. Food he douvered weekly, most of it kind of nauseating, I thought.

When Michael comes on stage, that innate aura of confidence shows in his steps; he lights up the bare setting like a candle and I think, he is perfection. In the two months that I know Michael I had hoped for a deeper, more solid connection, and yet I still find myself clinging to this hope. I push away the idea that it's just plain sex, along with the comfort of his extravagant spending.

I've avoided discussing Michael with Howard because whenever I do, I notice a change in Howard. He shrugs, his body language fills with deep distaste. Suddenly I see him as powerless, without authority, and I become uncomfortable or insecure with our relationship. Now I question why do I need Howard to be in authority. Why do I feel I need his permssion?

The play is tedious, too intellectual, not enough drama. Ironically, last week, when I asked Michael what the play was about, he said, in a obviously practiced tone, after clearing his throat and pushing his glasses up along the bridge of his nose. "It's about the constricting limits of society and the inability of humans to communicate."

Across the aisle a couple of girls hoot with approval at his appearance. Even though Michael described the script as being abstract — underground—avant-garde, it still makes me feel inadequate. I don't get it. Am I so stupid, or is everyone just pretending to get it? That sinking feeling of not measuring up starts to twist inside me. My mind tumbles in and out. I tell myself, pretend to like it. Is it Michael's feelings I'm worried about or my own inadequacies? Afterwards I wait for the crowd to disband around Michael and Mark. Freshmen are all over him. "Where did you learn to act that way?" Another even asks for his autograph. After a while, Michael says, "There you are," pretending he was looking for me. "How was I?" he asks, instead of asking how was the play, while wiping the sweat from his forehead and neck with my neckerchief.

"Great," I tell him. "Wonderful. How did you manage to memorize all those lines?" Dumb me. He looks at me with uncertainty. Already I've said the wrong thing.

"So, what do you really think?" asks Mark, his hands nervously fidgeting in the pockets of the windbreaker he has just tossed on.

"Very original, Mark," I say. He looks at me blankly, waiting for something more, anything.

"You've done something here — something that's so hard to do." Mark and he both wait to hear accolades while my insides begin to quake insecurities.

Last Sunday I had read a review of a new poet. The book reviewer said that the best writing grows organically, and that this particular poet did it with fervor and a passion he hadn't seen since Theodore Roethke. Instinctively I always knew about "organic" and "fervor" in writing, but never put it into words. "Your lines — well — they — seemed to grow organically, right up to the climax. It had such — fervor, such passion. And Michael's delivery — well, how can I say it —"

The crowd has dispersed from the theater, my voice seems to be the only sound, "— Michael's deliverance — well — he gave it the intensity it deserved."

My little lies races inside me stomach, but I am successful. Michael throws his arm over my shoulder, and all three of us walk up the aisle seemingly happy.

Two hours later, the debut party begins. Michael's off campus apartment is newly decorated. It is the first time I see it, and strangely, I can't remember if it's because I've been too busy with classes or because he hasn't invited me. The white plush wall to wall rug looks as if it was never walked on. Little fuzz balls of carpeting attached themselves to my black faille high heel shoes. A woman in a white ruffled apron is walking around with hors d'oeuvres on a silver tray. Word of the party is out. Frat girls dressed in lace empire dresses, and mini skirts that seem to go beyond mini, command the very center of the room. Their long straight hair pieces annoyingly flip each time they laugh. After hours of drinking and pretentious loud conversations over the blasting music, I decide to get sick and go home. Michael is already so drunk, and it's three in the morning, so I call myself a taxicab.

I lay in bed restless and tired, struggling. Shame grips me. *Tell them what they want to hear — especially if you want them to like you.* This behavior is old. Each time I think I'm changing, I take a step back. Michael's party has upset me. The whole evening held a strangeness. I feel as if I've lost my footing —floating about, uncertain where to land. I don't fit with the crowd he runs with. I don't understand why he's with me? I want to call Howard, but feel too much humiliation and shame. Why do I sell myself short. I think I drank too much. The fact that I lied seems out of proportion, all blown up. Is it really about the lies? In my mind I've committed a small disaster. I wish the Waverly Square Market were open. I want to buy a tub of ice cream, stuff my face with it, then throw it all up. I picture myself slipping a package of thin mints into my pocket. I still haven't told Howard I take things. I fall asleep despising myself.

The Oak tree outside Howard's building is beginning to bud. The weather is so nice we decide to sit on the park bench outside his office. Crocus circle the small fountain that trails along the concrete flower boxes. I feel free for the first time in my life. Howard likes that I use the word "free."

"What does freedom represent to you?" he asks with a relaxed smile, almost as though he doesn't care if I answer or not. His red hair is lighter in the sun. Splinters of short gold pieces move in the breeze around his forehead. Only recently I began to understand, began to connect the dots: I am completely drawn to Howard in a way I was never drawn to anyone. Now my mind turns to Wanda for a moment. Our adolescent fumblings—only the beginnings. Not together long enough for any real history, although we managed to share the blunt of our mother's pain. And Wanda's betrayal, how I thought for sure it would kill me. I had asked

Howard, "Is the core of love pain? Is it only through pain that we discover love?" He had just smiled and said, "That's not love, Emily. That kind of love we leave for the artist, the poet. The tragic."

This thing with Howard, I can say is just plain boring. Caring. Genuine. No games or antics or false skins to climb in or out of. I am altogether at peace with him, and I know on some level he cares about me. And I about him. Yet that familiar chill of distrust still runs through me, and I wonder how will I be hurt?

My bare feet under me, on the park bench, some fragment of thought makes me laugh.

"What's so funny?"

"I was just thinking that to me you're like my grandmother's babka; safe and warm."

Howard puckers his lips, and slowly moves his head up and down, indicating some approval. "Well at least it's not her Kapusta, or sauerkraut."

I love that he is completely untroubled by my analogy. The sun is so strong, I find myself closing my eyes, turning my face towards it.

"So tell me, how does freedom feel to you?"

"Breathing clean fresh air, or like taking a good shit." I say not hesitating.

Without a flinch, he says, "So freedom, therefore is a physical matter." Quick and playful.

"No," I laugh. I know he wants more of me. "I feel carefree, without burden. I only have me to think about."

"So you're no longer worried about your mother?"

The hedges along the brick wall have turned a light pea-green. I take a deep breath. "I can't help her, so why should I kill myself over something I can't change?" I say this because it's the way I want to feel, the right, healthy way to feel. And if I keep saying, thinking it, it might come true. Besides, holding onto my wounds I hold onto my anger, and anger I've come to know is my anchor, my strength. Although Howard is seated to the right of me he turns and faces me fully. The whites of his light blue eyes are blood-shot as they sometimes are. He is about to say something but changes his mind. His sunglasses hang from the neckline of his tee shirt, caught on a thread, he pulls slightly and puts them on. "Babka, huh!" he smirks.

A light, early spring-like breeze passes between us bringing back a texture, a smell, a long ago memory of grandmother or mother but I don't want to examine it, so I push it away to wherever memories go, knowing it will return again.

Sunday mornings I like to sleep at least till noon: Irma, the Resident Advisor wakes me by knocking on my door. When I open the door she's standing there in her lean nightshirt. "Em. I'm just informing the building that a girl was found almost beaten to death last night."

"My God, who?" For a moment I think it's a dream. I pad back to my bed and sit, dazed, bare feet on the cold floor.

"They found her on campus, behind the library."

"Jesus."

"They don't want to tell us who she is until they're sure the parents are notified. So awful. I'm asking all the girls to keep their doors locked." Irma sounds nasal, as if she's been crying. "Especially you singles."

I feel numb and queasy. How many times I walked that route, cutting through the library, out the back towards the quadrangle and food court.

"I'll let you know when I find out who she is."

I get up and lock the door behind Irma.

The day builds on this knowledge.

Going to the food court, I notice the concrete planters along the pathway continue to flood with rainwater. Newly planted seedlings float on the surface. By the time I reach the cafeteria my sweater is soaked to my blouse. A strange kind of blur penetrates the campus. Everyone is talking about the assault. A gold locket was found near her body. The beaten girl was on drugs. Tracks were found along her veins. Her ex-boyfriend found her with another boy and beat her silly with a baseball bat. I hug myself and shiver, feeling the hairs on the back of my neck rise. Fear drives the rumors the way thunder drives rain against the cafeteria doors.

Nora waves to me from a corner table. She sits with her knees drawn up to her chin. She is sick with fear that she'll be next. She drinks black coffee. "That's it," she says. "No more dope for me." Her normally spiked hair is flattened like a boy just getting out of bed.

"You've said that before, Nora." I say, feeling little compassion, suddenly not caring, feeling less tolerate.

"No. I mean it this time, Em. I heard that girl was doping up and fucking any Dick she could find."

"No one knows who she is — how come everyone knows what her life was like?"

"It makes sense, Em," she says, looking at me with her dull, un-stoned eyes, black kohl smeared along her bottom lid from the night before. "People just don't get beaten for no reason."

"Maybe," I say, sensing Nora's fear. "I guess there has to be a reason."

I visualize a girl, long blonde straight hair, on the first day of admission, unloading the family car, placing boxes on the ground outside her dorm, a crisp new comforter still wrapped in plastic on top of her stereo. I see a patch of bloody grass behind the library, and then I see her neck, twisted into this position by the force of the bat across her shoulders. And then I see the small gold locket her high-school sweetheart gave her, half buried near the tree roots. I gulp down a glass of orange juice and try to shake the vision from my mind. "I hope she'll be all right," I say.

The heavy rain has turned to drizzle. On the way back to my room I check for mail. Even though it's daylight the room is dark. I turn on the light and tear open the letter.

We are please to inform you, "Night Glimpse" will be included in our Poetry Anthology. Upon publication we will forward two contributor copies. We congratulate you on this achievement, and hope you will continue to let us see your poems. Sincerely, the editors.

I huddle in my chair and read the letter again, then again. I had sent the poem to them over a year ago. Until now it was only something I dreamt about. "I don't believe it," I say. Clutching the letter to my chest, I float to the telephone and call Michael; he answers in a stupor. "We were cel-bratin," he says, his voice drowning into his pillow. I glance at my clock,

"It's three in the afternoon."

"Hmm . . . " he moans.

The need to tell him dissipates. "I'll talk to you later," I say.

Going through my small folder of poems, I come upon "Night Glimpse." I think of Grandmother, the time we went ice-skating on Paumanok Lake. The way she was up on her skates in no time, extending her arms in wild gestures. She looked awkward and peculiar. Was she trying to balance or was she performing her own unrehearsed dance? She called out to me, "My swan imitation," her arms flopping about like clumsy heavy wings. "I'm moving into the swan's home for the winter," she said. I was tightening the shoelaces on my skates. I remember the cold, already stunning my toes, and my laughter drawing in breaths of iced air. Then, years later, after her stroke, when she could no longer walk or talk, I dreamt we were back on that lake. The dream was so vivid; the brown liver spot on her cheek. Strange details only dreams are allowed. I called out to her, but she didn't respond. Her skates cut into the frozen lake, screeching, like a train hugging a curve. She spun in circles; flames of ice began to shoot up around her feet. She was delirious. Faster and faster she twirled until the 'spot' on her cheek became a series of dots at the end of a movie film. She was fascinated, pleased with her style, with her behavior — it was the only time I recognized her as a woman. Not a mother or grandmother, but a woman. I woke from the dream shouting something inaudible. Aunt Eva had burst into my room. She was afraid I'd wake Uncle George. At breakfast Aunt Eva said, "Dreaming about your mother." More of a statement than a question. I never told her the dream was about grandmother, and that afternoon in school, in Mrs. Staver's English class, I began to write the poem.

I spend the rest of the day and night going through my poems. I pull out a few that I think have potential, and put them aside for revision. Michael doesn't call until sometime in the early morning hours, waking me from a dream so deep, I couldn't recall any part of it. "Did I wake you?" he asks.

Even though we've agreed on "no commitments," his late night phone calls always make me feel wounded. But then I remember my poem, and try to brush my feeling aside. "I've had a poem accepted," I mutter.

"A what?"

"A poem," I repeat more clearly.

"Wow, that's groovy. Can I come up?" He sounds high on beer. "Mark and I have been working on something new. Jesus, it's going to blow you away."

"Did you hear about the girl?"

"What girl?"

"The girl who was beaten."

"Oh yeah. I heard."

"Isn't it awful?" I say.

"Hey, yeah — well, you know she didn't go here."

"She didn't?" I am becoming more alert. "How do you know?"

"She's a pro."

"A what?" For a moment his term escapes me.

"You know. A hooker, a whore. Most of the guys know her. She works the campus." Michael has a hard time being still. I hear feet shuffling, then a tinny sound indicating he's at a pay phone.

"You know her?"

"Listen, Em, go downstairs and unlock the door for me. I'll be there in two minutes."

I recognize the pattern that's formed: I find it difficult to resist Michael, then afterwards berate myself knowing he's using me, calling me whenever he needs, no matter the hour. His sculptured Roman nose and plush lips, deep gray eyes, and his alabaster skin tone all contribute to his beauty, and now emptying his pockets of cash machine slips, money he gets from his parent's account daily, and blue breath mints on top of my desk, not even noticing the scattering of poems purposely left to entice, I wonder would he be less self-absorbed if he weren't so good looking?

"Where are your eyeglasses?" I ask.

"I left them at the house."

"How come, don't you need them?"

"Nay," he says, unbuttoning his shirt. "I just like the way they look."

"And," he moves to take me in his arms, "I also like the way you look."

Later, our naked bodies pressed together. "I like coming home to you." He says

"Home?"

"Yeah, you feel like home. Maybe we should get married." He was talking through weed, and even at this late hour, still smelling of department store cologne.

"What do you want to do with your life?" I ask.

"Play." He nuzzles in my neck. "Play, and more play."

"I'm serious." I say.

"So am I." he says, "Too much beer, be right back." He pulls up his Jeans, opens the door and looks both ways before padding across the hall to the bathroom.

Michael's late night phone calls have gotten to me. Three days after not hearing from him he calls me at 2:30 in the morning. "Hi Baby," he says, "come down and open the door for me, I'll be there in a few minutes."

"No." I say, having just gotten to sleep, and once again feeling injured. "How the hell can you be so inconsiderate? I ask. I have a test in the morning."

"Boy, you're in a lousy mood," he says and slams the phone receiver hard enough to startle me.

I feel violated. His waking me, then hanging up.

Do I expect the impossible? Howard says I purposely gravitate to those that will hurt me. Trying to build self-esteem is like taking baby steps, he says. One small change builds on another. I feel the end of my relationship with Michael is near. The disagreements, fights, excuses — lies — and now this inkling I have of him cheating on me. Lately there have been no dinners, or gifts or flowers, as there were at the beginning. Endings come into existence in quiet, mundane ways — you can't tell when it's happening, somehow it sneaks up on you. I promise myself, no more relationships. Even when you think they won't hurt, they do.

A few days later another surprise comes in the mail: Legal documents from a lawyer. It appears Grandmother left the house and its belongings to me. A summer memory comes quickly: I see the house as it once was; clematis vines blooming along the fence; the brick walk hosed down, pinched clean of the insistent weeds that grew in between the cracks. The lion's head doorknocker, shiny, with one brass screw missing. Inside, Mother and Greta nap in the parlor chairs, in front of a too loud television. They have taken over. I forget what I'm trying to remember, and place the papers in my top drawer under my underwear. What will I do with the house? I would never go back to live in Maine? Is this Grandmother's guilt gift for keeping a secret from me? I think of George Junior. His name doesn't appear anywhere in the papers. Still greedy for her love, I feel victorious, triumphant. Now they'll know the capacity of Babcia's love for me, I think.

Out of nowhere that poor beaten girl comes to mind. How, in a way, it could have been me if it weren't for Grandmother. She had saved any penny she could snatch up to send me to college. I recall her coal-miners widow's pension check arriving by mail each month, the way she'd throw a kiss towards heaven and say, "God bless you, Antoni," and sometimes she'd add, "and you too, Boris."

Then there were the yards of white silk and lace running under the pulsating needle of the sewing machine, billowing over on her lap. The small pearls she hand-sewed onto the bodice and sleeves seemed lost in her broad thick fingers. A gifted seamstress, who sometimes also took in laundry, and cleaned 'rich people's homes' when there were no bridal gowns to be sewn. Never once did she stray from being the savior, the protector, from the hugeness of her role as mother and grandmother. In my spiritual, surreal world, even though she kept this secret of another daughter from me, she remains the Icon, the God of all mothers, the one who was able to courageously point a finger and somehow makes things what they ought to be.

I do not tell Michael of Grandmother's will. His selfishness seems to have burrowed deeper than normal. Besides, would he care? When I tell Howard he is pleased for me. But he is even more pleased by the pending publication of my poem. "See how talented you are?" he says, his blue eyes glow, an expression so generous, so bloated with praise that it embarrasses me. "You've made no real effort in marketing — where did you send it —two, three places? Your grandmother, Em, she's smiling down on you." Like me, although unspoken, I know Howard believes in the afterlife.

When I leave his office, I feel good about myself. Better than I've felt for a long time. I feel myself growing stronger, more independent. Those doors people speak of seem to be opening for me. For the first time, I feel as though my life is taking on some shape. A shape separate from my families — I will not fade away after all.

Two days later, Michael sends me a bouquet of iris and tulips, mixed with Queen Ann's lace, and baby's breath. The note says, "I'm sorry."

Feeling that familiar weakness, and my keen resistance to change, I accept the flowers, and tell myself maybe a transformation has taken place. I call him and ask him to come over.

We embrace at the door. He kisses me full and deeply, and I realize how much I've missed him. I forget about disagreements and the small things that tend to destroy relationships. We leave a path of clothing from the door to my bed. Afterwards, before I have a chance to ask him about the note, he says, "Sometimes — not always," he chuckles, nuzzling in my hair, "I'm so selfish, so self-absorbed."

I am whole for a few moments, peaceful lying next to Michael. He lights a cigarette and puts it between my lips. I don't want to disturb the moment, but I can't help myself, plus I need to quell this issue that keeps popping into my mind.

"Did you sleep with that girl?" I ask.

"What girl?" he says, taking a puff from our shared cigarette, arranging the pillow under his head.

"Michael, no games, please. Did you?"

"Why do you have to know, Emily? If I did, it wasn't out of love." He puts the cigarette to my lips but I shake my head until he takes it away.

"It's getting hot in here," he says, and stretches over me to open the window. His body smells of sweat, of me and him, of sex.

"Michael, you slept with her, don't you have any inkling of sorrow — no emotion, no feeling? She was practically deformed, left for dead right here on campus."

"Jesus," he huffs, his face flushed with anger. "I wasn't the one who did it — I only let her — go down on me. I didn't sleep with her. Listen, Em, guys are different than girls — you know, we need . . . ."

"Down on you?" Suddenly I don't want him to see my body. I sit up and pull the sheet up.

"Christ — a blowjob. She gave me a blowjob. Once. For two bucks."

My mind visits the tree in back of the library — Michael standing up against the sprawling oak, groaning, his eyes rolling, his body on the brink of a tremble, that poor girl on her knees taking him in as though she were loved. Inside me, something clicks. Was he with me on that same day? I crawl over him, jump from the bed, and pull on my jeans. Michael sits up, "What is it with you? Didn't we agree, no ties? Anyway, she wasn't another girl she was a whore. I paid her."

The air in the room is cool. "Close the window," I say, and pick up my shirt from the floor and put it on.

"Guys, we like to experiment — to try things. It didn't hurt anyone."

I nod. "I'm confused." I say, trying to put 'no ties' in a proper place and trying to figure out what part of this scene I hate most; his attitude that she was only a whore, not another girlfriend, or this deafening awareness of his callousness towards another human.

"One day you let her take you in her mouth — the next day she's found beaten to a pulp. But it's okay; she's only a whore. Would you feel the same about me?"

Michael approaches the chair I sit in; I turn from the sight of his genitals wobbling against his thighs. "Don't say that, Em. Hey, kiddo, it wasn't a big deal. And besides, she's going to be all right. I hear it was her pimp who got her. These girls are used to it."

"Get dressed," I say sharply, my body shrinking so far from his, I suddenly feel such disgust I think I may vomit. He kneels before me and tries to stroke my hair. He speaks to me as if I am a young child. I push him hard and he falls over backwards. "Damn you, Emily, the truth isn't always necessary—you get hurt when you push. Some things you have no business knowing."

"Get, get out." I scream.

"You'll feel better about this in a day or two."

His patronizing tone inflames me. "Don't tell me how I'll feel." My voice in a shout, "God, Michael, she's a human being — just go."

"Fuck," Michael says, as he scrambles for his clothing, "enough. No way I'm gonna beg you."

I feel myself about to cry, so I reach for a book on the desk and pretend to start reading. At the door, Michael says, just as if nothing has happened, "I was thinking — now that you're a published writer, you could help Mark and me with the new play we're working on. Think about it," he says and closes the door.

"You sociopathic prick." I scream at the door. "User. You never even read my poems."

I find myself wanting to stay in this chair forever. To melt into the fabric, dissolve to where I can't be touched by any outside force. Emptiness fills the room. Cold, it reaches back inside me to where it has grown familiar. I know it's over. I can't do it. Not any more. It all seems too hard, too painful. I think of all the bad: Spoiled rich kid. Rotted. Never earning his way, cheater, liar, ego manic. Drowning in all the negativity, I slowly begin to feel myself unravel from Michael's clutches. For a long time I knew I wasn't myself with him. There was no room in his heart, I think, if he even has one. In a couple of weeks the semester will be over. It will be easier then, not seeing him on campus.

When I think of the semester being over, I feel unguarded, jolted by change, the very thing I foolishly thought no longer could touch me. Howard had suggested I stay for the summer and work in his department. I try to evoke an image of myself filing papers, answering the telephone in the Counselor's office. Moving my stuff into one of the faculty rooms for the summer, but it doesn't come easily to me.

The usual sounds of doors slamming, students shouting in the halls, the background noise soothes me until my eyes close. Moments later, when Kimberly, from down the hall, knocks at my door, I drift back to the present. I only met Kim this semester when I moved into this dorm. I like her candid approach to everything. She wants to go into town for some pasta. Tonight Kimberly feels like a blessing. I don't want to be alone. She stands in the threshold of the doorway. I'm still sitting in the chair.

"Why are you sitting in the dark?" she asks.

"Nothing — I'll tell you later," I say, still uncertain if I will ever tell her, or how close a friend she will be.

I wash my face with cold water and prepare to go to dinner. I must keep busy. Push myself. On my desk, under the lamp, I see Grandmother's obituary. It is yellowed, except where the base of the lamp sat. I have read the obituary so many times, and now I read it once again. How did this woman, this Paulina know? How did she know Grandmother so well — *and she lives on in those that truly knew her.* The words are prickly on my skin, and now suddenly I know these words can only be written by someone who really did love. Words even I might've written. Four months since the burial and only now do I realize by ignoring this Paulina, I am behaving like Aunt Eva and Mother: Don't think about it dear, it will go away. Where do you get these ideas, Emily? Stop making trouble — pray dear, pray. When I think of Mother and Aunt Eva, who live their lives of pretend, who twist truth because they are afraid or cowardly, I feel repelled. I am caught off guard by a hot rush. That same ferociousness I've felt when I had to turn away from Mother's illness, her gross insanity. I cannot ignore this Paulina. Nor can I ignore the truth. My stomach growls from hunger. I slip the obituary back under the lamp. My intuition tells me to move forward. I have nothing to lose.

EMILY & PAULINA
JUNE 1966
CHAPTER FIFTEEN

Almost four days have passed since Emily left Maryland. The bus ride to Tucson is relentless, exhausting. When she arrives at the bus station the dry heat overtakes her, so she immediately takes a taxicab to a motel. The motel is drab, with a worn rug and faded drapes. Still the room is clean; light pours through the picture window. She struggles to remove her boots, then lies on the lumpy bed, grateful there is no movement.

She has a virus of some sort, which has been hanging on longer than she expected. Thirst overcomes her. She gathers a few coins and steps outside into a hologram of light. Squinting, she shades her eyes with her hand and follows the scorching concrete path to the vending machine. Her stomach feels too queasy to eat, so she will drink some soda and sleep; certain she'll feel better after a good night rest.

The bedspread with its faded swirls of brown-orange print makes her feel tipsy. As if that isn't enough, it also smells fruity, like an apple fermented in the sun. A gas bubble rises in her throat; she burps a sour taste, feels some relief, then pulls the bed cover to the floor and lies face down on the thinning yellow sheet blanket.

Howard insisted she call when she arrived in Tucson, so she picks up the telephone and dials his number. After several rings, just when she is about to hang up, he answers. "You must be exhausted," he says. She strains to hear him over the rumbling sound of the air conditioning unit that juts out above the doorjamb, occasionally releasing a drop of water on the carpet.

"I am," she says, now closing her eyes. "My stomach is a mess."

"Nerves," Howard says. "It's natural, Emily." She sees his forehead crease to a smile. "Try to remember how polite and accommodating Paulina was on the telephone." She recalls the deep raspy voice; *I'll be here Emily. Waiting. Whenever you want to come, just let me know, Pumpkin.* Pumpkin? What kind of person calls someone they never met pumpkin? She tells herself she's in for another Aunt Eva, yet knows it isn't so.

"I'll call and tell her I'm here in the morning."

"We miss you," Howard says softly.

Emily is surprised by his words, but not by the tenderness in his voice.

"The papers are piling up already," he says with some exuberance.

Still processing "we miss you," she hears Chevy, his yellow Lab, bark in the background. "You remind Chevy I'm not getting paid to be picking up after him," she says suddenly, and then feeling a flicker of warmth, she realizes she misses them too. Howard's voice continues to soothe her, readies her for sleep.

Paulina stares at herself in the mirror. Why, suddenly, does she care about the way she looks? She finds an old compact of rouge that is cracked and dried, and wipes a tissue over the top, then awkwardly pats the apples of her cheeks until they appear pinkish. A couple of glasses of wine would look better, she thinks, but it's too early in the morning. She sent a car for Emily at the motel. When the hour had come to pick her up, Mr. Bowles waited in the driveway for directions from Paulina. Paulina handed Lourdes a piece of paper with the name of the motel and Emily's room number. "Give this to Bowles," she said, already aware of Lourdes discomfort with the situation.

"You're not going in the car?"

Paulina turned from Lourdes' accusing look. But now she feels she may have been wrong not to go.

Under stress, Paulina feels the need to turn inward. This is all she has. Herself, without pretenses. Besides, Emily's hesitant tone of voice, telling her she wasn't feeling like herself, she might not even show. The car should arrive at any moment, Paulina thinks, yet she walks out back to her studio to check on Bird.

Emily felt relieved and somewhat significant when Paulina told her she was sending the car to the motel. "Mr. Bowles will be there at ten thirty. Is that okay?" she said.

Emily had a restful night's sleep, but was woken by a wave of nausea around seven in the morning. When she vomited she thought how ironic, she had been working with Howard on the bulimia and hadn't forced herself to throw up for months. Now sitting in the back seat of the big black Buick, she is no longer nauseated, just a gnawing emptiness in her stomach.

"First time in Tucson?" Mr. Bowles asks.

"Yes," she says, uncertain if Mr. Bowles is a hired car or part of Paulina's staff. She feels tingly — excited; she doesn't want any more information just yet. She is simply thankful Paulina is not that bag lady living under a bridge.

"Miss Paulina said you're her niece."

How odd to think she has another aunt, a hidden relative. Hidden, but why?

Mr. Bowles' gray hair touches his shoulders with a short ponytail tied with a frayed leather string. He laughs. "She's quite a lady. Says it the way it is."

Gradually, the highway begins to open, spreading out on both sides like colossal wings stretching towards the foot of the mountains. She begins to notice the giant cacti, and the lemon-yellow flowers growing on thorny branches, and low lying bushes sprouting pink flowers. There is light everywhere. It makes Emily happy, somehow mysteriously blessed.

Mr. Bowles swerves around what appears to be a dead tortoise, the largest turtle Emily has ever seen. "Another one bites the dust," Mr. Bowles says.

"Are there a lot of turtles here?" Emily asks.

"Used to be," he says, his hoarse laughter rattling inside the car.

The vegetation around the house is greenish, lush in contrast to the surrounding desert. White stucco arches shape the exterior walls of the house. Yuccas line the flag stone path to the front door.

A short woman with light brown skin and black hair stands under the middle arch and waves her hand. Can this be? She is not what Emily expected. The woman is Mexican or Indian, and although heavy, she moves quickly and nervously. She ushers Emily into the house and waves off Mr. Bowles.

"Sit," she says. "Sit here," directing her to one of the sofas. "I'll get Miss Paulina." Emily finds herself sitting on the edge of a couch, alone in this room with an odor of what? Peppermint, citronella, vanilla, or patchouli? Then she notices the candles; all sizes and shapes, all once lit, with charred wicks.

Across the room on the fireplace mantle, she sees a photograph of Grandmother and herself. Before her next thought can slip through, the short woman enters with another woman. She is tall, and buxom, with hair straight to her waist. As she draws closer Emily sees her hair is blonde, mixed with heavy streaks of white. The woman surprises Emily by embracing her. Nervous warm moisture envelops her. When Emily looks up at Paulina she is lost in her grandmother's eyes, in a reflection of light that seems to penetrate her the same way Babcia's did. She feels a quickening of heat in her throat, in her stomach, and fights the tears. She must take this slowly. She doesn't want to show her vulnerability. She tries to pull away gently, but Paulina's hands cup her face. "*Ty Jestes piekna,*" she says, her voice breaking, and the words, like an ancient memory plays in Emily's head; *Grandmother stoops, they are eye to eye. She feels the pads of her rough fingers on her chin. "Ty Jestes piekna. You are perfect, like a small doll, my little Laleczka."*

The short woman is sitting on the ottoman, now crying. Paulina turns from Emily, "Lourdes, it's okay—we should be happy."

Smiling, Paulina wipes her own cheeks with a tissue she slips from the pocket of her ankle-length dress. "Please — make us a pot of tea," she turns to Emily, "or coffee?"

"Tea will be fine," Emily says, somehow feeling lighter now.

Small talk about her bus trip, and the difference in the weather in the Northeast as opposed to the Southwest desert, feels awkward. When the telephone rings Paulina leaves the room. Suddenly music, classical music, comes through speakers some where behind the couch. Music she hasn't heard since she was a child when Grandmother played her records on Sunday mornings. The estrangement she feels begins to narrow as she walks towards the fireplace and picks up the photograph of Marishka and herself.

"Your grandmother brought me that one summer. I believe you were thirteen or fourteen," Paulina says entering the room with a bowl of pistachio nuts.

"I was thirteen." She felt herself both cautious and curious. Did grandmother have a good relationship with her? Was this a daughter she could trust? But why would she give her a photograph if she didn't care for her?

When Paulina sits on the couch once again, Emily notices her glowing skin, her wide cheekbones and large dewy eyes. She is radiant, unexpectedly beautiful, like grandmother, only taller, with gestures more similar to Mother and Aunt Eva. This woman is not an imposter. Emily is certain of this now.

"How is school going?" Paulina asks, then quickly dismisses her question. "I should be asking how your summer is going."

Paulina has a hard time concentrating on what Emily is saying. She watches the way Emily speaks, the way her eyes dart about and the way she nervously tucks her black curls behind her ears. There, there in her bone structure — squared jawed, with high cheekbones and a small forehead, and the widow's peak, she sees Francesco. She can't help but feel that after all this time she is dreaming, that this sweet child is not really sitting here in her living room.

Emily tells her of her summer work with Howard but doesn't mention how they met. She feels Paulina's gaze on her. She thinks she sees a smile form on Paulina's lips. Emily finds it both difficult and pleasing — this kind of concentration just for her. Instead of looking directly into Paulina's eyes, she focuses on the grouping of candles on the table behind Paulina's shoulder.

Nodding towards the photograph once more, Paulina says, "Actually, it was your babcia's last visit — that she brought me that photograph — when she had her first stroke."

Babcia. When was the last time she heard the word? Emily feels like a dry riverbed knowing the waters will come, excited and afraid she may not be able to handle it all.

Lourdes brings tea on a hand carved wooden tray; the china clatters as she places it on the coffee table. Emily doesn't know who or what connection this woman has to Paulina but hopes Lourdes will join them, and she does. Pouring tea, Lourdes asks, "How are the astronomy classes coming along?"

Emily is taken back by the question. "How did you know I was studying astronomy?"

"When you were little, Marishka would tell us how you loved the stars—she said you were going to be astronomer."

"Aunt Eva told us." Paulina corrects Lourdes.

"I've dropped it. This last semester. When Grandmother died."

"So," Paulina says, fumbling with the turquoise and silver necklace around her throat, "My Mother — your babcia — used to say that one shouldn't push so hard to find the truth—it can change your life forever. How . . . " she brings her hand to her throat once again and nervously clears it, "How do you feel about that?"

The question feels like a test of sorts — so straightforward that she is reminded of the frustration, the attempted talks with her mother, with Aunt Eva, and the power of their silence eating away at her. Now this blunt, straight forward question blocks her for a moment. Her gaze falls on the angular design of the Navajo rug at her feet.

"Grandmother and I — we agreed most of the time." Sucking in the air-conditioned air, locking eyes with Paulina, she says, not knowing where this new found courage has come from, "And besides, I am here, aren't I?"

"Good," Paulina says, feeling an unfamiliar discomfort, as though she is forcing something unnatural to take place. *Let it flow*, she thinks, "Have your tea and let me show you around. If you'd like?"

Emily finds the hallway leading to the bedrooms narrow and cool-white with clay floor tiles, not like her house up north with the wide-planked wood floors covered with braided rugs.

"This is where your babcia slept when she visited," Paulina says moving to the side allowing Emily to look inside the room. White walls with a white crocheted bedspread, and a chaise lounge covered in a thick leopard pattern. Books, many art books in baskets and shelves. She notices a medal of St. Anthony strung with a tea-colored piece of lace tied to the footboard post and recognizes it as Grandmother's.

She tries to see the room, the hallway, through Grandmother's eyes, her daughter talking with her in this bedroom, Grandmother in what she called her kangaroo nightgown with the bulky pocket that had been darned so tightly that the fabric appeared puffy. Grandmother sits on the edge of the bed, her bare feet resting on a footstool. Her daughter sits with her legs dangling over the footboard. They are both laughing about something that happened a long time ago, perhaps when Paulina was only a baby.

For a moment the vision is alive, full and textured, wrapping Emily's mind in gauzy detail. Surprised by the comfort and peace she feels Emily takes a noticeably deep breath.

"Are you all right?" Paulina asks.

All of a sudden Emily needs to ask questions. She starts with an easy one. "How often did Grandmother visit?"

Paulina feels a tightness in her throat. What does she have to lose? She didn't have anything before, what does it matter? "She used to visit once a year. I'm her friend Mary."

"So, there never was a Mary?"

"There was, but your grandmother lost touch with her after the first year they were in this country."

Cat Claw startles Emily by dashing between them. Lourdes chases after him. "Oh he woke from his coma. You allergic, Emily? I'll get him and throw him out." She rushes towards them. "Where'd he go?"

"No, I'm okay," Emily says.

"No. I know you're allergic. And if you're not, you will be. Where is he?"

"Lourdes, Emily said she's fine." Although Paulina is glad for the interruption, she feels annoyed at Lourdes' insensitivity to the situation. Taking Emily by the elbow, she says, "Let's go into my studio."

Outside the studio, Emily watches this woman who seems both orderly and yet unruly. "I always leave the key here in the planter," Paulina says.

Lifting the hem of her dress she starts to search the ground cover around her feet.

Emily tries the doorknob and it turns.

Paulina feels embarrassed, flustered. "I forgot. I was in the studio when you arrived," she says apologetically.

Canvases are piled against one wall. Only their backs showing. Two easels covered with paint-stained cloth stand back to back. Tubes of paint, rags, and large coffee cans filled with brushes line another wall. To the right of the sink, leaning against the wall, is an old mirror that catches Emily's reflection when she passes. The image of herself seems odd, unreal, like in a dream.

"I would like you to see what I do," Paulina says, thinking, *this is good, show her the best side of you.*

"This is what I'm working on now," she says, pulling the paint-stained cloth from the canvas. She feels her stomach turn. "If you don't understand it, it's okay, neither do I," a nervous laugh, "It was a dream I had."

Emily takes a moment to register the fact that this woman who has just come into her life is not only her aunt, but a painter who apparently dreams the way she does, allowing her dreams to be part of her life.

Emily takes a few steps back from the square shaped canvas. A nude stands against a background of sky, looking through a window, which is suspended in the clouds. One cannot see her face. Her clean, cherubic flesh glows and seems so real that Emily feels the urge to touch her. A light wind lifts her hair to the side. Her arms rise lightly as though she is about to move forward. Floating high above the woman, caught in this breeze is a small-framed picture, a portrait painted in brownish-gold tint. Emily moves closer to the canvas. The painted photograph has age cracks and the edges are torn, like a sepia that had been lying in a drawer for years. "Is that grandmother?"

"Yes," Paulina says. "The way I want to remember her, when she was young." She coughs, *not now* she thinks, and clears her throat. "It's the only thing that seems to ground the painting." She coughs again.

Approaching the easel, Paulina lifts the large canvas and with little effort turns it upside down. She backs away from the easel, squints, and continues to stare at the painting, concentrating so hard she is unaware of the light movement her fingers make tracing the crease in between her generous breasts.

In a low mumble she says, "The brick wall," and turns the picture right side up.

On the lower left hand corner of the canvas is a wall made up of bricks, a child's hand, gropes, rises up out of the bricks.

"The wall," Paulina repeats, flushing with excitement, "I hadn't realized. Of course the hand, it's yours . . . " she says. "It's you." She takes in a deep breath. "Yes, it is you," her voice quiet, thoughtful.

Her excitement is infectious. Emily senses the passion, the intensity and the pulse of her work. She feels overwhelmed by Paulina's generosity, by this invitation to know her, so brazen and courageous, it makes her feel cheated, angry it was never offered to her before.

A scratching noise breaks her thoughts. Paulina hears it too. "Don't worry, that's just Bird." She turns to find where the noise is coming from. "He's been here for weeks. I think I've spoiled him. He doesn't want to leave."

"Bird? Another cat?"

"No," Paulina laughs. "A small bird," she says, scooting down behind a bench full of old newspapers. "Here he is." Paulina cuddles the bird close to her breast. "He's a Cactus Wren. Cat Claw injured his wing. I doctored it up for him. I know he can fly a little. He flies back and forth across the room. Don't you?" she says to the bird.

Lourdes knocks and enters the studio. Three worms dangle from her fingers. "Lunch time," she announces. Paulina gently takes one from her hand and feeds it to the bird who slurps it up so quickly that when he is finished it doesn't seem enough.

Paulina touches Lourdes' arm, "Thank you, Lourdes. You're timing couldn't have been better."

An exchange of friendship, fine like crystal. This life, Emily realizes is a free one. This woman lives the way she wants. Emily thinks the smell of turpentine is getting to her. She feels heady. Amazed by the beauty of Paulina's canvases, by the bird in her arms, a small piece of gauze still clinging to his wing. And now, watching her with Lourdes she knows why she was confined to a life without her family. *Paulina is trying to tell her; she is gay, a lesbian. That's why they disowned her. Of course,* she thinks, *Anna and Eva wouldn't know how to tolerate such a life style.*

Placing the bird down on the floor, he quickly scatters a few feet away. Lourdes is talking about lunch, but Paulina watches Emily. She hopes she isn't scaring her away. Goodness knows they need time to get to know each other. Maybe she isn't ready, she doesn't ask many questions? She will have to wait. Wait for Emily to open to her.

Lunch is a smorgasbord of taco's and guacamole, rice and beans with escarole. Paulina is amused by the amount of food this slim girl takes in. The conversations have been going so well, Paulina can hardly believe her good luck. But she wants to get to the core, to have it all out on the table.

"How did you learn to paint so well?" Emily asks.

"I've been drawing and painting all my life." She doesn't want to seem egotistic. "I studied for many years."

"You're the only one in the family," Emily says.

"What?"

"With talent."

"No. Not true. You have talent. Babcia said you write poetry. Besides I got the gift from my mother—babcia."

"Grandmother?"

Yes, your grandmother."

"She painted?" Suddenly remembering the obituary: *She was a wonderful artist who chose. . . .*

"Yes . . . " Paulina almost flies from the chair. "Come, let me show you." Emily follows Paulina back outside to her studio.

Paulina rummages through sheets and sheets of papers until she comes to what appears to be a large thick pad.

Emily is aware of the bird racing along the perimeter of the room.

"When Babcia first came to this country she wanted to keep a diary of her life. Because she was determined to learn English, she didn't want to write in Polish unless necessary, besides, she claimed she wasn't much of a writer, so she decided to record her experiences in drawings, in paintings."

Pulling out a sheet of paper, she places it on the bench and flattens and smoothes it out with her hands. Paulina feels full inside as if the start of a celebration is about to begin. "This is a painting of the ship that took your grandmother and grandfather to America. And poor Uncle Felix, mother's brother who was never allowed to go further than Ellis Island."

"Oh God," Emily cries with excitement. "I know Uncle Felix. I remember him."

"You remember him?"

"Yes, when he came to visit us. I must've been ten or eleven."

"Oh yes! I'd forgotten. He was traveling with the Budapest Orchestra."

"I can't believe grandmother did this. I never knew. She never said."

Surprises, small gifts start to materialize before Emily's eyes.

"There they are." Quiet overcomes Paulina, as though something sacred is going on.

On the deck of the ship there are three figures, small, hardly recognizable. Emily sees Uncle Felix right away, he is the smallest one, holding onto the railing, and his violin case fixed on the floor between his legs. Grandmother Marishka wears a white blouse with a lacey collar, and a wine colored skirt to the floor. She has a flowered shawl wrapped around her shoulders. And the man, the Grandfather she never knew, with a tan hat tilted to the side, is dressed like a gentleman, and carries a book in his hand.

Emily is amazed by the boldness of the painting. "I can't believe this. Why didn't she continue to paint?"

Paulina silently brings out another drawing.

A woman, apparently Grandmother, sits next to a coal stove. A little girl sits on her lap, while another brushes her hair. The colors are warm reds, gold, and browns. The details are mesmerizing: A black iron pot on the coal stove, steam evaporating through the slanted cover. A doll lying on the cement floor with only one braid done, and the small rug at her feet is worn with holes. The rocking chair she sits in has long curved arches to rest your arms.

"Is this mother?" Emily asks pointing to the child on her lap.

Paulina nods, afraid if she speaks Emily will hear the emotion in her voice.

"Did you really brush grandmother's hair?"

"Uh huh," she mumbles.

Emily remembers grandmother brushing her hair. The quick tug of her hair front to back, front to back, until her braids or ponytails were so tight that Emily felt numbness on the scalp. "I hated when she brushed mine. I think that's the only thing Mother did better than her." A small throb in her chest signals her disloyalty towards Mother.

Paulina carefully returns the drawings to their original space. As she closes the drawer, she pulls in a deep breath, and suddenly feels so complete. She hasn't felt this way since Francesco, so long ago. "I'm so happy to have you here, Emily," she says unexpectedly, her hand rising to touch the soft dark curls that fall on Emily's shoulder.

Later on, Paulina is on the telephone again. Emily hears her voice, clear, positive with a sense of purpose. "Sorry," she says, as she enters the living room carrying what appears to be an exotic succulent flower floating in a bowl of water. "The Women's Club. They want to meet at my house this month." She places the bowl on the low pine table between them, moving aside a book.

"I guess you got that from Grandmother too."

"What?"

"The flowers, plants, growing things."

Paulina thinks for a moment then nods reminiscently.

"Is it a Feminist group?"

"Well, not really—perhaps. More about women having economic and political power. Just trying to get the word out there. You know there was a poster during WW11 which showed a woman flexing her arm muscle. It said WE CAN DO IT. It inspired many women. I'm sure you being in college, you're more aware than most."

Emily gestures a half-truth by nodding yes.

"You know your grandmother, she was the one, way ahead of her time. She always said a woman could do anything a man can do. That we were equal — with one exception."

"One exception?"

"Oh, well—I hope you don't mind my bluntness, but you're a young woman." Paulina takes a book of matches from the mantle piece and begins to light the candles on the deacon bench and the high table behind the sofa. "Let the angels come into our lives." When she turns her head to smile at Emily the sweep of her long hair seems threatened by the candle she has just lit.

The candles soften the light in the room. Emily has the sensation of being adrift; a sort of spiritual comfort blankets her.

"Yes, Babcia said a woman was equal to a man until they laid together." Paulina returns the matches to the mantle. "They can both leave the bed, but only one of them could be pregnant."

No one in Emily's family had ever brought up the idea of sex so easily. They both watch Cat Claw glide across the floor and jump on the sofa next to Paulina.

"Was Grandmother the only one who accepted your way of living?"

"My way of living?"

Immediately, Emily is sorry she spoke. The silence drawing around them makes her feel more uncomfortable.

"Well, yes, you living with Lourdes."

Paulina frowns. "Why shouldn't she — accept?"

Just say it, Emily thinks.

Lourdes enters the room like a lightning bug looking for a place to perch. She brings a bowl of fruit to the table, finds a crumpled napkin on the floor, lifts the seat cushion from the club chair she sat in earlier, and with her hand sweeps whatever she finds onto the floor.

"Lourdes, if you want to join us, do so. Whatever you're doing is distracting and unnecessary."

"No. It's okay. I keep myself busy inside. It's too hot to go out today." Lourdes flashes a quick look at Emily. She seems to be teary eyed; her mouth softens to a quiver of a smile.

"I think Lourdes has been looking forward to your visit as much as I have."

Feeling a bit worn out suddenly, Paulina waits as Lourdes heads for the kitchen.

"How long has Lourdes been with you?"

"Oh at least — goodness — almost your age." Thoughts of the time of

Emily's birth tumble back to Paulina. The desire she felt for Francesco, and the desperateness, and then the loneliness, all of it seemed tightly woven in her chest as it has been for years. It was like Cat Claw's fur ball churning in her throat, waiting to be spit up.

"Are you a lesbian?" Emily just blurts it out, "A homosexual? Is that why Mother and Aunt Eva don't speak to you?"

"A lesbian?" Paulina laughs. "Oh my God." She holds her face in her hands, laughing. She glances at Emily. "Lourdes? Oh no. But maybe I should've been." She continues to laugh.

Emily feels gullible — almost stupid. She should've waited to be certain. "I'm sorry, I . . . ."

"Oh, Pumpkin, don't worry about it." Paulina reaches for a tissue on the table behind her. "We're all human. What does it matter. Two women living together. It isn't the first time, I'm sure that someone may have thought that."

"Then why?"

"Why what?" Trying to delay the moment.

"Why don't they speak to you? Why were you never part of the family?"

"Because what I did was, I guess you could say, it was bad."

"Bad?"

Paulina sees for a moment, no, less than a moment—Francesco about to put his lips to his saxophone. He plays one long vaporous note—his face wrenching in passion. That same aching look he endowed when they made love.

Cat Claw repositions himself on Paulina's lap.

"Sometimes, things happen in life. Unexpected things . . . unplanned . . . " Her voice heavier than usual.

"What could be so bad?" Emily asks.

Paulina looks up at Emily sitting across from her. She seems adrift, harmless and innocent. "I had an affair with your father," she says.

Emily has to swallow a few times, to record these words carefully. "My father?"

"Yes," she says, "your father."

"When? How?"

"Before you were born, and during the first year of your life."

"But my father died when I was six weeks old."

"No, Emily. That's what your mother told you. That's what the family plan was. For us to just disappear — to kill us softly. Strip us from their minds."

Emily allows Paulina's words to filter, to come to her slowly. The toxicity of the past wears heavily on Paulina's expression.

Emily has always wanted to be like Polaris; constant, never changing. She had told Howard once, "Polaris is safe, it has a position, guarded and fearless."

"But without change, we wouldn't grow," Howard said, "it's human nature."

Paulina sits next to Emily, and touches her hand.

"When did he die?" Emily asks, feeling Paulina's hand grow large around hers.

"He's not dead, Emily. He's alive."

It takes Emily a moment to understand what she's heard. "Alive?"

"Yes," Paulina says.

Tears roll down Paulina's face. Suddenly she appears bewildered and lost, crazy, like her sister Anna. Emily pulls her hand from hers. She rises from the loveseat her shield of protection, now in place, rises with her. The numbness settling in. The years flash by; Mother, Grandmother, Aunt Eva. How could they keep it from her? And what about him? What kind of man is this?

"I don't feel well. Excuse me." Emily rushes towards the bathroom. She locks the door, and sits on the closed toilet seat. "What the fuck is this? What a fucking crazy family."

Paulina is outside the door. "Are you okay?

Emily doesn't respond. She hears Paulina and Lourdes talking in whispers as if they're at a funeral. *My mother. I hate her. How could she lie to me about something so important?* Her stomach is worse now; she needs to eat something, she thinks. *Father? What kind of man would allow such a thing?*

She hears movement outside the door.

"Where is my father?" she shouts towards the door.

"He's in Italy." A pause, then more whispering. "He lives there now."

Italy. Well he's safe. Far enough away. And her, Paulina, what kind of sister is she? Answering her own question, Emily thinks, *the kind of sister Wanda would've been.*

"How am I supposed to understand this?" Emily reaches for a towel, holds it under the running cold water, and presses it to her face.

"Emily, please come out. Are you okay? Come, let me make you a cup of tea."

"What's with this screwed up family? Every time someone's upset, they want to feed you."

"Okay then, we'll talk." Paulina tries to hide the panic in her voice and thinks, what have I done. Oh God, don't let her be like her mother. A cold sweat grips her. Lourdes stands behind her wringing her hands.

And Grandmother, why did she keep it from me?

"How could Babcia not tell me?" she says quietly, more of a thought than a question. The genuine love and truth which binds her towards her grandmother, is this too a lie? It is this thought that reigns —shakes through her body. Lies tear you open — what you thought was real becomes nothing. Lies can change you forever. She doesn't know how long she sits there, while the sounds beyond the door remain dreamlike.

When Emily finally rises from the seat she realizes she has to take a pee. Her black eye liner is smeared under her eyes. She tries to wipe it away with toilet paper. "Call me a cab. I have to go now," she says through the door. "I need to be alone for a while." She needs to call Howard.

When she opens the door, she feels embarrassed, as though she were the one who had done something wrong.

Paulina's eyes are red and swollen. Lourdes has her back to Emily, carrying a kitchen chair down the hall, which they apparently used outside the bathroom door.

"Stay a while longer, Emily. Let me try to explain."

Emily can't seem to look at her. She looks down at her boots. "No. I can't listen right now. I need to go." And not knowing where it came from she lies, "I'll come back tomorrow."

EMILY
JUNE 1966
CHAPTER SIXTEEN

On the way back to the motel Bob Dylan is singing, *Like A Rolling Stone.* Guitars, tambourines, and a lone harmonica fill the taxi. Suddenly I want to get high, so I ask the driver to stop at the Quik Pik where I buy a gallon of ice cream laced with cherries and nuts, potato chips, and a large package of crème sandwich cookies. I forget to ask for a spoon, so back in the motel, I use the cookies as a tool to lift the ice cream to my mouth. As the ice cream becomes softer, I am able to use the potato chips, one by one. At one point I even use my fingers. An instant of euphoria; dipping, scooping the cream until my hand forms the five finger lakes, running between my fingers, down my forearm. The television blasts in the background. The telephone receiver is off the cradle, and the food soothes me into heavy sleep.

Slamming of car doors outside the motel window wake me in the morning. My stomach gnaws and burns, I promise myself to not binge any more or force myself to throw up again.

As soon as I place the telephone back on the receiver, it rings. *I don't want to speak to her, not now.* The man at the other end has a low squeaky voice. "Someone was trying to reach you all night. You must've had the phone off the hook."

"Okay," I respond dully.

"Don't you want the number?"

Relieved that it was only Howard, I start to get myself ready to leave for the bus station. I feel as though I have a hangover, sluggish and slow. My cuticles are raw, all bitten and craggy. Mother is haunting me; last night I dreamt of her again.

When I arrive at Howard's office, he holds the door open for me as I enter. He's wearing a tee shirt once again; Los Angeles Dodgers is printed across the front. When he hugs me I smell his familiar Old Spice. His embrace is warm and meaningful. Now more than a confidant, he is my only true friend.

He takes the news of my father being alive as a positive; a door opening; an opportunity. "But," he says in his professional voice, "the chance of rejection is high." Chevy has his soggy tennis ball and is trying to work his way under his arm. "You won't know until you try — that's the hard part."

Tired and drained, I feel over sensitive since finding out about Paulina and my father. I sit on the sofa and try desperately not to bite at my cuticles.

Howard fusses at his desk. He is looking for something. Chevy stands next to him in "treat" pose.

"I want you to really look at this." Howard says as he sits next to me. "Look at this as if you've never seen it before."

He hands me a greeting card. Henri Rossi's Sleeping Gypsy is on the cover. I open the card. A black and white photograph of me is taped inside. I am three or four years old sitting on the stoop of the old apartment house where Mother and I lived. The white wicker doll carriage I took everywhere is by my side, and the baby doll whose name I can't remember now is posed on my lap for the camera. My curly hair parted down the center refused to be contained in the loose braids resting on my shoulders: Wisps of hair escape and are lit by the sun.

Howard moves closer. "Look at this child." His after-shave isn't Old Spice after all. New, it smells of cloves and pine, which makes me uncomfortable. "Notice her eyes, her smile. Do you really want to continue to hurt this child? His voice is hoarse, scratchy. "She never hurt anyone, Em."

The photograph still in my hand, I look closer. Behind me, I see Mother's feet. Her high heels with white anklet socks. And then I see the words, Howard's words, under the photograph: *Love Me, stop hurting me.*

The innocence and purity of that four-year-old expression comes tumbling down. I want the impossible. To touch this child, to go back to that time and hold her in my arms. Pressing the card to my chest, I begin to cry. I cry from a place that seems fertile, a tranquil, more intimate place.

Howard holds me and inside I feel as if everything is breaking into small pieces of glass: Mother's drinking glasses on the tiled bathroom floor; a crashed vase lying in a puddle of water, dead flowers strewn around it; a tea cup flung to the kitchen floor: Glass cold and sharp, everywhere.

"Get rid of it — let it go," Howard rocks me in his arms. "Sweep it up, sweep it all up," he pleads, and I begin to sweep whatever I can, but I know there are hidden pieces so sharp, so piercing that they will always hurt.

A month has passed since my visit to Paulina. At a surprise birthday party for George Junior, Aunt Eva, knowing I had been to visit her sister, never mentions our meeting. She is happy I could be there to celebrate with what she calls "the family." Aunt Eva says my skin is glowing and I look well rested.

My secret solid inside me, I recall the doctor's words when I telephoned for the test results; "Well my dear," he said, "the rabbit died. Looks like you're going to be a mother."

For a while I felt confused and uncertain, but glad that Michael was no longer in my life. I thought of Nora. She knew someone who performed abortions. But now, only a week later, I feel intoxicated with my secret. Here I am talking to Aunt Eva and thinking; I have another human floating around inside me. A skull, two eyes, a spine, ten bony fingers and toes, and she has no idea. "I am a miracle yet to be discovered," I say out loud while Aunt Eva is cooing to a woman standing next to us. Aunt Eva turns to me and says, "That's nice, dear. Run along and see if you can find George Junior for me. Tell him we need more ice for the punch."

Howard sits on the edge of the heavy coffee table in the center room of our dorm. "The problem is not just going to disappear." The large windows are all open and the breeze moves through the rooms like a welcome guest. Over the summer months Howard has allowed his hair to grow even longer and he today he wears his wrinkled shirt unbuttoned to the middle of his hairless chest. He has a slight tan from taking Chevy to the beach each morning before starting work.

Searching for a package of sugar for his coffee, I suddenly have the urge to be playful. I sneak up behind him and poke him in the ribs. He jumps, Chevy barks then begins to lap the sugar on Howard's sandaled foot. Howard is ticklish and we both laugh. "I must admit, I've never seen you this happy." His smile forms small lines around his eyes and his whole face lights up.

Howard feels good to me. Since I've confessed to binging and shop lifting, no lies or pretenses have gone between us. Lately, we've been spending lots of time together. After work sometimes we go out to Spanky's for dinner, and then Howard insists on treating me to a movie. I've imagined making love with Howard. There is no fire in his eyes or in his touch. He lacks mystery, yet he is illuminated by this uncanny intuition and an incredible sense of generosity.

We talk about Paulina and my father, and how much I really don't know. We speak of Grandmother, who I naively thought kept no secrets from me. I marvel at the fact that I wasn't so off when I referred to Mary as Mysterious Mary. Howard says my intuition is strong like Babcia's and I must find someway to forgive them all. But this baby growing inside of me takes precedence. One evening over a serious cup of coffee at Cappuccino Joe's, Howard says, "This wasn't a choice you made, Em. You don't have to accept it."

"Isn't this what you call fate?" I say half joking. Even though I feel anxious, I feel strength and certainty. "I know it's crazy, but for the first time in my life I feel substantial, as if I have a direction." In my mind it seems nothing can stop me from having this baby. "Almost like—like I finally have a purpose."

Howard looks away from me and leaves for the men's room. On return his eyes seem watery. "Are you okay?" I ask.

He reaches for my hand across the table and pulls me closer. "Where are we going?" he asks. "I can't believe I've allowed myself to care for you as much as I do." For a moment he is a young boy. "I've broken the first rule of being a good therapist." He laughs, "It's a good thing I'm not a full-fledged therapist yet!"

I am not surprised at all. I saw it coming, but didn't care. I am getting what I need.

Howard bites on the inside of his cheek, the way he does when he's tense. I pat his hand "It's okay," I say. "I won't tell anyone." He smiles a little.

"Emily, I have to know if you still want me in your life."

"Of course I do," I say without hesitation, realizing how dreadfully selfish and needy I've become. "Let's just give it more time, Howard. Is there any reason for us to rush, to define our friendship?"

"It's more than friendship, Em. At least on my part. I know that you know this on some level."

I do know this, and it feels good like Marishka's warm hands smoothing the blanket over me, pulling the covers up to my chin. "I do care for you Howard, more than you think."

"Where or how does the father of your baby fit in?" He refuses to say his name.

Just thinking of Michael makes me feel uneasy. "He doesn't." I say. "Even if he knew, he wouldn't give a damn. I don't want anymore selfish people in my life."

"Don't you feel there is some moral issue here? I'd want to know if it were my baby."

"Howard, you don't understand. Michael isn't like you. He probably has lots of babies out there that he doesn't care about or want to know about." I no longer have to grapple for words, these thoughts have become my own standard mantra.

"I need time. To think. I'm going to a conference in San Francisco. I'll be gone for two weeks. I'll leave you the number at the hotel, if you need me, but I'm not going to call you. Not until I sort some things out."

The second day Howard is gone, I already miss him. But I concentrate on me. Day by day, I'm aware of changes in my body. Oddly, I feel myself growing stronger by the moment, as if this baby is nourishing me, instead of me nourishing it.

The word comes down from Portland, through Aunt Eva, that Greta can no longer handle Mother. Mother has lost her desire to eat, making her too weak to walk. I call Howard in California and he puts me in touch with a social worker who helps me find a place where Mother will get the proper care. "Rehabilitation" is a word I hear over and over. She may be overmedicated or under-medicated. Her symptoms of schizophrenia are increased.

When I arrive at the house I find Mother's bed has been moved into the living room. "The stairs were getting to be too much for her," Greta says.

The neck of an empty Vodka bottle sticks out from under her bed. When I bend to remove it, I discover several others. Greta, it seems, is not a believer in alcoholism. "I tried, but she was so difficult if she didn't get her schnapps every night." She stood with her arms folded, resting on her belly. "A little booze never hurt anyone."

I pack Mother's personal things for the nursing home. "Bring her hobbies, the family photographs, anything that will make her feel more at home," the short chubby woman with her clipboard had said. There is little for me to take.

I watch as Greta assists Mother to a wheel chair. Relief seems to settle around mother. She no longer has to do anything, but sit. A wave of shame rolls over me. How willingly, how easily she accepts this sentence.

I have the desire to strangle both Mother and Greta, to shake them until they break from the slovenly lazy cocoon they've managed to wrap themselves in.

Upstairs I find a small seashell in Mother's dresser drawer. Strange, she would never allow something so foreign to be mixed in with her underwear. The seashell is pink like a baby's fingernail, delicate, almost translucent. Had I given this to Mother? Did Mother draw it from the moist sand herself? Who is this woman? Had she once captured an awareness and love for living? Before my father and Paulina? The thought suffocates me. It is too painful. There are only sad memories here to hold, pieces scattered about—fragments of a woman's self-imprisonment. How, just how, does a child rescue a mother? "She doesn't," I finally say out loud. Yet now I torture myself with something new; would her life been saved had she married a man who was faithful to her? I take the seashell with the hope that one day I'll know why or how it got there.

I call Paulina and tell her the news: "My mother has moved into a nursing home."

"I'm so sorry," she says. For some reason I really believe her.

"Does this make you feel guilty?" I say.

She is quiet for a moment. "No. I don't feel guilty. Not anymore. I didn't cause her illness. Em, your mother was always troubled."

"Troubled? What a nice word for mentally ill."

"Emily can you come out so we can talk? I'll send you an airplane ticket."

"How can you be so sure that you and my father didn't cause her sickness?" Toxic words are not comforting to me, but I keep it going especially when she doesn't answer. "What kind of man was he to leave his baby? And screw his sister-in-law?" I hear her heavy breathing, but silence reigns. "He left me with a sick alcoholic woman. Doesn't that say a lot about him?"

"You'll have to ask him that question. I can't answer for him. You talk to him yourself." She is saintly in her new honesty.

For a long while we listen to the low hum of the telephone wire. "Emily, you may find this hard to believe, but I do love you. You're all the family I have — I want to try to make it right."

I decide to test her love. "I'm pregnant," I say.

"Pregnant. How far along?" She asks this question as though she is used to hearing this statement.

"Ten, eleven weeks," I say.

"Oh—is there, give me a moment," and then doesn't take it, "Who is the father? Are you serious?"

"There is no father."

"Emily, now we must talk. Don't do anything foolish."

"Foolish? Oh yes, that's a subject you know a lot about."

"I do," she says almost in a whisper. "Oh, I find this so difficult by telephone. I'm going to fly out so we can talk."

"Suit your self," I tell her.

Howard returns from his conference just in time. Paulina will be arriving in late afternoon. I scramble up some eggs and find I'm not able to eat anything. Even though a part of me wants to meet her at the airport, I stay behind. Howard understands my pain and anger, but says I must stop playing games with my feelings. I tell myself it's the "process of healing."

I ask Howard to be with me when she arrives at the dorm. He looks rested, lines vanished from his brow, he seems more confident. "You need the time alone with her." "Afterwards," he says, "if you want, call me and we'll meet for dinner at The Quarry."

There is no time to discuss what he's thought about over the last weeks, but his embrace is loving-almost joyous, and the timber in his voice unflustered.

Paulina arrives in a long dress, brown and turquoise Aztec design. Her hair is clipped in a loose bun. She appears flushed from the heat, and with eyes that seem hurt, grown deeper since we last met.

"Well, dorms have certainly changed. This is quite roomy," she says, looking towards the other room.

"It's a suite, for four girls," I say. "It's mine just for the summer."

She breathes heavily as she makes her way to the desk chair. Her movement or a gesture stirs a memory of Grandmother. Once seated, she looks directly in my eyes. "How are you feeling?"

"I'm fine," I tell her.

"Good." She smiles.

I think about saying something cruel, but I hold back.

"Have you made a decision?" she asks. I want to be the one to ask questions, but I sit quietly listening to her breathing. "Have you ever heard of Margaret Sanger?"

She doesn't wait for an answer. "She was the woman who fought for birth control. She said, `no woman can call herself free until she consciously makes a decision whether she will or will not be a mother."

"Are you saying you think I should have an abortion?"

"No. Certainly not. You have to do what you feel is best for you." She looks around, still trying to catch her breath it seems. "May I have a glass of water?"

I retrieve a glass from the drain board on the sink and fill it from the tap.

"Why didn't Babcia ever tell me about my father? She knew he was alive."

She takes slow sips. "When your grandmother found out your father and I were together, she already knew Anna was sick. She had known of your mother's mental illness for years; that's why she lived with you and your mother. Believe me Emily, your grandmother always was there to protect you."

Another sip.

"Your mother wanted me and your father never mentioned again. She told everyone she only had one sister. That your father was dead. Grandmother was caught in the middle of one daughter who was ill and weak, and another more tenacious daughter and, well, more like herself, so she decided to live this lie in order to protect your mother from further harm." She places the glass on my desk on a piece of paper. "Your grandmother said any other way would've been like trying to drive a car straight on a twisted road."

My life whirls around me at unmentionable speed. I want to hear more stories. I want to know everything that happened.

"At first your father spoke with Babcia, trying to find some solution, but she felt it was better to leave things as they were. Your grandmother was very forceful, Emily, especially when it came to her children. I think you know that." She makes accordion pleats with the hem of her dress. "Eventually your father stopped trying."

Now that Babcia is no longer here, its possible her "story" was so artfully played out through the years that even if it wasn't actually this way, it is now?

The glass makes a water stain on the paper. Paulina takes a pen from my cup holder and outlines what she sees, then stops just as quickly. Looking at the wilting philodendron, she says, "Oh, that plant needs water." She walks over to the bookcase and pours the remainder from her water glass in the plant.

"I've spoken to Francesco since I saw you last. He wants to see you. I've given him your telephone number."

"Francesco?"

"I'm sorry. I'd forgotten. That's your father's name."

"Babcia told me his name was Frank."

"That's what your mother called him, but his name is Francesco. Francesco Ferruggia. Don't turn him away, Emily. Give him a chance, especially now. He can help. I know he wants to."

"I don't need his help. I'm going to sell the house."

"That's fine, but what if you don't sell right away? It could take a year or two. I don't know the market up in Maine. Think about it, and if it doesn't work out for you, having your father in your life, I will be here for you." With both hands she smoothes her hair back, behind her ears. "What am I saying? I'm here for you no matter what. I want to be part of your life."

Standing inches from where I sit, she fumbles with her hair once more and fingers the brooch at her chest. Her eyes glisten.

The core of her secret exposed, she is a vision of vulnerability. She wants forgiveness; she wants to embrace me, and me to embrace her, but I stand awkwardly. Turned from her gaze, I feel as if I had waited all my life for this warmth, for this genuine attention, yet now that its here, I feel paralyzed. There doesn't seem to be a decent or right way to accept it.

EMILY
EARLY OCTOBER 1966
CHAPTER SEVENTEEN

Howard and I spend two weekends looking for an apartment for me. "It must have a good shower," I tell him, "not like those pathetic dorm showers, where they teasingly sprinkle a little water at a time." He is patient and puts up with my childish whims. When we enter the apartments the first thing I do is turn the shower on. Lately, I've been obsessed with cleanliness.

In the new shower stall warm water rolls over my belly. My hands caress my stomach. My body has changed and is still growing. For the first time I realize what it means for skin to be an organ; it is alive, overzealous and vigorous; I cannot imagine it stretching any more than it already has. The baby kicks strong now. I watch as the heel of the baby's foot moves under my swollen breasts. I try to picture what she will look like. I worry sometimes that maybe I won't love her. Maybe I'll find a baby a burden. What guarantee is there that I will love her? How much did they love me? Then I feel something like a bubble, a kick, a scratch, a hiccup, and I begin to feel uneasy, wondering if the baby's all right, if it's normal.

Two and a half months have passed since I found out my father is alive and living in Europe. For a while I stopped answering the phone because I didn't want or wasn't ready to talk to him. Once, when he called Howard spoke to him. He had asked for Amelia, and Howard told him there was no one by that name living here. He then excused himself, and said, "Amelia," is Italian for Emily. Unfortunately I'm one of those people who can only think in their native tongue." He left his name as simply Francesco. Howard said his accent isn't very strong, that he was quite informal and friendly given the circumstances.

When Paulina telephoned the last time, I told her I was ready to speak to him, but since that time he hasn't called.

Howard brings fried chicken and biscuits and cranberry jelly for dinner. We set the small bistro table in the kitchen, but there isn't enough room, so I take the folding snack table I bought at a yard sale and lay the food out on it. The table is the perfect height for Chevy. He sniffs the air, doesn't touch the food, but we know not to turn our backs.

Howard tells him, "You better behave yourself. You don't even belong here. If the superintendent catches you here, poor Emily will have to live in the street." Chevy tilts his head and lets go of a long rumbling sigh.

These last months have been filled with tranquility. The calmness that resonates is difficult for me to accept as commonplace. There was an article in a magazine at the doctor's office that said there is a natural pattern to "waiting. *Waiting gives the mother time to rest, to reflect, meditate and plan for her new life.*"

My "New Life," has sent Aunt Eva to her priest, to ask him to contact a priest in my area and have him come and visit with me. She had called to ask me to come home for Thanksgiving. When I told her I didn't think I could make it, that I was pregnant, she was stunned. After a moment of stillness, she said, "I knew no-good would come from you visiting with Paulina!"

"Paulina had or has nothing to do with this."

"Emily you must go to see your priest. Pray for forgiveness." She was panicked, urgency in her tone; "A child born out-of-wedlock is born with sin."

I believe that was the beginning, or at least of my awareness, of religion settling in me. I felt the weight of the little one move, floating — butterfly wings. The baby's movements seemed to be more vigorous than ever. How can such innocence be sinned?

"Why would God, if he is a good God, allow a newborn baby to be born sinned?" Why, why would He?" I asked, howling into the mouthpiece, trying to force an answer.

Instead Aunt Eva was whispering, reciting prayers into the phone. "Hail Mary, full of grace, the Lord is with . . . ."

I never waited for her answer. I just hung up. Crying myself to sleep that night, all I kept thinking was, the more things change, and the more they remain the same.

The fried chicken is greasy, but delicious. Chevy concentrates on the chicken in my hands and barks so loudly that we both jump. We feed him small pieces to keep him quiet. Moments later the doorbell rings. "Shit" Howard says, "Must be the Superintendent," and he goes to open the front door. There is a priest standing in the hallway. Car keys jingle in his hand as he tries to read from the index card he is holding. "Is there an Emily Mikulski here?"

Howard turns to me with a look of surprise. From where I sit I can see the priest. "May I come in?" he asks.

Howard looks towards me once again. I nod yes, even though those old feelings of fear and intimidation come rolling over me.

"I'm Father Jorgenson." He takes Howard's hand and shakes it.

"Ah yes." He sees that I am pregnant. "You are most definitely Emily," he says as he approaches me with an extended hand. "May I sit for a moment?"

I again nod and look at Howard so he knows not to leave.

Howard pulls a folding chair over to the table.

"Your Aunt Eva in Maine requested a visit from our parish. She said you were in trouble."

My pulse reaches its maximum speed. "Well, she is wrong, Father Jorgensen. I'm not in trouble."

"I know the whole story. Do you want to discuss any of it with me?"

Aunt Eva doesn't know anything. Yet he knows the whole story?

"There is nothing to discuss. I'm simply having a child." My heart beats so quickly, I think it will leave my chest.

"Yes, I know. And that's a lovely thing. Are you the father? He asks Howard.

Howard looks bewildered. "Isn't that a personal question for someone we've just met?" Even though Howard is right, that old Catholic guilt rises, and there is a piece of me that wants him to be respectful towards the priest.

"Listen, I know this is hard, but I would like to see this child and its mother be blessed, to free themselves from sin." Turning towards me, he says, "You cannot turn from God's will."

"It's God's will for me to have this baby."

"Of course. But not out of wedlock. You know that with this type of disobedience towards the church, and until you marry, I cannot bless you or the child."

I keep telling myself that this is just a man with a job to do. A rotten job at that. "That's okay." I say, "I'll work it out."

"Emily, do you believe in God?" His eyes are young, filled with promise, yet he has small creases around them.

"Yes, I do. But not in the same way you do."

The priest sits back in the chair with a smirk on his face. Here comes the patronizing, the condescending attitude. I look at Howard and he surprises me with a warm therapist smile and I remember that I'm not thirteen, alone, and confused.

"Emily, we'll be late for our appointment," Howard says.

That old intimidation still lurking in my bones, I say, "Okay. Just a moment."

Father Jorgensen goes on about my sin, comparing it to the original sin.

He speaks of the will of God, repentance, confession, and the benefits of the blessing of the lord.

Inside, I am smoldering, dying to tell him that religion is made by desperate men seeking control of others. That my God does not live in a building constructed by man. My God is portable; I carry him with me. He is within me, and will be within my baby. I want to tell him that Babcia was the most spiritual person I ever knew, and she believed in a Cosmic God. A God that doesn't condemn innocent people; a natural God, a God of nature, not only of this earth but of the entire universe, but my argument would have been senseless, full of holes, because, after all, he was schooled to have all the answers.

"I'm sorry, Father Jorgensen, but I must get to the doctor." Another sin freshly committed.

"Okay, my dear, but you come and visit me. Here's my card. And bring the father of your baby with you, if you can." He slips a look at Howard. Howard puts on his fake smile. "God bless. And, young lady, remember you can't go to communion until you right this."

Once the door is closed I feel calmer. We walk back to the kitchen to finish our meal and find that Chevy has finished it for us. Cleaning up the plates, Howard says, "Scolding him isn't going to help." And then he says, "I'm proud of the way you handled that. You didn't get all emotional. Great progress, Em." He pats my belly, "Even baby is proud of you."

"Inside I was an earthquake ready to explode."

"I'm beginning to think your Aunt Eva is a little passive aggressive."

I search the cabinet for something else to eat and find peanut butter and crackers, and then I turn on the radio to remove Father Jorgenson from my thoughts. I'm in the mood for some sugary music, but all I seem to get is static and a talk show about the one-year anniversary of the Watts racial riots in Los Angeles. Thirty-four dead, thousands injured. The commentator wants to know what Congress has done to prevent further rioting. Howard and I are both listening to the political jargon of the senator, when the telephone rings.

Paulina has been constant in her attention towards me. I'm beginning to feel comfortable around her. More comfortable than I've ever been with anyone, except Marishka. I realize now that both Paulina and Howard have allowed me to be myself.

I tell Paulina about the priest Aunt Eva sent over and our conversation. She says I should've thrown him out. "Easily said," I say, "but you know how this religious thing marks you for life. It's difficult to cut it off entirely without feeling superstitious and guilty."

Paulina laughs and says, "That's how the church operates. Guilt is their number one inducer." She starts to cough. I want to ask why she is still smoking.

"Have you heard from your father?"

"Please don't call him my father."

"I'm sorry."

"No, I haven't, not since we last spoke."

"I think its only fair to warn you. He said he would be coming to the States."

Howard sees my expression of surprise, "What's wrong?" He whispers.

I shake my head and wave him off like its nothing. When I hang up I tell him,

"She says Francesco is coming to the States. He wants to meet with me."

Moments later when the doorbell rings, my heart quickens. *He wouldn't dare come here without calling first.* Howard rushes to the door to keep Chevy from barking. "We have a delivery for Mulkuski." A short wide man with a baseball cap is at the door.

"A delivery?"

"Yup," he says, "Furniture."

"Furniture?"

"Yes, lady, furniture."

"But I didn't order any."

He looks through the bill of lading. "Someone bought it and paid for it."

"Who?"

"Listen lady, I'm already late. This is Saturday, I'd like to be home with my wife for dinner."

"Does it say who sent it?"

He fumbles through the papers once more. "Says it's a Francisco something."

"Francesco Ferruggia?"

"Yea."

I look at Howard in surprise.

"You want me to take it back?" the driver asks.

"What should I do?" I turn to Howard.

"What is it?" Howard asks.

The man rattles off: "A crib, a dresser, and a . . . " swishing papers, "kitchen table and chairs." He taps his foot impatiently.

"Take it," Howard says. "You can use it."

There is no time to think with two men waiting at the bottom of the staircase and the one with the baseball cap ready to go home.

The men bring the crib up in pieces and put it together in my bedroom. It is white with little lambs playing on the headboard. The dresser matches the crib. I feel relieved when I see the baby furniture in place. I was worried about the money and didn't want Howard to give me any more money.

The kitchen table is so big it is more like a dining table. We can barely get it into the kitchen. "Enough room to seat eight people." No sooner than I tell this to Howard, in come the eight chairs. Nice pine ladder-back chairs, with cane seating.

"He has good taste," Howard says as he tries out one of the chairs.

"This is ridiculous," I say. "It's so big."

"Maybe he thinks you're more Italian than Polish, and you're going to have a big family and feed a lot of people."

I frown at Howard.

"You knowa, those biga spaghetti and meatball dinners! Yum . . . .me."

Ironically, Rosemary Clooney starts to sing among the static of the radio: *Hey Mambo, Mambo Italiano.* Howard jumps up and says, "Just in time," and grabs a hold of me to dance. He takes some awkward steps with me, then stops and shakes his head. "I shouldn't have any time off from work," he says. "It makes me too . . . weird . . . silly."

"I like the chairs," I say and then look at the highly polished tabletop, "but not the table."

EMILY
OCTOBER 31, 1966
CHAPTER EIGHTEEN

The morning, the sun red like an organic egg yolk, I walk to the bookstore and purchase a book I had originally seen fanned out on Paulina's coffee table the day I met her. The book is about a dark-haired Polish child who lost his parents in the chaos of World War II and his struggle to survive.

Lately I feel as though I've got Grandmother's disease, wanting to keep up with Polish Americans. Except now at this late age, I find I am not just Polish, as I was raised to believe, but half Italian.

When I leave the bookstore, the sun is gone and huge snowflakes spin around in a confused state. Babcia would've loved the thought of snow in October. Now that I'm in my ninth month, and ready to have this baby in a few weeks, I feel drawn into a lull, a perfect stillness where there is nothing for me to do but wait. The idleness finds me missing Grandmother more. I wonder how she would have responded to being a great grandmother. Would she have sewn baby clothes and knitted blankets and hats? Would there be a christening dress handmade by her, even if I didn't believe in the church? Perhaps there would've been our own private ceremony on the beach or on a patch of grass when the moon was full and so bright that the billions of stars we knew were there could hardly be seen?

Two blocks from my apartment and the snow is patchy, coming in intervals of light twirls and heavy gusts. Nearby three girls laugh and shout. One is dressed as a pumpkin, another a witch, and the third is wearing a mini skirt with black net stockings, heavy makeup, four-inch heels, and a silver feather boa thrown over her shoulders. They giggle with excitement and then I see why. Across the street two boys, dusted in a white chalky substance, swing their flour socks at each other pretending not to notice the girls. Then they call out to the girls and start to chase them. When I turn the corner, I still hear their yelling and laughter.

On the stoop of my apartment building, fueled by the desire to be with Grandmother, I stop and move in the direction of the wind and pretend to collect snowflakes on my tongue. When I turn to enter the vestibule, I see a man through the high windowpane of the door. He holds open the door for me. Caught at my child's play, I feel myself blush. He is a tall man with big shoulders and a staggering smile. He wears a long black overcoat that seems excessive for October, yet appropriate for today. He is carrying a shopping bag. He looks at me and his smile wanes to sadness. I'm about to ask what apartment he wants, but then I look into his face and suddenly I feel as if I'm in that instantaneous atom of time when one wakes from a dream and reality is fused with fantasy.

"Emily?" he chokes. "Bella Amelia."

I can't answer him. I feel myself tear up; my breathing is heavy and uneven, my lungs want to close down. The wall where the mailboxes are supports me.

"I'm sorry to surprise you," he says. "I didn't want to telephone. I was afraid you wouldn't see me."

The ground floor neighbor tries to enter the vestibule. With the door open three people can't fit into the cramped hallway. Struggling to get words out without too much emotion, I say, "Come." Legs shaking I climb the two flights and he follows.

Once inside the apartment I can't even decide if I want him to remove his overcoat. "Have a seat." I tell him. Unsure of what to say or do I think about calling Howard for an instant, but know he would refuse to come. "Face your demons," he would say.

"I am pleased you accepted my small gift," he says, looking at the table crowded in the kitchen. "Oh, I see it's not as small as I thought." He smiles.

I feel mute, as though I've now been hit with a stun gun.

"This is so hard for me," he says. "I don't know where to begin." He rubs his palms together. Such big hands, unmarked hands of a would be warrior.

I don't make it easy. I sit on a chair far from him.

"You look well. Are you feeling good?"

I nod yes.

"I saw you . . . once — at your grandmother's funeral. You sat in the back. They wouldn't let me get near you." I find his accent thick, charming. He must attract women easily, I think.

"They?"

"Your Aunt Eva thought it would be too much for you, after the loss of your grandmother."

My memory is in front of grandmother's coffin where a man and woman are talking with Aunt Eva. Their voices raised in anger. Too young to be friends of Grandmother's, so I had settled they were friends of Aunt Eva's.

"There is a lot I would like to say, Emily, or do you want to ask me questions."

Ask questions? He acts as if this can be cleared up with the right answers like some sort of TV game show.

After a moment of silence he says, "Let me tell about myself. Cara Mia."

He is a vigorous man. Powerful square jawbone, full lips, and his left eyebrow raises when he speaks. He is almost too good looking to be someone's father. I find I am not ready to look into his eyes.

"What makes you think I want to hear?" I say bitterly.

He shifts in his seat and crosses one leg over the other, the way a woman would, except his right arm spreads to the back of another chair. "We must to start somewhere."

He clears his throat, "and I believe it starts with my story, because as the older, the father . . . if you don't mind."

The word father cuts into me with fury. "Oh my God," I cry out, jumping from the chair. "Do you have any idea how much I wanted, needed to have a father?"

He uncrosses his legs; his head now hangs between his arms. "I tried to think of ways, Emily. Really, I tried my best."

Your best? I look into his eyes; they are hazel green like I knew they would be, and his widow's peak, flecked with gray now, but still like mine.

The lost years tumble upon me. "Do you know that I went to a fortune teller, a gypsy, when I was just five years old. I looked for you everywhere. On some level, I knew you were out there even though they said you were dead. I remember looking behind the radio whenever a man's voice came on. I thought you were hiding in one of those little pathetic fucking tubes. *Your best?* God, it wasn't close to being good enough."

I feel myself out of control, bitter. "Your best was nothing. You left me with that crazy lady! You have no idea what you did to me."

Sobs rise from him. At first I think it's a child outside in the hallway playing trick or treat, a ghost moaning, but then he sucks in his breath. Holding his face in his hands, he says, "I know, Io conosco, I shouldn't have . . . ."

He has a spot balding on the top of his head; irregular like the molting spot Paulina's bird had on his chest. I feel so worn. Sorrow overtakes me. I never knew him as a younger man. He never held me as a small child. In my frenzy to be alone, to get to the bathroom, I accidentally kick his shopping bag and a stuffed cow with a bell around its neck jingles across the floor. When I return, the cow is propped on the table and Francesco's face is buried in his hands once again. I put a tissue box next to him, after taking some for myself.

He looks up; color drained from his face, no longer the solid man who walked in with me. I notice dark bags under his eyes I didn't see before. "Your mother, she made me feel — I was choking. I was suffocating living with her. I would've stayed, but she threw me out when she found out about Paulina."

I don't believe he would have stayed. He was going no matter what. "Oh my God. What was she supposed to do while you were sleeping with her sister? Why the hell can't you be honest?"

"This isn't coming out right." He wipes his eyes, blows his nose, an intrusive sound cutting into the sensibility of the moment. "And your grandmother. She was from the old school. Powerful . . . she —"

"Did you know that mother was also a drinker, an alcoholic?" I'm breaking into a cold sweat.

He nods yes.

" . . . and you never came for me?"

"Your grandmother was there. Emily, I didn't know the first thing about raising a daughter. You're a girl. You needed a mother or grandmother more than you needed a father."

"No. What I needed was one parent who was normal, one parent who loved me."

He stands and puts his arms out to me, "*T'amo, t'amo . . .* " he tries to speak. "Your grandmother . . . ."

Even though he evokes sympathy from me, I won't let him finish. "No one. No one could ever make me leave my baby." Suddenly I knew this to be the stabbing truth.

"I want you to leave. Now," I say, my voice trembling so much I think I will faint.

"*Momento, cara mia. So bene che per te e`difficile,*" he says to himself.

"There isn't anything left to say."

He walks towards me as though to embrace me.

"We must give this time." His voice is soft and hoarse now. The whites of his eyes splattered with red veins. When he gets near me he smells of wet forest, pine or cedar mixed with nicotine. I want so much to embrace him, for him to hold me against his chest, but am paralyzed by fear. Afraid that I finally have a life, afraid someone can take it from me. The way he did once, the way Paulina did and the way Mother did by not caring enough for me, by not helping herself to get better.

"I hate all of you," I cry. "You're all so fucking selfish." My legs begin to shake—weakness takes my body, and I sink downward. When I reach the floor, I feel wetness between my legs.

"Forgive me, bella mia, I ask your forgiveness," he pleads, kneeling on one knee before me, his overcoat fans out like a cloak.

The wetness seems to spread. I put my arms out for him to help pull me up. He thinks I want to hug him, but once standing, I push him away.

In the bathroom I take a towel and roll it between my legs. There is lots of blood, crimson black. "No, God, please," I pray. When I open the door, hunched over with my legs spread by the thickness of the towel, Francesco's expression is one of fear and surprise. "Dio mio, forgive me," he says, "What can I do?"

"Take me to the hospital," I say.

I am lying down in the back seat of Francesco's rented car. I check the towel in between my legs, and my fingers come away bloody. I'm so afraid I'm losing my baby. "Hurry," I tell Francesco. Even though the hospital is only ten blocks away, I think we should've called an ambulance. I feel like vomiting, and I cannot stop shivering. Moments later we get to the emergency room, and I'm afraid to stand because I know the bleeding is worse. Francesco goes in and comes out with a man in a white coat. "Are you a doctor?" I ask. "I need a doctor."

"You're okay, little lady." He checks the towel between my legs, then calls out some name or initials that I know is not good. Suddenly I'm panicked, and I start to cry, "Please save my baby."

I am holding onto Francesco's hand as though I've held it before.

Even though they put me on a stretcher and rush me into a room, everyone seems to be ignoring my plea for help. Walls of green tiles and huge bright lights sprint pass me. They ask Francesco to leave. When our eyes meet he issues a sorrowful helpless gaze, like a young boy being led away from his mother, yet his black coat, his massiveness moving away from me, I think maybe he is like an angel of death.

My clothing is peeled from me and when they sit me up, I begin to vomit. It is not the vomit that once warmed my insides; it is fear coursing through my body. The nurse cleans me with my blouse and says it will be okay, while another begins to insert an intravenous needle in my arm. They talk about toxemia, or a tear in the placenta. I am shivering. Towel gone, legs spread apart, I feel the blood trickling out of me. Strangers touching, fingers inside me, voices, unfamiliar medical terms alarm and scare me; make me think my baby is dying. "Please help my baby," I repeat over and over.

After what seems like hours, a doctor is at my bedside. I am already sleepy from what they've injected into my veins. "Emily, this is Dr. Gomes." His voice is loud, as though what's happening to me is also harming my hearing. "We're going to go in and take the baby." He holds my hand in his, I startle at the coldness of his fleshy fingers. "The baby is in trouble and so are you. We have to move fast. Do you understand?"

I just shake my head yes and cry.

I dream mother came to see the baby and me for Christmas. She brought gifts she purchased while visiting Francesco in Italy. She brought baby Marisa a Renaissance rocking horse, and for me a hand painted Venetian mask that I held with a stick. She had on her brown wool dress with the shawl collar. It was a happy dream.

I lay flat in a hospital bed unable to move because of a spinal injection. Howard is holding my right hand and this strange, hulking man gripes my left hand and says, "Cara mia, she looks just like you did when you were born. This much I know," he says triumphantly, "this much I know."

When Paulina visits me I am still groggy from anesthesia. I feel her caress my shoulder. She leans over the railing on the bed; "There was a full moon last night, the Hunter moon, Emily." She speaks in a whisper, as though it is our secret and no one else knows. "A bright pumpkin of a moon." Her eyes are moist and dreamy. "Born on Halloween, under the Hunter's moon, she will be a wise child and never go hungry. And most important," She catches her breath, "she will always be blessed." In my daze I think she is Babcia.

Marisa is now three months old. Her face is round and open like a glowing light bulb. She radiates happiness. When she was born, I immediately knew she was the soulmate, the reincarnation of Marishka. She has powder blue eyes like Grandmother's, eyes that own my heart.

I want to be the rare mother who makes no mistakes, but I know that's impossible. From the moment of conception, Marisa was already marked by my errors. Yet I know I will be an ample, generous mother. More worthy than my own, perhaps equal with Grandmother, or maybe even better, because one day Marisa will know Howard is not her biological father. I have chosen to forget what Michael looks like, but I've made a note of his name and birthday in my journal in case Marisa needs to find him, for I know now that secrets run in the bones and the blood of those who came before.

Paulina visits often. She has painted giraffes and baby elephants on the walls of Marisa's room. She loves Marisa dearly and takes on the grandmother roll with exuberance. I am more deeply rooted in family now. Francesco visits frequently. He leaves his older saxophone in the closet so he can play for the baby and me. He never comes when Paulina is here; I still feel disloyalty towards Mother should I see them together; but Howard is here to gently roll me over the humps.

Caring, considerate Howard who really feels and acts like the father of Marisa, who has since moved in with me, and patiently awaits the day we will marry.

At night in that small pocket of time when I'm between breast feedings and I cannot return to sleep easily, I think of the strangeness of my new family. We are a nuclear forced family, I think, each of us driven by a desperateness to not be alone.

Then some nights a picture stretches across my mind: We have a large house with a courtyard, like grandmother's house in Maine. Mother is no longer institutionalized, but sleeps in the back room. On those nights when she's too tired to come down for dinner, Marisa looks up at me, her focused innocence, her brilliant smile reminding me it's time to bring Mother her dinner.

In a vertigo of silence, strength has a way of penetrating cells. I have learned to forgive, to let go of destructive thoughts, yet when I feel Marisa's tiny hand wrapped around my pinky long after she is asleep, I remember. There is no *real* forgetting. Memories retreat, yet, hold me at haunt.

Miriam Polli is a native New Yorker who now lives between Key West, Virginia and Greece. Her short stories and poetry have been published in various commercial and literary journals. This is her first published novel. Miriam lives with her husband Jim Katsikis, who loves to grow things and is now a wine maker.